The Miracle Branch Line

Cenarth Fox

Dedication

To Peter Raymond Beck
Lover of railways and history

Chapter 1

Every morning Lord Randolf Fitzsimons and his gamekeeper went riding. As usual, they rarely spoke. Ever since His Lordship disowned and disinherited his only child, Stephen, for being a conchie and refusing to fight in WW1, Randolf became a shell of a man. He and his wife lived separate lives in their sprawling manor house, Ripley Hall near the village of Whittleton in East Anglia.

When railway porter, George Miracle, informed Fitzsimons his son not only served in the war but did so with enormous courage in the Friends' Ambulance Unit, risking his life to save wounded soldiers, the father wallowed in misery. It was easier to pull his teeth without anaesthetic than for His Lordship to tell his wife their boy was not a coward but in fact extraordinarily brave. Randolf's pride stopped him from asking forgiveness of his son. His Lordship hated life and worse, hated himself.

His morning ride took its usual route through the west pastures into the woods to the bridle path above the river. Fitzsimons always led the way. Heavy overnight rain made conditions treacherous.

'Ride slowly, my Lord,' called the gamekeeper.

Fitzsimons ignored the warning; he ignored everyone, and instead used his hands and heels to urge on his charger. Even the animal was unsure but did as ordered. In the woods and at a solid trot, both the animal's off legs slipped and the beast toppled and fell. The rider screamed, his fearful yell bouncing off the trees. The rider hit the ground and rolled. He would have copped a drenching in the river had not two saplings blocked his way.

The gamekeeper was off his horse and scrambling after the master. 'My Lord, are you all right?'

This was clearly a stupid question. Of course he wasn't all right but at least he had another reason to feel sorry for himself.

Trying to help Fitzsimons to his feet produced howls of pain. The alternative was to put the injured man out of his misery as the gamekeeper did countless times to injured animals. That thought actually crossed the gamekeeper's mind. It would stop the moaning.

With exceptional strength and much slipping, the employee carried his boss up the slope to the gamekeeper's steed. Draped over the horse, Fitzsimons maintained a constant wail.

Back to the Manor House they went with Randolf's loyal horse following, head bowed, cowed by his brute of a master.

A doctor declared the patient alive but his riding days dead. The crippled Lord was confined to his bed or a wheelchair meaning his self-pity finally reached a gold standard.

On the first day of January, 1923, the *Railways Act* came into force and the Great Eastern Railway, the GER, was no more. Its employees, rolling stock, stations, trolleys, brollies, pickets, tickets and tea urns were now the property of the London and North Eastern Railway, the LNER, the second-largest of the Big Four.

George Miracle, the newly appointed station master at Whittleton, was up early. His bedroom was now his alone following the death of his beloved uncle, the former Whittleton SM, Fred Carmody.

George didn't need any prompting to wake or hop out of bed. His sister's dog, Spike, waited at George's door. The canine knew the first human up and about is the first port of call when seeking an early breakfast.

'Good morning, Spike. Did you sleep well?' George headed outside. 'Come this way my fine fellow.' Despite his permanent hip injury thanks to a piece or two of WW1 German shrapnel, George learnt how to walk and negotiate steps with a minimum of pain.

Spike enjoyed his own spot for ablutions and both returned to the still warm kitchen thanks to last night's fire in the stove.

George got the kettle on the go then, in the sink, splashed his face with the coldest water in Whittleton.

Today was his first as station master working for his new employer, the LNER. He shaved and dressed. His new uniform gave him goose bumps. His overcoat sported two lines of impressive buttons. He left it undone so the chains of his watch in the pocket of his waistcoat could be seen. His shoes were shiny and spotless. His tie nestled perfectly inside his collar, and the pièce de résistance and his crowning glory, was his cap. The mirror in his bedroom didn't offer a full length view so he bent and swiveled to check his image—in parts.

In the kitchen, his mother, Connie, was making breakfast.

'Good morning, Ma. Did you sleep well?'

'Let me see you,' she said making her 24 year old son stand still and be inspected as if he were age 5 and about to start his first day at school. At least she didn't place a handkerchief against his nose and tell him to blow.

'I'm fine, Ma, and ...'

'Stand still,' she reprimanded and the son obeyed the mother.

Trixie the cat entered and rubbed against George's leg.

'You never know if a person from head office might call in to inspect you,' said Connie.

'We're a small station in the country, Ma, and now with hundreds of stations in the LNER, we'll be lucky if we're *ever* inspected.'

'Turn around,' said the domestic inspector and George felt the back of his coat being brushed. Connie checked her handiwork. 'You'll do. Your father and uncle would be proud of you, George, very proud.'

Thanks, Ma,' he said wishing those two men could see him now.

'Now eat your breakfast.'

He was scoffing his porridge when his 20 year-old sister arrived.

'My goodness,' said Emily, 'who's a pretty boy?' She gave the cat a saucer of milk. 'I feel I should be saluting the new SM.' She gave an exaggerated salute.

George ignored the teasing and announced his news. 'The two new porters arrive today. You know Eric's been here forever, but now the LNER has sent us a new porter, Gordon and a new lad porter, Phillip. I think he's thirteen but the other porters are both older than me.'

'You know what your uncle would say,' said Connie.

'Yes Ma.'

What would he say?' asked Emily.

Connie and George spoke as one remembering the late SM's advice. 'The passenger's your boss, and never be late.'

'Tell them that and all will be well,' said the lady of the house.

'Yes, Ma.' George gulped the last of his tea. 'I must dash.'

'You haven't finished your breakfast,' complained his mother.

Heading towards the front door, George called. 'I can't be late on my first day as SM for the brand new LNER.'

He left and the women heard the door close.

Connie stared at her hard-of-hearing daughter and waited till the young woman returned the stare.

'You have to tell him, Em.'

'I know, I know.'

'He has a lot on his mind right now but he needs to be told.

The young woman nodded and repeated herself. 'I know, I know.'

The walk from the front gate of the station house to the Whittleton station master's office took about 23 seconds on a slow day. The first Up train wasn't due for an hour but George loved being early. He unlocked his office door and a wave of sadness washed over him. The pain and grief of his uncle's sudden heart attack and swift death still lingered particularly in this, Fred's former office.

The thrill of being appointed the youngest station master in the GER and now the LNER faded, and was replaced by the fear of making a mess of the job.

He lit the fire, checked the two platforms, ticket supplies, the contents of the safe including the cash box, and examined himself in the full-length mirror in his office. He heard a knocking and turned to see a small boy in the doorway.

'Mr Miracle?' asked the lad in a voice in the throes of breaking.

'I am and you must be the new lad porter, Phillip. Come in.'

George extended his hand and couldn't help think back 12 years when he first worked as a station lad at Liverpool Street station in London. *Did I look as young as this boy?*

'They all call me Pip, sir.'

'Do they? Well I think we can keep that tradition going, Pip.'

'Thank you, sir,' he said with excitement in his voice.

George warmed to the boy. 'I see you're from London.'

'Yes sir, do you know it?'

'Born and bred. Now how are you fixed for accommodation?'

'My Grannie lives in Whittleton, sir, Mrs Enid Clough.'

'I know Mrs Clough, a lovely lady. Now, I have some paperwork for you to complete. Sit over here.'

As Pip filled out the forms, two men arrived at the same time.

Eric, Whittleton's long-serving porter, met the newcomer outside the station and did the introductions.

'Mr George Miracle, station master, meet Mr Gordon Littleton, porter.

The men shook hands. 'Littleton of Whittleton,' said George smiling and introduced the lad porter to the two new arrivals.

'He's okay for digs, sir,' said Eric. 'The poor chap's boarding with Monty and his missus.'

'You won't go hungry there, Gordon,' said George. 'Now please do the same as Pip and fill out this paperwork.'

George enjoyed his new role and gave his team "the passenger's your boss and never be late" speech. 'Now I want us all on duty at the same time for the first week. Eric will give you new chaps a tour of the signal box and the gatekeeper's hideaway. Afterwards, Eric and Pip can start on the Down, and Gordon, you'll be with me. We can all have a cuppa after the 11:05 Up. Now I'm off for a chat with the crew on the Crabbie, which is something else for you to explain later, please Eric.'

'Right you are, sir,' said Eric who chose to call the new SM, young enough to be his grandson, sir instead of George. The porter enjoyed respecting rank and long admired George ever since the young man, and his uncle, arrived at Whittleton.

George crossed to the island platform, the far side of which was the terminus of the branch line to Crabbwell. It was never a busy line and with the arrival of the Big Four, and their new employer the LNER, the Crabbie footplate crew of Madge and Bobby both reckoned their days were numbered. They were preparing their workhorse, a chunky Class J69 0-6-0T, a good old tank engine, for its first run of the day.

'Good morning, gentlemen,' said George.

Both men respected their new SM. They used to take the mickey out of young Miracle the porter but always in good humour. They knew about his war record, and saw him in action working hard for his late uncle and the passengers. The crew snapped to attention and gave a soldier's salute speaking as one.

'Good morning, sir.'

'Enough of that nonsense; the locals will think you're being disrespectful.'

The crew was instantly serious. Their banter was harmless and meant to be humorous. 'Sorry, boss,' said Bobby.

'Like the new uniform, boss,' said Madge. 'What's happening with the new rolling stock for the branch? We've been driving this lot since Queen Victoria was a gel.'

'I know nothing, gents, but as soon as I do, you'll be the first to hear. Now my uncle used to complain about the amount of paperwork every SM handles, and I can tell you it's true. I'm swamped with reports but I need details from our friendly Welshman at Crabbtree. Tell him I want last month's freight and passenger figures as soon as possible. Okay?'

'Will do, boss.'

'Safe travels,' he called, and walked back to his office.

Passengers arrived on the Up platform. George greeted them. Having worked as a porter here for several years, he knew just about everyone in the village and copied his uncle by greeting people by name. They appreciated this courtesy and all admired his change of uniform. When porter George Miracle became the youngest station master at Whittleton, and anywhere in the GER which then became the LNER, he became the talk of the village and amongst railway men near and far. His appointment raised a few eyebrows.

The first Down pulled in and Eric noted how well the new lad porter related to the passengers and to the guard. Having hard-working and courteous colleagues meant the world to George. All four members of the platform staff gathered in his office to enjoy their tea.

'I'll make no bones about the situation, gentlemen,' said George. 'The reason more than a hundred companies were amalgamated was all about money or the lack of it. Being on the line to London, we seem to be fairly safe. But the branch could be right in the firing line for closure.'

Eric said his piece. 'There's been talk about closing the Crabbie even before you and your uncle arrived, sir.'

'I know, Eric, but now we have a serious competitor.'

'Road transport,' said Gordon.

'Correct,' said George. 'I served in the army in the war when the government ran the railways and bought huge numbers of trucks and vans. Those vehicles became surplus to requirements. Haulage companies have bought up big. Chaps returning from the war have snapped up a vehicle and gone into business for themselves. Companies and individuals are out-gunning the railways left, right and centre.'

'They're killing us,' added Eric. 'But this new LNER is huge, the second biggest railway company in Britain. We now send trains up to Scotland so why can't we use our vast network to offer cheaper rates?'

George knew why. 'Because the government controls our rates.'

Silence settled in the SM's office.

'Are we in serious trouble?' asked Gordon.

'Perhaps,' said George taking out his pocket watch on its gold chain tucked inside his flash new waistcoat. 'The next Up is due in 6 minutes, gentlemen. Let's be ready.' The team scattered.

Once the train departed, George returned to his mountain of paperwork when someone knocked on his door.

'May I enter, Mr Stationmaster?' said his sister sporting a cheeky grin. 'I have a letter and some news.'

She handed her brother a letter addressed to him care of the Station House, Whittleton. George opened it and read with delight.

'Good news?' asked Emily.

'Indeed,' said George, 'and I'm going to keep you guessing till tonight.' Emily glared at him. 'Although I could reveal all if you do the same for me first.'

She shook her head. 'You always were the brainy one in the family, George.'

'I disagree. Anyone who lost their hearing age six and can understand and speak as you do is clearly intelligent and clever. But enough of the back slapping, tell me your news.'

Emily checked to be sure no-one was listening. 'Ma says Bert needs to ask you for permission before he can ask me to marry him.'

George produced a huge grin. 'What? You're pulling my leg.'

'No I'm not,' she replied indignantly.'

'I'm your brother, not your father.'

'If Dad was alive, Bert would have to ask him.'

'Oh come on, Em, Queen Victoria's dead. That ask-the-father routine's a bit old-fashioned. It's 1923.'

She became annoyed. 'So you refuse to let him ask you?'

George dropped his guard. 'Of course I don't refuse.' He paused and beckoned. 'Come here.' She moved to him and they embraced. 'I'll give my permission tonight.' She hugged him again.

Porter Littleton of Whittleton appeared, and looked embarrassed. George spoke to his colleague.

'Gordon, come in and meet my sister, Emily.' The couple shook hands. 'Please be aware she's already spoken for.'

Emily gave her brother a friendly slap, and Gordon relaxed and smiled. 'Sorry to interrupt, sir, but there's a cart stuck on the crossing.'

Gordon left with George following. Emily called. 'Hang on. You promised me *your* news.'

George stopped and gave her a fearful stare. 'I'm going to be a father.'

He left to help push the cart while Emily's eyes and mouth opened simultaneously and were never so wide.

Chapter 2

When Emily went home and told her mother what George said, Connie didn't believe her. 'It's one of his pathetic jokes and in the worst possible taste. I thought him becoming a station master would see an end to all that silly nonsense.'

'But it was in the letter I gave him. He opened the envelope, read the letter and then grinned.'

'So? It could mean anything.'

'It could mean all those trips he used to make to London were to see his sweetheart.'

'What sweetheart? He doesn't have one, and as long as he's living in this tiny village he probably never will.'

Emily fought back. 'I found a husband in Whittleton, why can't George meet a girl here?'

That knockout reply flattened Connie who regretted her comment and worried. *Is my son really about to become a father?* The women were forced to wait until George came home for his supper.

Having cleared the cart from the crossing, George spoke to both Desmond the gatekeeper and Monty in the signal box. He liked to keep in regular contact with all his team. Then he headed for the island platform and waited for the Crabbie to return. It was on time.

'The SM at Crabbtree said he'll send the reports tomorrow, boss,' said Madge.

George wasn't happy. 'I'll come with you, gentlemen, on the next Down. I need a face-to-face chat with our friend.'

The crew knew Owen Griffith was a porter and played along with the game of pretending he was the SM at the tiny terminus.

There was more than an hour between departures on the branch, and with the young SM on board in the only carriage, the Crabbie started with three passengers and a package destined for a Mrs Tring at the unmanned Bridle Hill station.

Perfect weather made the trip along the picturesque line a delight. Both farm animals and wildlife seemed to welcome the train.

Bobby, the artistic fireman, hopped down at Bridle Hill and placed the package of clothing, all the way from a specialist shop in Dulwich Hill in London, in the waiting room, an old carriage on the empty station. No chance of the goods being pinched and Mrs Tring's unmarried son would wander to the station and collect the goods. This was a typical transaction on a quiet country railway, a branch line with the sword of Damocles dangling from its water tower. Mind you there was no water tower.

In Crabbtree, Owen Griffith performed his bowing and scraping routine at the sight of the new SM. 'Oh boyo, so pleased to see you I am, and to congratulate you again on your marvellous promotion.'

'Thank you, Owen, your kindness is appreciated. Are you well?'

George forgot he should never ask Owen about his health. The pretend SM delighted in listing his ailments in great detail giving strength to the claim he was never happy unless he was miserable.

After a description of his teeth being so sensitive, he claimed they became itchy; George called a halt to the personal and switched to business.

'Tell me, Owen, if you would be so kind, how is the freight side of the line?'

'I have your report nearly complete and will send it by express service on the 10.10 Up in the morning.' It would be quicker to walk.

Excellent,' said George, 'but can you give me a verbal report here and now? A rough estimate will do.'

The porter grimaced, finding it impossible to make a silk purse out of a pig's ear. Business was close to non-existent. 'I'd have to check the paperwork, sir,' said Owen knowing full well the figures were terrible.

'Well can you give me a list of traders in the village who have done business with the line in say the last twelve months?'

Owen could and furnished his boss with the names. It was a short list. George went to the crew.

'I'm off to the village, gents, and will be back for the 13:10 Up.'

George bade the footplate crew and Owen farewell and set off on foot the mile or so to the village. On such a glorious day, the surrounds gave his spirits a lift. He paused on the foot bridge over the river, the waterway which prevented the line continuing into civilization at Crabbtree. At the time of construction, a rail bridge was deemed too expensive to build.

On his first visit to Crabbtree station more than five years ago, George saw how that decision left the station far from the madding crowd in the village. Who wants to travel by train if, in the pouring rain, you have to traipse a mile because the line and the village ne'er shall meet? Here was a perfect illustration of how to kill a railway.

The river's cleanliness meant you could see the grasses growing on the river bed. They danced as the gentle current inspired their choreography in this green and pleasant part of England.

George walked into Crabbtree and using his list of traders, approached the first business, Thomas and Son, bakers.

'Good day, Mr Thomas,' said George entering the business.

'Good day to you, sir,' said the baker wearing plenty of his basic ingredient.

'I'm George Miracle.'

'I know who you are.'

George worried although was not sure why. 'As I've recently been appointed as the new station master at Whittleton, I thought I'd see if there is anything the new and much larger London and North Eastern Railway company could do to help you and your business.'

Thomas the older shook his head sending fine ground flour into the air. 'There is nothing at all you or your new company can do for me, young man.'

'Nothing?' said George with a sense of disbelief.

'No, those road haulage chaps have you beaten every which way. They're cheaper, more reliable and damn convenient.'

George expected a negative response but winced at the brutality of the facts. Things grew worse.

'If I have my flour delivered by train to the Crabbtree station way out there across the river, it's a real pain pushing the hand cart all the way there and back. It's murder in the rain. Your freight charges are pretty steep and you never seem willing or able to negotiate a better price. Oh and there's that Welshman, the one with verbal diarrhea.'

George went to speak but the businessman wasn't finished.

'I pay a cheaper rate to the trucking company who are happy to talk finance, they deliver to my front door, and the driver even hops down and gives me a hand unloading and placing the flour in the room out back. Now I ask, can you beat their price and service?'

With not a hope in hell of even coming close, George left. He remembered his uncle Fred explaining how the government fixed the charges railway companies could charge for freight allowing no room for negotiation. No such rules for trucking companies. Unfair!

George looked at his list of six business names but gave up after the second. The message was clear. For all the rail companies and especially the one he worked for, the situation with freight was dire. The Crabbtree branch was withering on the railway vine and it was only a matter of time before it died. He walked back to Crabbtree Station and returned to Whittleton with a heavy heart.

This SM lark ain't all it's cracked up to be.

He spent the rest of the day studying figures—passenger numbers and freight traffic movements. Whittleton held its own, just, but Crabbtree was a lost cause; few passengers and the odd item of freight. How long before the new company, the massive LNER stepped in and cut its losses? George said nothing to his staff on the platform and not a word to the boys on the Crabbie footplate.

With only two trains to and from London still to deal with, he sent the lad porter home to his Grannie in the village, and ducked home for his supper. He'd forgotten about his promise to Emily about her beau, and his cheeky comment about becoming a father. She most certainly remembered and told their mother. Both females waited.

In a sing song fashion, George entered the station cottage calling, 'Stand clear, train now departing on Platform 1!'

He heard nothing and reached the kitchen to see the table set for supper, his sister sat with a cat on her lap, and the dog sat in its basket wagging its tail. George's mother played with the cloth she used to take dishes from the oven. The women stared in silence.

George removed his overcoat and cap and paused. 'Somebody die?' he asked in jest.

Connie repeated his words. 'I'm going to be a father.'

George twigged. 'Ah,' he sighed, 'it's Emily the singing canary.'

'What's it all about, George?' demanded his mother. 'I can't believe it's true but if it is, you may be in serious trouble. If it's not true, your sense of humour is a disgrace.'

He begged his mother to go easy. 'I'm starving, Ma, I could eat one of your steak and kidney pies all by myself.' He grinned.

Emily didn't and snapped, frightening the cat. 'George!'

'Oh all right,' he surrendered and produced an envelope. 'You remember my friend, the former 2nd Lieutenant and now Lord George Carruthers.' He took out the letter. 'He and his wife have a baby boy and have asked me to be the wee lad's godfather.'

'That's not a proper father,' snapped Emily feeling cheated.

'It's a type of father,' protested George tossing the letter on the table with both women eager to read.

'Oh George,' snapped Emily, 'why are you so awful?'

'This is wonderful, son,' said Connie reading the letter. 'What will you wear to the christening?'

George blinked. 'I haven't a clue, Ma, but I'm sure whatever it is, you'll have me brushed within an inch of my life.'

Connie presented him with a warm plate and an even warmer meal. He salivated and began to eat. Emily honed in on her brother.

'Bert's coming around tonight.'

Despite having his mouth full, George managed to groan.

Someone knocked on the front door, and George groaned again.

'It can't be Bert,' said Emily distressed. 'I told him not before 8.'

'You wanted the job, son,' said Connie. 'In a village, the station master's cottage is home to anyone and everyone.'

Wiping his mouth, George tossed his serviette on the table. 'I reckon they watch till I come home, wait five minutes then knock on the door.'

'Please be kind, George,' begged Emily, starting to shake.

He headed up the hallway and opened the front door.

'Good evening,' said an elderly man with a weathered face overloaded with worry lines. 'My name is Gardiner and I wanted to make an appointment with the station master.'

If the saying about a dog looking like its master is true—or is it the other way round?—here was proof positive. The beagle was a dead spit for the elderly chap beside him, and they both had big ears.

'Good evening, sir' replied the SM. 'I'm George Miracle the new station master. How can I be of help?'

'Oh, forgive me for not recognizing you. I would like to speak to you about the garden at the railway station.'

George hesitated. 'Ah, there isn't a garden at the station, sir.'

'Which is why I'm here. Would you like one?'

'Oh,' said George not normally stuck for an answer.

'Forgive me calling at this hour but if you could grant me a few minutes any day this week, I'd be happy to explain my proposal.'

'How about in fifteen minutes at the station?'

The old chap was taken aback. 'Are you sure? It can wait.'

'I like to strike while the iron's hot, Mr Gardiner. Shall we say, 14 minutes and counting?' George smiled, his visitor smiled and the beagle studied both his owner and the SM. The men parted not knowing who was the more excited. George entered the kitchen.

'Who was that?' asked Emily.

'A local elderly chap I've not met before; said his name was Gardiner. I thought I knew all the residents of Whittleton.'

'With a beagle?' asked Connie replacing her son's plate she'd popped back in the oven. He tucked in trying not to speak with his mouth full.

'Yes, he wants to talk about a garden on the station.'

'He never goes out but works in his garden. He's been caring for his wife for years. She went into hospital recently and died last week.'

George stopped eating feeling rotten. 'Oh Lord, I wish I'd known.'

'His garden is magnificent.'

'I'm meeting him at the station in 10 minutes.'

'No!' cried Emily. 'You have to be here for your meeting with Bert.'

The sister's face oozed sadness and George felt terrible. He loved his sister and wanted to help her in any way he could. Her wedding was hugely important and he seemed to be treating it with little respect.

'Tell you what, Em, send Bert up to the station and we can sort out this permission business, and while he's there we can plan your wedding and honeymoon at the same time.'

She seemed ready to explode then saw his grin and wink and knew he meant well. 'Promise me you'll be serious, George.'

'I promise and I'll make sure *he's* serious. No bloke gets to marry my baby sister unless he's up to the mark.'

Emily put down the cat and went and hugged her brother. She went to her room with her eyes glistening. Connie couldn't stop her own tears.

'Your children are growing up, Ma,' said George finishing his supper. 'Smashing pie as always; thanks.' He put on his coat and station master cap. 'Wish me luck with young Bertram. This is new territory for both of us.'

As he headed back to work, Connie thought about her life's situation. It was changing again. Her husband and brother were dead, and her daughter would soon marry and move to a farm in the surrounding countryside. Connie picked up the elderly Trixie thinking at least the cat would never leave her alone.

Each of the amalgamated railway companies, the Big Four, wanted to be the best; the best looking, the best financially, publicity-wise and to be the fastest and safest. They planned and worked to win the crown. George Miracle's LNER made a terrible start.

The finest railway signaling systems in the world don't prevent driver error. A freight train in Nottinghamshire was slowly moving off the mainline to allow an express passenger train to race through. Crash! There were three men on the footplate of the express; driver, fireman and an inspector. All three died.

The report listed the cause of the accident as "Driver error". It was assumed none of the three men saw the red and at full speed, the express ploughed into the rear of the freight train.

Many passengers were injured with dozens suffering shock. The headlines appeared all over the country.

When George read the newspaper reports of the tragedy, a shiver ran down his spine.

Chapter 3

After leaving the railwayman's cottage, the elderly couple of Horace and Melville headed straight to the station. The master sat on an old GER platform bench with his beagle by his side.

George arrived and spotted them. 'Come through, Mr Gardiner, please.' Horace and Melville shuffled forward.

'I'm a bit stiff I'm afraid,' said the septuagenarian.

'I know the feeling, sir,' replied George patting his hip, and who had decided to do away with his walking stick and make light of his shrapnel-carrying injury. It was a sort of out-of-sight, out-of-mind self-improvement course which didn't always work. 'Take a seat please, sir.'

They settled and George met Melville who didn't say much.

'This is extremely kind of you, Mr Miracle. I thought I might be lucky to be granted an interview sometime next week so I'm grateful for your prompt attention.'

George worried about raising a certain topic. 'Mr Gardiner, I have only recently heard of your wife's passing. Please accept my condolences.'

A tear appeared in Horace's right eye. He grimaced and nodded, struggled to speak and managed a hoarse whisper, 'Thank you.' His raw grief remained close to the surface. George changed the topic.

'Now please tell me about your garden idea. I'm eager to learn.'

Horace sparked into life. 'I've long been a keen gardener, sir, and whenever I've travelled on the train, it seemed to me your platforms are the ideal setting for a garden with flowers and shrubs. With my wife being poorly and my own garden keeping me busy, I've never spoken about my thoughts before now.' He paused not wanting to elaborate on the loss of his wife of 54 years. George helped him.

'So you'd like to see Whittleton station have its own garden?'

'Exactly,' beamed the old man whose breathing became shorter as his enthusiasm and anticipation grew.

'I'll say two things, Mr Gardiner. I think your idea sounds wonderful but any decision to go ahead will rest with my employer, the London and North Eastern Railway.'

'Of course, we must do as our masters decree.'

George caught fire. Seeing this elderly man, obviously still grieving, but getting on with life and in an activity which gave him much pleasure, warmed the cockles of the SM's heart.

'My mother told me about your garden, sir, and was full of praise. To my shame I have not discovered its beauty but I will make sure that omission is quickly repaired.'

'You would be most welcome at any time.'

The station telephone rang and George went to answer it. 'Please excuse me.'

Horace stood. 'I'll leave you, sir, and send you something in writing.'

Before George could ask him to stay, Gardiner the gardener led Melville out of the office with both showing a spring in their step. It seemed the pooch was a good reader of his master's moods.

'Whittleton station, how may I help you?'

'Barclay here, head office.'

'Good evening, sir.'

'To whom am I speaking?'

'Station master George Miracle, sir.'

'I'm working late tasked with finding ways to cut costs for our new company.' George copped a sinking feeling in his stomach. Was this the bad news already? 'Your branch line to Craptree is listed as a possible closure. But reading recent reports, it would appear results are improving. Is that the case and, if so, how have you done it?'

'Actually the branch line runs to Crabbtree, sir, that's Crabb with a double b.'

'I can spell, my good fellow. Now if you've found some magic formula to turn around passenger numbers and boost freight turnover, we at head office want to know about it. You can send in a written report or we could have an inspector come out and give you the once over. Which do you prefer?'

George sensed a vision of being both the youngest station master and the shortest serving. *How on Earth does he think the Whittleton branch is improving? Chuffing hell, man, the opposite is true.*

'I could send you a detailed report, sir, with your permission.'

'Good show. Mark to my attention at Forward Planning. You could do your career a bit of good with this, Miracle. And stop hiding your genius in the engine shed. Good night.'

What genius? The telephone line went dead, a bit like the branch line, and George wished he was back being a porter without a care or responsibility in the world. He slumped in his chair feeling wretched when his future brother-in-law arrived.

'Hello, George,' said Bertram Culpepper dressed in his best and only suit, and all to ask a chap only three years his senior for permission to marry the station master's sister.

George stood and smiled. 'Bert, come in.' They shook hands. 'Come and take a seat.'

'I'd rather stand, if you don't mind.'

Shock hit George. Bert became a man with the weight of the world on his shoulders.

'Look old man, there's no need to be so formal,' said George aiming for a relaxed situation.

'My mother gave me strict instructions on how I should behave.'

'Oh,' said George with a twinkle in his eye. 'I've got one of those mothers.' Not a ripple or a titter from Bert who could have been mistaken for a man on death's row the night before meeting the hangman.

Right, thought George, *I guess we play by Mrs Culpepper's rules.* 'Please, Bert, ask away.'

The farmer remembered his well-prepared speech. Was it written by his mater? Did she require him to rehearse it before he was let loose on the village station master?

'Mr Miracle, ...'

Mr Miracle? He's only ever called me George.

'I would be deeply honoured, sir, if you would allow me to ask for your daughter's, *sister's* hand in marriage.'

George was about to say, "Of course, and good luck with her answer," when a bell sounded and the last Up was heard approaching. George hopped up. 'Sorry Bert, I must pop out and see the train departs on time.' He patted the poor fellow's arm. 'Be back in a jiffy.'

George stood on the platform as the train came to a stop. No passengers to embark or disembark and nothing in the way of parcels. The guard called.

'Can't you find something for me to do, Mr Stationmaster?'

It was said in jest, both the title afforded to George and the request for freight, but still George struggled to return fire. How could he joke about his tiny empire when part of it was about to disappear?

'We'll soon have plenty for you to do. Whittleton's due to thrive,' called George, giving the guard the nod to set the train on its way. The SM returned to the Coliseum and to his continuing bout with the nervous gladiator.

Bert stood there mute. He'd become a nervous wreck trying to make his speech. No sooner did he start then he stopped. His distress screamed. George took control, leading Bert to a chair. 'Sit'.

George sat opposite and smiled.

'Let's forget the speech, mate. I know Em loves you and wants to marry you. Your Mum is old-fashioned and wants to maintain the traditions. To save you the worry and stress of making a speech, let me say you have my permission to ask for my sister's hand. Okay?'

A mightily relieved Bertram Culpepper nodded although George sensed a flash of fear in his eyes. Bert whispered, 'Thanks.'

'You pop along, old man, and rest assured I have given a firm order. If the lady in question doesn't say "Yes" she'll be in serious trouble.' He paused and stared into Bert's eyes. 'Are we good to go?'

Bert still struggled to speak but did manage another nod.

George stood. 'Good show.' Bert stood. 'I'll be working here for an hour or more so you'll have no interruptions from me. Mind you, your future mother-in-law may well be lurking in the kitchen but you'll be fine. Off you go and good luck.'

Bert again whispered, 'Thanks,' then left sans enthusiasm.

George stared at the paperwork on his desk hoping some magical document would appear proving his rail empire had turned the corner and was blossoming. Nothing appeared. As he despaired about the situation, he heard a door knock and turned. Bert stood there looking bereft.

'Bert,' exclaimed George whose mind exploded.

Has he asked her and been knocked back? No, there wasn't enough time. So why is he back looking like his world has collapsed?

'I don't know who to ask,' whimpered Bert. George hopped up and ushered his future brother-in-law inside. They sat.

A sensitive young SM spoke softly and did away with any attempt at being funny. 'You're okay, Bert. Pop the question with a simple, "Will you marry me?" and Em will be the happiest girl in the village. Go on, away you go.' Bert froze. *Is a shove appropriate?* Bert's face now screamed fear. *What's the matter with the man?*

'You don't understand,' whispered Bert.

He was right. 'You don't know who to ask what?' asked George.

Bert took his time as he obviously struggled. 'I don't know anything about having sex.'

Chapter 4

What a night. George faced many problems. His future brother-in-law, the man who saw, even helped sheep, horses, cows and pigs mate, not to mention dogs, cats and rabbits, seemingly lacked any knowledge of human intimacy. Of course he knew the ins and outs of the process but didn't know the language, technique or etiquette.

His mates teased him and gave their cock-eyed descriptions of copulation but none satisfied the bewildered young man.

He couldn't bear hurting his true love and making a fool of himself. His father would laugh if his rugged son asked for help.

Bert's last and only hope was the station master. He would know and he wouldn't tell anyone about Bert's ignorance. "Come on, George, give us the good oil" was what he wanted to say.

For the SM, the funniest part of the request was the assumption that he, George, knew the facts of life. Again, of course he knew the basics but with a war and a war wound, he wasn't exactly prepared for much in the way of romance. In the language of love-making, if George wasn't Mr Ignorant, he was certainly Mr Inexperienced.

A terrible thought flashed into George's head. If anyone's been outside on the platform and listening to this discussion about sex, the SM and his sister's beau would be teased for a bit longer than eternity. He checked and they were alone.

George pretended he knew what he was talking about without being specific. If Bert twigged to the fact his teacher knew probably even less than the student, his sister might never receive a proposal.

After who knows how long, George reckoned Bert's fears were fading and to bring their torture to an end, urged him to take action.

'Listen, Bert, Em was expecting you half an hour ago. Get cracking and stop worrying about sex. You have to get married first.'

George winked and Bert relaxed even more, his heart pumping faster. 'Thanks so much, George, for all you've done. I'll be honoured to welcome you to my family.' The SM reckoned it was the other way round and gently directed the budding fiancé to the platform and then to the twenty yards or so leading to the station house. The light in the front room glowed bright. There sat Miss Miracle awaiting the new "fully-educated" Bertram Culpepper.

George quickly forgot the family marriage situation. He faced a major crisis. How on Earth did the chap from HQ in London come to believe the Whittleton branch was booming? Busting more like.

Where did he get the impression we're flying?

George drew up a list of possibilities.

1. Head Office has confused Whittleton and Crabbtree with another station and its branch which is doing rather well.
2. Mr Barclay at Head Office is a simpleton and doesn't know what he's talking about.
3. Owen Griffiths at Crabbtree has been writing reports which contain wildly inflated figures, and is sending such reports direct to London so as to try and save his job.

The station was quiet and the lamp on George's desk cast an eerie glow around his office. He gave himself some advice.

Forget family issues, George; solve this lack of business crisis or your branch line will be closed and your career as an SM damaged forever.

He didn't know which of his three theories about a supposed booming station was correct or even if there was another possibility, and went home hoping a new day would bring better news.

Opening the cottage door, he was surprised to see the kitchen well-lit, and wandered down the passage.

'Where have you been?' demanded his mother.

Before he could answer, his sister ran to him and hugged him with a ferocity he'd never seen before.

'Hey, what's all this?' he protested trying to remove her arms.

'Thank you, George. I knew you would say the right thing.'

He twigged. 'Ah, so Bert turned up did he?'

Emily held up her left hand and waggled her finger displaying an engagement ring.'

'Blimey!' exclaimed George. 'What a beauty. So you said yes?'

Emily slapped his arm and grinned again, her cheeks now aching from constant smiling.

''Well come on, son,' said Connie. 'What did you say to Bertram? He was like a new man. Tell him, Em.'

'He was so happy and confident and made the most wonderful proposal. I was shocked until Ma figured it out.'

George blanched. 'Was Ma there when he proposed?'

The indignant mother snapped. 'Of course I wasn't. They were in the front room.'

And you were listening from the kitchen.

Connie popped on her indignant face.

Emily kept badgering her brother. 'It must have been George, said Ma and of course it was. So tell us please, what did you say?'

At least this happy family event took George's mind off the difficulties with the branch line. But now he was in another quandary. There was no way he could tell his family what he told the young farmer. So switching to porkies it was.

'I told him the best thing that could ever happen to a chap was to find the right girl, and when he did, he should tell her how much he loved her and how he couldn't live without her and then ask her to marry him.'

The women were staggered at such romantic and poetic words from a railwayman, a bachelor and a romantically shy one as well, and moreover, someone they knew. Both females instinctively moved to the SM and hugged him as one.

If only they knew, thought George, *if only they knew.*

Next morning, a Wednesday, the first Crabbie pulled in with its regular passenger, Freda and her much-loved Irish wolfhound, Rufus.

The woman George walked through the rain to rescue from her outhouse spotted her hero on the Up and yelled.

'Hello, George!' She waved with gusto. Rufus barked with gusto.

With far less enthusiasm, George waved and waited for his number one admirer to cross the tracks. Rufus was released and leapt upon the embarrassed SM. Was it George's freshly and expertly shaved cheeks that prompted such licking?

Freda arrived and kissed George with nearly the same enthusiasm as Rufus. This was witnessed by the new members of staff, Gordon and Pip. Their minds raced. *Is she the SM's girlfriend? She's a bit old for the SM. Is this how passengers behave in this village?*

After settling the arrivals, George asked about the farm, and Freda gave him chapter and verse. As the platform was empty, he led Freda to a bench which still had its GER logo, and asked her to sit.

'What's happened?' she asked sensing a problem.

'There's nothing to worry about, Freda. I'm asking people who travel on the Crabbie how important the train is to them.'

She appeared aghast. 'They're closing the Crabbie!'

George panicked. He didn't want to shush her so tried to pacify her instead. 'No, no, no, it's the new company wanting to know more about their branch lines.'

Freda was on a roll. 'If they close the Crabbie, George, I'm sunk. I'll have to walk to Crabbtree and find a taxi which will cost a fortune.'

'You could catch the bus.'

'Bus? What bus? This isn't London, George, we're in the sticks.' She jabbed a finger towards the tiny loco across the platform and then at Mr Miracle. 'George, you've gotta keep the Crabbie.'

He understood and escorted Freda and Rufus from the station.

'Give my regards to your sister,' he called and waved her away making a mental note of when she'd return, planning to be absent.

His mood turned darker and he struggled with paperwork. When the next Down was due, he happily went over to the platform to try and take his mind off the problems.

About a dozen passengers alighted and George nodded to people saying, 'Good morning,' when he saw a face he knew. His smile was returned.

'Stephen,' said George, pleased he recalled the chap's name.

'Good morning George M,' said the passenger.

Some years ago they met at a reunion of World War 1 comrades being introduced by George Carruthers, now Lord Carruthers and father to George Miracle's godson, soon to be christened.

'Welcome to Whittleton,' said George remembering Stephen once lived here before being disowned by his father, Lord Fitzsimons, the man now in a wheelchair. 'Or should I say, welcome back.'

'Thank you, and may I say you look resplendent in your station master's uniform. But what's happened to your walking stick?'

George made light of the matter. 'On a railway platform, I'm as fit as a fiddle.'

Their laughter subsided when Stephen revealed the reason for his visit. 'My mother has asked me to come home because my father is unwell. I'm pretty sure he's dying, George.'

'I'm sorry to hear that. I did hear about His Lordship's riding accident. Please give him my kind regards.'

'Thank you and I understand you too have experienced sad news of late. George C and my mother keep me abreast of local news.'

'Yes my uncle, my mentor and the man who once ran this station has sadly passed away.'

Stephen indicated George in his uniform. 'To be replaced by the best looking and youngest station master in England.' George smiled. 'Many congratulations.'

'Thank you. Will you be staying long?'

'Not sure. But we must meet up for a drink. At least I know where to find you.'

They laughed, shook hands and Stephen walked out of the station to the manor house, Ripley Hall, once his home and inheritance.

Eric, the most experienced porter, was starting later that morning, and even though Gordon the porter and Pip the lad porter were new, George decided he would leave them in charge. He could hear his uncle. "What a damn silly move, George. If anything serious happens, you need to be there or at least close by."

He told his two new colleagues to contact Monty in the signal box and Desmond the gatekeeper if there was anything serious which needed attention.

'I'm going to Crabbtree on business. I'll be back on the noon train.'

The two new boys accepted their roles although the lad porter worried that without his boss he might fail to do the right thing.

Madge and Bobby were ready to depart. 'Morning boss,' they spoke as one. George climbed onto the footplate.

'I'm going to Crabbtree,' said George.

'It's awful mucky in here,' said Madge. 'There are plenty of seats in first class.' He grinned, revealing teeth which appeared much whiter given his sooty face.

'I want a word in private.' The crew exchanged glances. 'Will we be overheard as we travel?'

'As you're the only passenger, boss, and the Crabbie is famous for its misfiring and snorting sounds, there's not much chance of any eavesdropping,' said Madge.

The men worried. They knew George was being serious. He glanced along the island platform. 'Take it away, gentlemen.' With a healthy toot from the tank engine and a solid surge of steam, they departed.

Nobody likes to have the boss looking over their shoulder while they work but this was different. They weren't being assessed but rather quizzed. As the 0-6-0 settled at a steady 14mph, George let rip.

'Gentlemen, the powers in our new LNER have asked me about our beautiful branch line.'

Madge and Bobby took their eyes off the line and the firebox. 'Are we closing, boss?' asked Madge. 'Are you here to tell us we're gone?'

'No, at least not yet,' replied George spreading his feet to maintain his balance. 'Some chap in head office wants to know why our passenger and freight results are, wait for it, so good.'

'What!' exclaimed both driver and fireman as one.

'You mean why they're so *bad*,' said Bobby shovelling coal.

'Can either of you think why London has the wrong idea? Why would they think the branch is booming when the opposite is true?' The crew said nothing. 'This gent from Head Office was sure we were improving and setting an example for other stations. Why would he say such a thing?'

'No idea, boss,' said Madge and slowed as they approached Ruby, the small Halt and closest stop to Whittleton. No surprise there was an empty platform if you could call the carriage-length line of packed earth a platform. The train picked up speed.

'I'll have a word with Owen and see if he has any ideas.'

'You sure about that, boss?' asked Bobby.

George eyed him. 'Meaning?'

'Oh come on, boss, Taffy can talk underwater. He'll have a hundred ideas and excuses and not one of 'em will make any sense.'

George nodded. He knew all about Owen's tannin-laden tea.

The SM tried to enjoy the scenery. It was beautiful. He turned to admire a bird and his eye caught sight of a shotgun hiding in the corner.

'What's that?' he asked more in shock than ignorance.

Madge acted in a calm manner. 'Oh it's for any injured animals, boss.' George didn't follow. 'If some silly sheep runs on the track and gets hit, it's cruel to leave it there with a broken leg so we put it out of its misery.' There was a pause. 'We send a message to the farmer when we arrive back at Whitty.'

George decided the less he knew the better.

The next stop was Marlowe, a pretty little station and shock of all shocks, a woman with two children stood waiting on the platform. The Crabbie stopped and the woman nearly died when a chap wearing a uniform and a cap with the word *Stationmaster* thereon stepped out of the loco, greeted her and opened a carriage door.

'Good morning, madam.'

'Good morning,' she replied and herded her youngsters aboard. George went to close the door when the woman bellowed. 'Sidney!'

From the bushes behind the old carriage with no wheels, which served as a waiting room, a man, presumably the husband and father of the other passengers, hurried out buttoning his flies.

'When is you gunna build proper facilities on your station?' he enquired of the SM doubling as porter and guard.

George wanted to say, "When we find some passengers," but failed to answer, closed the door and rejoined the crew on the footplate. Nothing happened and the train sat in the station.

Madge quizzed the young SM. 'Are you the guard, boss?'

George twigged, peered along the empty platform, produced a whistle and blew it hard. 'Take it away, driver.'

Madge sounded the engine's whistle, the first time at Marlowe in ages, and grinning, set the Crabbie on its way.

The four passengers and the SM alighted at Crabbtree. Owen was stunned to see paying members of the public but more so when his boss stepped off the footplate.

'Good morning, boyo,' said Owen doffing his cap, the one without the word *Stationmaster*.

'Good morning, Owen. Please attend to the passengers.' They soon disappeared and Owen returned. 'Can I offer you a fine cup of tea, boyo?' he asked and George, without hesitation, declined.

'I'd like to have a chat, Owen.'

'Of course, this way, this way indeed.'

They settled in the porter's office which was more of a lean-to, and George cut to the chase.

'I've been contacted by head office in London who seem to be under the impression this branch is doing excellent business both in passengers *and* freight. Can you tell me why they have such an impression?'

'Well we have dropped a little of late,' explained Owen in all seriousness.

George remembered his uncle's attitude about always behaving in a professional manner and never allowing his temper to run free. 'Owen, please show me the passenger numbers for the last three months.'

'Three months,' said Owen searching for his reports. He stopped. 'Would you mind moving, sir?' George was blocking access to the only piece of furniture Owen used for paperwork. It was an old chair with loose folders piled in the *No particular order* formation.

George stepped aside noticing Owen's change of attitude. Gone was "boyo" to be replaced by "sir".

'Here they are, sir,' he said handing George the documents. They were inspected. George read what he already knew. He studied the porter. 'I know I've been a bit tardy in sending them up the line, sir, but it won't happen again.'

George looked at his colleague's face. 'Tell me one thing, Owen, and I want the truth, the whole truth and nothing but the truth.'

'Certainly, sir,' replied a now nervous porter.

'Have you ever sent any reports direct to head office in London?'

Owen's head shook. 'Never sir; I would never do such a thing.'

George experienced mixed feelings. He believed Owen but still couldn't solve the mystery. Why did London think this part of the rail network was thriving?

The Crabbie was ready for the return journey. George now carried Owen's recent paperwork covering both passengers and freight. It should have been sent earlier.

Surprising all four railway employees, three adults boarded the train. George went to the crew and told them he would leave them alone for the return trip.

He settled in the carriage and started to study Owen's reports.

They pulled in at Bridle Hill in case the passengers wished to depart. Nobody moved and so on they went. They passed the Halt at Pickling where Freda and Rufus embarked and disembarked on Wednesdays. No stopping today.

A few minutes later, George was deep in reading when he heard a gunshot. Startled, he came alive. The other passengers carried on chatting as if nothing happened. He stared out the window and nearly died. There was Madge, the driver, scampering into the adjacent field, grabbing a recently deceased rabbit, presumably his stew for tonight, and turning to run, well hasten back.

One of the passengers called out. 'There's a man out there.'

George knew there was and studied the reaction of the passenger. But to George's horror, the passenger wasn't looking at Madge but at Bobby the fireman. He too was off the footplate but on the other side of the train. He'd spotted a flower he long wanted to paint and jumped down to pinch a sample.

Never mind that taking certain flora might be against the law, the footplate on a moving train was unmanned. Unmanned! Railwayman free! George believed he was about to have a fit.

The train, the branch line train over which he as station master exercised control, was travelling its normal route as a runaway; it was a driverless train.

Now to be fair, the Crabbie didn't have any mountains to climb, and by setting the regulator to maintain its slowest speed, the humble engine would probably just about overtake any strolling ramblers.

George looked from one side to the other as both men headed back to the loco and disappeared from his view. He was decades younger than his late Uncle Fred but reckoned experiences like this could give the young SM a heart attack in the near future.

They reached Whittleton and George waited for the passengers to alight. He approached the locomotive.

The crew was relaxed. Their little escapade was a regular occurrence for both men. No harm done and normal goals achieved.

George paused trying to control his emotions. The men didn't blink. 'I'll see you both in my office in five minutes.' He stormed off, his limp more marked than ever as Madge and Bobby admired their recent acquisitions.

Eric came into George's office and collided with the boss's wrath. 'Do you know what I just saw on my Crabbie trip?' Eric copped both barrels. At the end of George's diatribe, he asked the experienced porter for advice. 'What should I do to them, Eric?'

'Nothing, sir.'

George stifled his rage. 'Nothing!' he spluttered.

'This is the countryside, sir. We do things differently here. Those two men have been on the footplate for more than 20 years, and do you know how many accident reports they've filled out?'

George couldn't stop his anger retreating. 'Let me guess; none.'

'We're on our knees already, sir. Why say anything when the line is finished anyway?'

George couldn't answer those questions.

'Knock, knock,' said Madge as he and Bobby arrived.

'You wanted to see us, boss?'

George considered them. 'Good trip, gentlemen. Thanks for the education. Now don't be late for your next run.'

The crew grinned and departed reckoning this young SM was a jolly fine chap.

Chapter 5

Christening Sunday for baby Carruthers drew ever closer. Connie approved George's choice to wear his station master uniform for the occasion. This was mainly because his military uniform showed signs of wear and tear, would not be appropriate, and his only suit was his late uncle's over-sized, out-of-date hand-me-down.

The plan was to meet at George and Valerie's massive home in Hampstead and travel in cars to the church as one group. George remembered their wedding consisted of eight people in total and guessed the christening party would draw a similar crowd.

He sorted staffing for the Sunday, the quietest day of the week timetable wise, and planned his trip. Up to London, try and avoid any mates at Liverpool Street, and then take either the Underground or Overground to the Heath and walk to Tudor House. Pray for no rain was the last item on his list.

He wrote to George Carruthers giving him the correct greeting of Your Lordship and asking about dress code. The father suggested the railway outfit stating, 'You'll be a hit, George. The girls love a man in uniform.' The last sentence gave the SM a few stirring thoughts making him both excited and worried. The book, *George Miracle's Love Life* was yet to receive an offer from any publisher.

Connie did her usual over-zealous brushing routine before George fled the cottage and wandered into the station knowing the next London Up was due in four minutes.

Eric, the senior porter was in charge. 'You're looking smart, sir. Will you be catching up with former colleagues at Liverpool Street?'

'Not if I want to be at the church on time,' smiled George who resisted the temptation to say anything about staff doing their best in his absence. The train arrived with George surprising the guard by climbing aboard the last carriage.

He alighted at Liverpool Street and tried to hide amongst the passengers.

'George!' cried a voice and in a minute, three former colleagues descended on the youngest station master in the LNER, in England. He received welcome slaps and a fair bit of teasing as to his new position. Mind you, when the news of his SM appointment was first announced, not everyone raised a glass to celebrate.

Men who'd served longer, much longer than young Mr Miracle, were still battling away at porter class. How come he rose to be an SM so soon and at his age? The word *nepotism* was bandied about.

One railwayman in particular was furious. He was a porter passed over for promotion several times, and now working at Chatham. Ralph Topliss heard about young Miracle's extraordinary promotion and took out his anger and frustration at home.

'Twenty-six years I've been a porter,' he seethed, 'twenty-six. This bloody upstart's in the job five minutes and is made up to SM, and he's about half my age.'

The disgruntled porter, a widower with a son, lived with his in-laws. They put up with his whingeing still grieving the death of their daughter. Topliss avoided conscription in the Great War because of it. Widowers with issue were exempt. George Miracle's promotion built resentment. "I didn't ask to stay at home," was Ralph's cry if ever asked about his lack of war service.

His mother-in-law gave him an idea. 'If you can't win promotion, you could try upsetting this Johnny-come-lately's applecart.'

The porter liked the idea but didn't follow. 'Wotcha mean?'

She shrugged. 'There's more than one way to skin a cat. Why not help the company drag the wonder boy down a peg or two?'

'And how can I do that and not get caught?'

She shrugged again. 'Find his weak spot. Give the London bosses a reason to think they've made a mistake. Embarrass the blighter.'

Mr Jealous breathed easier. His mind buzzed with plans to topple the SM who enjoyed a meteoric rise to the top.

If I'm not promoted, let's have Nepotism Miracle demoted.

Mind you there were many colleagues who admired the young SM and never begrudged him his success. They knew his minor limp was because of his war service, and that combined with his diligent work ethic made him a popular figure. They congratulated him with sincere enthusiasm.

He escaped his former workplace at Liverpool Street and arrived at Hampstead. The sky remained clear. He strode along the streets feeling chipper. Mind you, striding for George was never straightforward. His war wound pinged from time to time and his efforts to disguise a limp often failed. His pride pushed him to ditch the walking stick.

He well remembered the Carruthers' mansion. Many years ago, as a lowly lad porter, he struggled to open the massive iron-gate before setting off through the park-like garden. Once inside the mansion, the interior of the house was even more intimidating.

In the glorious library, the former Lord Carruthers and his good lady were furious when George delivered the message about their son having sailed for France to fight in the Great War.

Today the SM went straight to the front door; huge, impressive and appropriate for the wealth of the property and its grounds. He rang the bell.

A gentleman of senior years opened the door and stepped back. 'Good morning, Mr Miracle. Please come in.'

George was already impressed but more so being greeted by name. Standing in the massive foyer was a new experience. Last time, he used the tradesman's entrance.

'May I take your coat and cap, sir,' said the servant. As George dispensed with his accoutrements, a female voice filled the vast space.

'George,' called Valerie, and Lady Carruthers, the mother of George's godson, floated towards him, kissed his cheek and squeezed his hands. 'It's wonderful to see you again. You look marvellous. George and I are thrilled you have agreed to be wee George's godfather.'

Wee George? Not another George, thought George the SM. *Hello George, I'm George, meet George.*

'It's lovely to see you again, my Lady.'

She politely rebuked him. 'Oh stop all that my Lady nonsense. For you, I'll always be Valerie. Now, come and meet your namesake.' She took his arm and led him to one of the many rooms.

They entered the library and George's heart raced. This was where he delivered the message which set his friend George's parents aflame. Was his message the tipping point and cause of the brutal murder?

'Look who I've found,' announced Valerie and the SM became the centre of attention.

George smiled struggling to know what to say to the group of twelve people. From the group and moving skillfully on crutches came his older namesake. Lord Carruthers approached with his one and a half legs and a smile growing bigger.

He balanced superbly and embraced the railwayman with his free arm. 'My friend, my dear, dear friend, thank you again so much for agreeing to be our boy's godfather. He is the luckiest child in Christendom with you to guide him through life.'

A sense of warmth and happiness flowed around the library. Most of the baby's family and friends were delighted with the choice of godfather. George managed to mumble a greeting to so many people and was overcome by the friendliness of the guests. The parents of his godson sang his praises long and loud. Lord Carruthers announced.

'For those of you who don't know, this is my dearest friend, a war hero and the best station master in England, Mr George Miracle.'

The others applauded.

Bloody hell, thought George wondering what to say and do.

His Lordship led George to the other guests. 'Come and meet your fellow godparents. The beautiful young woman, Valerie's bridesmaid at the wedding, was one godmother along with Valerie's maternal grandmother. George smiled and nearly bowed feeling the wealth and class of the others to be way above his humble upbringing and current status. The biggest surprise was the fact that he was the only godfather. Two godmothers but only the station master to lead and care for the lad from the male side of the family.

Goodness.

Sherry was served and George found himself the centre of attention. Valerie's parents and their son he'd met at the wedding during the war, and they wanted to know about his current life seemingly much impressed with his job status.

'You must be exceptionally good, young man,' said Valerie's mother, 'to be appointed a station master at such a young age.'

George tried hard not to sound too humble.

They were interrupted by Lord Carruthers' uncle, the MP he met at the wedding. 'I see now why you never needed to ask for my help,' said the politician. 'Congratulations on what is obviously a brilliant career.'

'Thank you, sir, but I do believe you may have put in a good word for my uncle a few years ago and I am most grateful.'

'Well my offer still stands. If you ever find yourself in a spot of bother, I will be disappointed if you don't contact me. Do you still have my card?'

'It's in the top drawer of my desk, sir.'

'Good man.'

A small bell tinkled and the elderly gent who welcomed George at the front door made an announcement about the cars being ready.

George waited to follow the others when Valerie approached holding her son in a mass of garments and a christening blanket.

'Now godfather George, may I introduce you to godson George.'

The baby stared at the SM and, as only a perfect newborn could do, flapped his arms and smiled. Under explicit instructions from his mother in Whittleton, George leant forward and whispered. 'How do you do, young sir? I'm looking forward to getting to know you better.'

Another smile from the babe saw his mother and godfather join the grinning game. Everyone headed outside.

There were several cars all large and solid. The drivers were well dressed and helped the party into the vehicles. George Carruthers had drawn up a list of cars and their occupants. George Miracle waited back until his name was called. He moved to the opened back door, entered a car and froze. Already seated in the back seat was a young woman who smiled and made him stare. He thought she was the most beautiful woman he'd ever seen.

'Hello,' she said and held out a hand. 'I'm Louisa.'

George could hear his mother loud and clear. "Do not shake a lady's hand, simply hold it for a brief time and do so gently.'

'How do you do, I'm George.'

He released his light grip but couldn't stop his insides jogging.

'I've been told I'll be travelling with the godfather.'

'You are,' managed George with his heartrate continuing to rise.

Their car set off and George couldn't remember a darn thing his mother mentioned about making small talk. It was no matter because Louisa took over.

'And a station master,' she said surprising George.

'You have me at an advantage, Miss. I did meet several family members at George and Valerie's wedding but you could not have been there as I would certainly have remembered someone so beautiful.'

George froze. *What the hell am I saying? Is that proper small talk? I can hear Ma yelling at me all the way from Whittleton.*

His companion smiled. 'You and I are probably the only members of the christening party who are not family.'

Why couldn't I say something sensible like that?

'I'm the companion to Lady Carruthers, and as the boy's godfather, I suppose we'll have to work together from time to time.'

George tingled and wanted to say, "I can't wait," but didn't and smiled and tingled again.

The christening service was short, sweet and successful. The photograph of the parents, the baby and the godparents came up a treat and when a copy eventually arrived in Whittleton, Connie and Emily pored over it for an age. All their questions when George arrived home were asked again as they pointed to the various people.

George said not a word about the lady's companion he met. He kept wondering when his first godfather duties would be required giving him reason to travel to Hampstead and to possibly meet Louisa whose family name he never discovered.

He considered asking George or Valerie about the young woman but shyness beat him back. *How can I discover more about her?*

The event in London was a wonderful distraction from his problems at work and, in particular, the failing branch line and its false and inflated figures. He alighted at Whittleton and went straight to his office.

On his desk lay a large envelope with his name clearly written in a beautiful Round Hand script. It wasn't official mail and there was no stamp on the envelope. Curious, he removed the contents discovering a hand-written covering letter, again transcribed in perfect Round Hand script, and then several pages each containing an illustration; some pages displayed two drawings.

Horace Gardiner kept his word. His letter explained the proposal for a station garden with detailed illustrations of his vision. What a gentleman. What a proposal.

A tear appeared in one of George's eyes. The illustrations were exquisite, the entire garden setting he thought was breathtaking, and all the woes of losing the Crabbie disappeared as the SM wandered metaphorically around his new station. *This is marvellous.*

During his trip to London, the Whittleton station and its branch to Crabbtree ran without a hitch.

Eric gave his boss a report. 'All trains on time, sir, and not a complaint or lost parcel to be seen.'

'Are you telling me, Eric, I am redundant?'

Eric smiled, well, moved his lips a tad. Eric was never big on grins.

'You have a couple of gifts though, sir.'

'Gifts?' asked George both curious and worried.

'There's a piece of art and a freshly skinned rabbit over there.'

Eric pointed and George inspected. The illustration, a water colour of a flower local to this part of the county, was superb. George knew little about art but loved the painting and wanted to display the work in his office; he wanted to show it to the whole village and beyond.

A more practical gift was the rabbit calling out to be the basis of a stew for his supper tonight. His main thought was about Eric who told him not to give the Crabbie driver and fireman a bollocking when they left the footplate while the locomotive was still in motion. Their response was heart-warming and George wondered if Eric played a part. He did.

George picked up both gifts, and the envelope containing Horace Gardiner's gardening vision, and headed home. The shortest of walks still gave him time to rejoice.

The reaction of his family continued well into the night. As if the report on the christening wasn't enough, the food, art and garden plans kept the conversation going for hours. The rabbit stew filled bellies and warmed hearts.

Emily's news about the banns being read for the first time next Sunday drifted in and out of George's mind. Right now it was filled with the image, clothes, words and scent of a woman called Louisa.

Chapter 6

George walked to Horace Gardiner's cottage situated on the edge of the village and facing open fields. George opened the gate and stopped to admire the layout and beauty of the garden.

'I thought I heard the gate,' said Horace coming around the side of the cottage wearing a huge sun hat and well-worn, soil-stained gardening gloves. 'I've been meaning to put some oil on those hinges all week.'

'Good morning, sir,' said George doffing his cap. 'I've come to thank you for all the work you've done in creating your wonderful proposal.'

'Do you like it?'

'No, sir, I love it. Your attention to detail is superb and I hope with all my heart we can make your vision a reality.'

The elderly gent seemed ready to cry. 'Thank you,' he whispered overcome with emotion. 'I am so pleased because I'm well aware my vision may not suit everyone.'

'As I mentioned when we first discussed your proposal, I will need to obtain permission from Head Office in London, and I wonder if we might discuss some of the finer points.'

'By all means, Mr Miracle; please come inside.'

Horace led the way to the back door, the usual entrance for country folk, and George followed him and Melville into a charming country kitchen. Horace made tea while George admired the quaint layout of the cottage. Its magnificent garden was on view from every window.

George took out a notepad and prepared to write. 'If you could give me an idea of the cost involved, sir, it will make my letter to the company complete.'

Horace became both shocked and surprised. 'Oh there's no cost,' he said.

George stared at him. 'No cost? But surely there are many materials not to mention the plants.'

'Yes but I will supply everything without charge.'

Now it was George's turn to be both surprised and shocked. 'Everything?'

Horace explained. 'It's my way of saying thank you to the village for being so kind to me and my wife over all these years.' George's mouth opened and stayed so. 'I have the soil from my garden as well as the shrubs and flowers. Over the years I've collected rocks and discarded railway sleepers for use in my garden, and some of the sleepers can be moved to the station.' He smiled. 'They'd be returning whence they came.'

'You are extremely generous, Mr Gardiner, but surely labour costs will be involved. You can't possibly transport all the material to the station. And there's the labour involved in construction.'

Horace placed a cup of tea on a saucer on the table. Mrs Gardiner admired fine bone china and cared for it with a passion. 'Help yourself to milk and sugar.' He opened some kitchen cupboards. 'I'm sure there are biscuits here somewhere. Yes, here they are.' He popped them on a plate and placed it in front of the SM.

'Thank you,' said George still wanting to talk money.

'I have another idea and wondered if you think it possible.' George found his admiration for the elderly man continuing to grow. 'It would be wonderful if we could have a working-bee; ask the villagers if they'd like to help create the station garden.'

George beamed. 'That's a brilliant idea, sir.'

'It would get the project moving and further develop a community spirit and sense of pride in our village. Do you agree?'

'Now you're asking a silly question. How could I not give my full support to someone who has a vision for something beautiful and the generosity and skill to make it happen?'

Horace struggled to speak. He was a gentleman in the old-fashioned meaning of the word. George extended his hand. Horace, surprised at first, turned joyful and naturally responded in kind.

After their tea-drinking, George left promising to give his new friend any news as soon as it came to hand. As he headed back towards the station he reflected on his life in the country. His greatest satisfaction came from the people he lived amongst and served, with Horace Gardiner being a perfect example.

He turned into a street he remembered well, being the scene of his first major incident at Whittleton. He lost a puppy, found another, and then found the lost one. Disaster turned into triumph and it was all thanks to an eccentric villager, Septimus Oldmeadow.

George stopped outside the gentleman's cottage and decided to bid the dear man good day. The first time he knocked on this door, its limerick-reciting resident appeared with fun and laughter oozing from his bewhiskered face. George knocked.

Silence. He waited then knocked again.

'Go away,' called a sullen voice from inside.

Go away? What happened to the hearty, welcoming bonhomie?

'Mr Oldmeadow, it's George Miracle from the station.'

Silence. 'You mean the former porter who lost a puppy? Didn't I hear you're now the station master?'

George worried. The puppy swap had remained a secret all these years and George wanted it kept so. He whispered. 'Yes sir, it's me.'

Footsteps were heard and then the door opened about halfway. Septimus peered around the frame, his face sullen and afraid. 'Come in,' he said without any warmth.

George entered. 'Are you all right, sir?'

'No, I'm in the depths of despair. Come in and tell me what you think of my latest, and I believe greatest, brew.'

George knew this routine from when he first called, and drinking alcohol while at work was a strict no-no but these were exceptional circumstances. The poor man obviously needed help.

Seated with a glass of homemade "poison" in his hand, George waited for the horrific news which had brought the man with an effervescent personality to his knees.

'My secret is out,' was all he said.

George's curiosity climbed even higher. 'I don't understand, sir.'

'My reputation as a bon vivant and creator of laughter-filled limericks is ruined.' Tears appeared in his eyes.

It's obviously serious thought George *but what has happened?*

'I've won the Currer Bell Medal.' Now he *did* cry.

George's face became blank. *What's the Currer Bell Medal? Why has winning something caused such sadness?*

'I'll be honest with you, Mr Oldmeadow; I have no idea what you're talking about.'

Septimus perked up. 'Really? Well that could be good news. If the rest of the world know as much as you, I might be all right.' He looked at George who thought he was being insulted. 'Righto, here's an explanation for a station master who's never read a book in his life.'

George reacted. *Fair go, I've read lots ... well, a few.*

'The Currer Bell Medal is a prestigious literary prize given to an author who has produced a body of work, over their lifetime, deemed to be an invaluable contribution to literature.'

'And that's you?' Septimus nodded. 'Well many congratulations, Mr Oldmeadow, and I for one will now seek out your books and read them with interest.'

'Really?' replied Septimus now genuinely pleased. 'You may have made me a happy old man.' Then in a flash he turned morose. 'But if they discover I'm the creator of nonsense limericks, instead of rewards, I'll receive ridicule. What sort of serious novelist produces such tosh?'

'Such tosh? I thought the limerick you recited the day we met was witty and funny.'

Septimus gasped with pleasure and surprise. 'You did? You do?'

'Indeed, and why can't both types of writing exist side by side?'

'Oh the joy of ignorance,' exclaimed Septimus. Somehow George still didn't feel insulted. 'My dear sir, the world of literature and publishing is replete with jealousy, revenge and schadenfreude. Some who didn't and never will win will delight in exposing my scribbles.'

George didn't understand the explanation and certainly not the word *schadenfreude*.

'I'm still a bit confused, sir. I mean how can you keep all your work a secret?'

'By using a nom de plume. All my novels are published under the non-gender name of P. J. Beaufoy. In that sense I'm like Currer Bell. My mailing address is care of the post office in Crabbtree. My publisher is under pain of bankruptcy should he reveal his client's identity. But don't you see? If P. J. Beaufoy is announced as Septimus Oldmeadow the limerick writer, I'll be a laughing stock. This literary prize will become a curse, a millstone around my neck.'

George blew air; the information overload whacked his brain.

'Well all I can say, sir, is the world should hear of your literary triumph, and I for one as a proud resident of Whittleton, will delight in shouting your success from the rooftops.'

This time Septimus sparked up. 'I say, what a splendid fellow you are, station master Miracle. Let me top up your glass.'

Without hesitation, George grew a backbone. 'No, sir, please, I am in uniform and drinking on the job is a sackable offence. You wouldn't want your greatest admirer to be forced from Whittleton in disgrace, would you?'

'Oh heaven forbid and please do forgive me, sir. Now, are you in need of a puppy or a kitten perhaps?'

George smiled. 'Thank you, but not today, and now I must depart. Again my heartfelt congratulations and I look forward to reading your prize-winning books, even if they were written by this chap Beaufoy.'

'Or woman,' added Septimus with the sparkle back in his eyes.

'Good day, Mr Oldmeadow.'

'Good day, sir.' He whispered. 'And you won't betray my little pen name secret will you?'

'I have no idea what you mean.' Their laughter was contagious.

As George returned to the station, his heart warmed to another resident of this small village where creativity and a love for life were alive and well. He heard the Crabbie whistle as the loco returned on time. He tried to hurry but his hip told him to forget such a move.

Madge crossed the tracks and knocked on the SM's door. 'There's some mail for you, boss, courtesy of the pretend SM at the pretend Crabbtree station about a mile from the real Crabbtree village.'

'Thank you, Madge. Is everything okay?'

'All good, boss.'

'Oh and thank your mother for the rabbit and tell John Constable I reckon he should give up his day job.'

Madge managed a smile of embarrassment and disappeared. George opened the envelope and studied the Owen reports. They did not make for good reading. Depression filled the office.

These are far worse than I imagined. Head office has got this seriously wrong. The branch should have closed yesterday.

As George considered pulling out his hair, lad porter Pip appeared holding the dirtiest kitten in East Anglia.

'Found it under the signal box, sir; could be abandoned. I'd be happy to care for it as our station cat, with your permission, sir. A good mouser will always do its station proud, sir.'

George's foul mood overwhelmed him. 'Yes, yes, whatever.'

Pip didn't hang around waiting for the SM to change his mind. The boy set up a bed in a box in the storeroom with two bowls; water and sardines. A small box with sand was for other essential activities. He wanted to name the cat Miracle but thought he'd be pushing his luck so settled for Whitty.

Pip put a sign on the closed door, *Cat Inside*, and then hurried back to the Down platform to greet the next train from London.

George faced two issues. The first was the dreadful mix-up over the status of the branch line where solutions seemed few, if any, and he now reckoned his first achievement as a station master would be to preside over the death of a railway.

The second was painless and filled with hope. He wrote to Head Office regarding the plan for a station garden. He described the proposal in great detail, listed all the positive outcomes to be expected, and finished by pointing out the entire project would be of no cost whatsoever to the company. He sealed and addressed the envelope and wandered out to the Up platform. He knew the next train was due in three and a half minutes.

Eric approached asking if everything was all right. George seemed a million miles away. The possible imminent demise of the branch bored a hole in the heart of the SM. Eric departed, confused.

To the guard he handed the envelope addressed to Head Office. 'It's important, Michael,' said George. 'Please don't lose it and please make sure it reaches its destination.'

'Right you are,' said the guard sending the train on its way.

The phone rang in George's office. 'Barclay here, Miracle. I've received the latest report from your little branch line at Craptree. Damn fine figures, man. You're setting an example for all the smaller lines to follow.' George didn't know what to say. 'Hello? Are you still there, Miracle?'

'Yes sir, I'm still here.'

'I've spoken with my chief and he agrees an inspection is needed. After that we may send a journalist and photographer to capture your little gold mine and tell the country how one small corner of the great LNER is setting the world alight.'

Once more George was struck dumb.

'Hello?'

'Yes sir, I am listening to every word you say.'

'Well you don't sound too excited, man. You station master chaps are supposed to lead from the front; rally the troops and all that bally malarkey.'

'Yes sir.'

'I'll arrange this visit and once we have the right people available I'll let you know the day. Cheerio Miracle, and once again, congratulations on your great success.'

The phone went click and George's heart went clunk.

I am a dead man walking.

Something was clearly wrong. Head office reckoned the Crabbie was booming when in fact it was bust. It was currently trading while insolvent. But why, *why* did Head Office think otherwise?

It's not Owen and it's not me. Where is this wrong data coming from and who is responsible?

To try and solve the mystery, George would have to take time off, go to London and how would he explain such a move? If someone discovered him playing detective, it could mean awkward questions. But if Head Office discovered the branch line reports were pure fiction, his career could be over. Either scenario could see him at least demoted and possibly dismissed.

Thank God Uncle Fred is not here to witness my demise. And worse, if I'm demoted or dismissed, I will lose the station cottage and my family will be living on the street. Talk about a spectacular fall from grace.

Chapter 7

Despair best described the young SM. His problems mounted. Was it always darkest before the dawn? He slumped at his desk when someone knocked on his open door.

'Can you direct me to the station master?' asked a young man.

George saw the smiling face of Stephen Fitzsimons, the disinherited son of Lord Fitzsimons. George's spirits soared.

'Stephen,' he cried shaking hands with the former local. 'It's lovely to see you again and welcome to the Whittleton inner sanctum.'

'I knew if I ever came home I would have to see the youngest station master in situ.' They laughed and George wondered what was meant by *in situ*.

'Please have a seat and tell me your news.'

Stephen hesitated causing the mood to darken. George continued to ignore his mother's advice about not asking personal questions.

'How is your father? I hope his riding injury is not too much of a burden.' George winced at his blunt words. Stephen didn't mind.

'Lord Carruthers told me you were a wise man. "Mr Miracle is a fine fellow and clever to boot," he said. "If ever you want someone beside you in a trench, George Miracle is your man".' The SM was lost for words. Stephen continued. 'And your namesake is right because you are spot on. As I may have told you, my mother asked me to come home because my father is, I regret to say, not long for this world.'

'I'm sorry,' said George thinking of the time when his father died without warning on his, George's 12th birthday.

'He's dying, George. The injury from his fall damaged his spine which has created all sorts of health problems but the doctor thinks he's dying of a broken heart. The poor fellow has never forgiven himself for ordering me out of the family home in disgrace only to discover, like you, I served my country in time of war.'

'That's very sad, Stephen. Is there any chance you might help your father forgive himself?'

'I'm hoping I can do just that but pride and self-pity are powerful foes. He's been moved to the cottage on the estate with a live-in nurse. My mother and I visit daily.'

George grimaced. It was a tricky and tragic situation. 'Good luck,' he whispered.

'You're a canny fellow, George Miracle. The families Carruthers and Fitzsimons have histories with Shakespearean-like tragic scenarios and here you are, a station master in a small rural village, privy to the hidden details of the aristocracy.' George didn't know what to say. 'So tell me, is a station master required to be an expert on the private lives of railway passengers? Are you an expert on all secret even intimate matters?'

'I hope not. It was a coincidence I met George at Liverpool Street in 1914, and I only met you through him.'

'And it's a happy coincidence for both me and Lord Carruthers.'

'So, may I enquire if you are to return to live in the manor house?'

'You may and I am, George, and I plan some major changes.'

George bucked up. 'I see.' He didn't see but certainly wanted to.

'You wouldn't know this but years ago the estate ran a successful winery. The vines are still there although in bad shape. I plan to restore them and resume the business of making our own vintage.'

The SM buzzed. 'How marvellous, Stephen. I wish you much success.'

'George, if all goes to plan, there'll be employment for folk in the district and possibly plenty of freight for your railway. How does that sound?'

George sensed tears appear. 'In a word, it's marvellous. I cannot tell you how happy your news makes me feel. Things are not going well here and particularly so with the branch line. And to make matters worse, I'm pretty sure someone is trying to bring me undone.'

Stephen's interest piqued. 'Why? What have you done?'

'Nothing, at least nothing I'm aware of.'

'Can I help?'

George hesitated. 'Thank you but probably not.' There was a pause and George decided to tell all hoping a trouble shared would indeed become a trouble halved. 'Between the two of us, Stephen, the passenger and freight results for the Crabbie are terrible yet some unknown person is sending reports to London with greatly inflated figures. Head Office reckons our failing branch is flying.'

'I don't understand.'

'Nobody does. It's the great unsolved mystery. Head Office is planning a visit to what they believe is a booming branch line and when they arrive, they'll discover the truth leaving me to explain the mess, which I can't.'

Stephen pondered the situation. 'Could it be someone is jealous of your promotion to station master at such a young age?'

George paused, thinking. 'Possibly but if true, I have no evidence. And when the company discovers the real situation, at best I'll look a fool, and at worst, I'll be seen as incompetent and could even be sacked.'

Stephen considered his answer. 'Well apart from uncovering the snake in the grass trying to do you over, have you thought about making the false reports true?'

George floundered. 'I'm sorry, Stephen, I don't follow.'

'Why is the Crabbie failing?'

'For two reasons; the line was poorly planned in the first place finishing far from its village, and now the road haulage chaps are offering cheaper rates and door-to-door service. We can't compete.'

'Okay then why not offer something the road haulage companies can't?' Still George didn't follow. 'Why not make the branch line a tourist attraction?'

George stared. *What is this man suggesting? And why does he have ideas, even if a bit loopy, when I have none?* Now George wanted details.

Stephen seemed to be thinking on the run. 'We're in the same boat, George. Your branch line and my winery are both down for the count. Let's combine forces and work together. I'll offer tours of the winery and you can offer trips on the Crabbie.'

George thrilled at his friend's enthusiasm but saw a multitude of problems.'

'But if your vines are in poor condition, won't it take years for the next vintage to arrive?'

'It will but we have hundreds of bottles in storage. They could and can be sold tomorrow.'

'You would do that for the Whittleton station?' gasped George.

'No, I would do that for the Ridley Hall estate but people have to get here and the railway is the ideal mode of transport. I could have picnic facilities on the estate and wine tastings in the cellar, and you could have excursion trains on the weekend.'

This time George's beating heart outpaced his thinking. 'I don't know what to say.'

Stephen kept going. 'If the LNER reckon the branch line is booming, why not make it boom? The bastard who's trying to stitch you up will have done you a favour.'

George endured mixed feelings of delight and concern. 'You mentioned excursions on the branch line. To where? I mean it's like many branch lines; it goes nowhere and the locals rarely use it.'

Stephen's brain came alive. 'What about the old Druid site near the Pickling Halt? You could run tours and have the curious discover how ancient Druids worshipped not far from Whittleton.'

'Once again, Stephen, I have no idea what you're talking about.'

'Freda will know. Have you met the rather fierce woman, always dressed in homemade clothes, who runs a farm out near Pickling?'

George nodded. He knew her somewhat intimately. 'She is one of the Crabbie's few and most loyal passengers.'

'Have a word with Freda. She knows the history of the place.'

'I will and thank you for all your ideas and kindness.'

'We can help one another, George. Two "old" soldiers with their problems could join forces and set the world aright. You set up a day for your station and I'll tag along and join the party.'

George couldn't stop grinning and thanking his friend. 'I could call it the Whittleton Station Day.'

'Not too flashy but it hits the nail on the head,' enthused Stephen.

They shook hands with vigour, with George's grip relaying his gratitude, enthusiasm and relief the visit brought. He loved the idea of a special day for the station, a Whittleton Station Day.

'Oh, I nearly forgot the reason for my visit,' said Stephen. 'Lord and Lady Carruthers are making noises about coming to stay for a few days. I'm under strict instructions to tell the godfather of their son and heir, his presence will be required and no excuses whatsoever will be accepted.' He grinned. 'Message delivered.'

George grinned. 'Message received and understood, sir.'

Stephen departed and George found his feet shifting despite his dicky hip. Was he dancing? *The Crabbie might yet survive and better still, Louisa might be coming to Whittleton.*

When George arrived for his supper, his mother looked him over. 'You look like you've lost a penny and found sixpence,' she said.

'It's been an interesting day, Ma,' he replied heading off to ablute.

Emily called. 'We need to start rehearsing, George. I don't want to leave it to the last minute.'

He returned, lifted the cat, Trixie off the SM's chair, sat and tucked a serviette under his chin. 'Rehearse what?' he asked knowing full well the answer.

'For the wedding, you rotter,' she hissed.

'What wedding? Who's getting married?'

Emily tossed a piece of bread which struck her brother's chest.

'All right, enough,' snapped their mother.

'It's only a walk down the aisle, Em. Since when has a walk needed a rehearsal?'

'With your limp, George, I don't want you standing on my wedding dress.' He knew she was serious. It was her big day and there were times when his balance could be described as wonky. Standing on the bride's train would be equivalent to derailing another type of train.

'So how is young Bertie boy? Still as keen as mustard is he?'

'Enough, George,' said Connie serving the meal of lamb chops, mash and peas. They launched into the food.

'Lovely, Ma,' said George.

'Yes, Ma,' said Emily. 'And tomorrow will you teach me how to make a steak and kidney pie please?'

Connie paused and turned serious. Her children tensed, sensing something important was about to be announced. They looked at their mother and then at one another.

'I want you to know I've asked Mr Beckwith to accompany me to the wedding. He has kindly agreed to do so and I'm telling you now so as not to surprise you on the day.'

John Beckwith was a deacon at the Whittleton church. Never married, the semi-retired solicitor lived alone in the Whittleton cottage, bequeathed to him by his parents, in which he was born 58 years ago.

Connie's children froze then overcompensated by speaking over the top of one another.

'That sounds wonderful, Ma,' said George.

'He's such a lovely man, Ma.'

'Good,' said Connie, 'that's settled then.'

The eating resumed in silence. Worried, Connie's children were thinking the same thing. *Does our Ma have a beau?*

Emily broke the silence. 'But what about you, George? You're playing the role of the father of the bride and you'll be all on your own?'

'I'll be fine, I'm a big boy now. I can take care of m'self, thank you.'

'It's easier for a man being on his own,' said Connie.

George paused. 'Any way, I may not be on my own.'

What? Cutlery hit the table as jaws hit the floor.

'Not on your own?' asked Connie using a Sherlockian-like voice.

'You *have* got a girl, George Miracle. I told you he did, Ma.'

'Have you, George?' fired back his mother.

George answered his inquisitors. 'I said I *may* not be on my own.'

Emily attacked. 'So there *is* someone. What's her name? Where does she live?' She turned serious. 'Have you kissed her?'

'Emily,' reprimanded her mother who paused. 'Have you, George?'

Mr Innocent answered. 'Have I what?' His stomach took unusual and unprompted action. He reckoned Louisa, whatever-her-surname-was, would be the perfect girl for him. But liking her was a million miles from her becoming his partner at Emily's wedding. Too late, he'd dropped a hint.

'We need to arrange the seating plan, George,' said the bride-to-be. 'You can't just bring some girl at the last minute.'

'Some girl?' retorted George. 'That's a bit rude, young lady.'

'Do we know her?' asked Connie. 'Is she from Whittleton?'

'No,' said George and instantly regretted his answer.

'Ah,' replied Emily, pointing. 'So she does exist. I bet she's from London. All those trips up to town were not always for work. Come on, George,' now pleaded Emily. 'You must tell me the name of my future sister-in-law.'

Both females stared at him. His pulse got busy. He knew the lady in question was coming to Whittleton soon and such news helped kick-start his heart. He might be able to ask her then. If she accepted his invitation, he would go to Hampstead and escort her to Ridley Hall then, on the day of the wedding, collect her and take her to the church. That would be the best thing ever.

She would be on her own for the short time he was involved in the service but then he could be by her side for the rest of eternity, er, the rest of the day.

'Her name, George, please,' begged Emily.

He drove his sister mad. He shook his head. 'Darn,' he said pretending to be annoyed, 'you know, I can't remember.'

Next morning he called a meeting with his three porters and gave instructions. 'I have some business on the branch. As you know, the situation is bad there but I'm fighting tooth and nail to keep the Crabbie running. I'll be a couple of hours, three at the most. Please make sure people and parcels are treated professionally. Remember a smile costs nothing and can do a power of good.'

He caught the first Crabbie, told the crew he was disembarking at Pickling and typically, enjoyed the carriage on his own; not a paying passenger for love nor money.

Before they set off, Madge politely enquired. 'Checking the facilities on the Pickling platform are we, boss?'

George glared at him. 'Actually I'm trying to save your jobs.'

Boy, did that flatten the crew on the footplate.

At Pickling he disembarked and waved the loco on its way. Not a passenger, not even a living soul within sight.

Chapter 8

As George arrived at Freda's farm, Rufus barked and bounded towards the SM. This was the best news for the wolfhound. His favourite railwayman had come a calling.

'Rufus,' bellowed Freda who stopped chopping wood when she spotted the visitor.

'Good morning, Freda,' called George.

'And to you but George, I've now learnt how to sit on the pan and remain upright. You've been given a bum steer, me lad.'

They laughed and Rufus grinned.

'I need your help, please Freda.'

'And a cuppa,' she replied and led him inside.

Once settled, he explained. 'Remember how I told you the Crabbie might be in trouble, Freda, well I'm afraid it's true.' She slumped on the table and groaned. 'But we're not giving up without a fight. Someone has suggested we might attract people as tourists if we can develop the site used by the Druids.'

'The Druids!' she exclaimed. 'What nonsense is this you're saying?'

George worried. 'You don't like the idea?'

'My dad reckoned them a bunch of silly old buggers. "Sacred site, my arse," he'd say. But then he'd say, "If people wanna believe in somethin', why not the equinoxes"?'

George didn't know the word. 'We simply have to find a way to encourage people to travel on the Crabbie. If the passenger numbers don't return, you'll be walking to Whittleton.'

Freda could no more walk to Whittleton than skip to Skipton.'

'So what's your plan?' she asked.

'I know nothing about the Druids or their site. Someone said you were the expert.'

'Who's this someone?' George waved a dismissive hand. 'The site where they met is on old Danny Wight's land an' he won't have a bar of anyone, especially tourists an' ramblers traipsing over his place.'

George's heart sank. His only plan failed before it began.

'But I know something about Danny Wight that'll shift him.' She winked at George. 'If you think back to your famous outhouse rescue, George, and multiply it by a hundred, then I've got plenty on Mr Creepy Wight.'

George's heart leapt back into the land of hope. 'You'll have a word with the farmer?'

'*We'll* have a word,' she snorted. 'I want the Crabbie firing and so does Rufus.' The dog barked his firm and total agreement. 'Let's go.'

All three—Rufus went everywhere with Freda—reached the Pickling Halt with Freda leading the way. 'It's only about 20 yards into the woods.' They reached a clearing with three large stones. One was huge. 'This is where the Druids came to worship.'

'It's certainly convenient to Pickling.'

'Which ain't got the best conveniences in the world,' said Freda and George worried. 'You can't have people coming out here as tourists and giving them next to nothing, George. Having the rocks is one thing, but you'll have to do some work on the privy.'

'Thank you, I'm aware of the situation.'

Ten minutes later George, Freda and Rufus arrived at Danny Wight's farm. It was as if God the Farmer shuffled a collection of ramshackle sheds and sprinkled them from above. They landed in odd places and conditions and so stood where they were today.

Which is his home? thought George.

'Danny!' yelled Freda.

The man appeared and George was stunned because despite his windswept appearance, unshaven face and unwashed clothes—*did he sleep in them?*—the man wore a tie.

'This is the station master at Whitty, Mr Miracle,' said Freda.

'Good morning, sir,' smiled George prepared to extend his hand.

Mr Surly didn't do polite or niceties. 'Wotcha want?'

'Tell him, George.'

'We would like to bring people to visit the site where the Druids used to worship. There would be a path from the Pickling Halt and no-one would be allowed to go beyond the site. May we have your permission, sir, to enter your land? It's all for a good cause. We wish to keep the Crabbie running. As station master, I would be prepared to offer you and your family free travel on the Crabbie.'

'What family?' sniffed Danny.

'Or freight conveyance at a greatly reduced rate,' added George desperate to gain Danny's permission.

'What freight?' from the still sniffing farmer.

Freda killed the chat. 'Danny, Christmas 1913,' was all she said.

George saw alarm and fear in the man's eyes. 'You keep 'em away from me pigs,' he sniffed, disappearing into a higgledy-piggledy shed.

'You're a lifesaver, Freda,' said George as they headed back to the Halt. They stood on the tiny platform with its basic amenities. Under the name PICKLING, George envisaged a smaller sign, *Home of the Druids*.

His heart rate gathered speed. Something was happening. Of course it may not work but having a plan gave him hope.

'The privy needs more than a clean, George,' said Freda.

'We'll do what it takes, Freda,' he replied with his heart overruling his head. Before he could add another word, the distinctive sound of a steam engine's whistle called from a distance. The sound penetrated across the fields as the Crabbie approached on her run home.

'I'll leave you to it, George,' said Freda who stepped towards him, planted a sloppy kiss on his lips and took off home. 'Rufus,' she cried and the poor hound despaired. He too wanted to deliver a kiss to his favourite station master but when the mistress calls, we go.

As the tank engine approached, George didn't extend his hand to hail the locomotive. Madge and Bobby saw their boss—how could they miss him?—and brought the train to a halt.

'Do you have a ticket, sir?' asked Madge with a serious face.

George pointed at the crew. 'You are going to stop at this station a lot more in the future. Mark my words.'

'Is it a station now?' asked Bobby. 'Has always been a Halt to me.'

George peered inside, saw the shotgun, carefully collected it and wandered back to the carriage. He opened a door, took out his whistle and blew it hard. 'When you're ready, gentlemen,' he called and climbed aboard.

At Whittleton, he returned the firearm, waved to Monty in the signal box and to Desmond the gatekeeper, and returned to his office. Eric knocked and entered.

'All clear, sir?' he asked hoping for news from his boss.

'Eric, I'm working on a plan to boost passenger traffic on the Crabbie. Nothing's been decided yet but I'll tell all of you as soon as I have definite news. Now if you'll excuse me, I have a letter to write.'

It was addressed to a Member of Parliament. Twice now, the uncle of the one-legged George Carruthers offered his help to George Miracle. Twice George didn't respond. Now he decided to cash in.

Without going into details, George asked for a meeting with the MP. 'It is,' wrote George, 'a matter of some urgency.'

He decided to use the Royal Mail and walked into the village and posted the letter. Coming out of the post office, he met Septimus Oldmeadow a.k.a. P. J. Beaufoy on his way in.

'Mr Miracle,' exclaimed the writer. 'What a joy to see you, sir.'

'Mr Oldmeadow,' smiled George. 'I trust you and your writing are both in fine form.'

The chap with the white whiskers dropped his voice. 'So far, so good, dear sir, so far, so good.' He patted his nose with a forefinger and disappeared into the post office.

Ever since Stephen Fitzsimon's ideas about the winery and the Druids, George wished for more ideas, more ways to draw people to Whittleton for his Whittleton Station Day. In the street, he found one.

Septimus Oldmeadow could be a drawcard for book lovers. They might flock to Whittleton to meet the award-winning author. He could sign their books and, once here, they could take the Crabbie out to Pickling.

Thanks to the shrapnel in his hip, George never skipped, but even so he bounced back to the station.

The lad porter occupied a bench with two children. They were patting Whitty the station kitten rapidly turning into the station cat. Pip worried when he spotted his superior but relaxed when the SM nodded and smiled; if the station cat amused the passengers then long may Whitty reign.

A letter lay on George's desk. It was from head office with the LNER address on the top left corner. *Not the date for the inspection* groaned George fumbling to retrieve the missive. *Not so soon, please.*

His fear turned to joy. It was advice approving the construction of a garden at the Whittleton station.

George shouted, 'Yes!' causing those outside to turn towards his office. The letter listed the restrictions such as not covering station signs and notices, not creating a danger for passengers, and requiring the company to not incur any costs including maintenance.

George couldn't wait to visit Mr Gardiner and share the brilliant news.

The 18:06 Down departed after which George would normally slip home for his supper. He popped in to tell his mother he first needed to run an errand. Knocking on Horace Gardiner's cottage door saw him start to shake. Giving good news was always exciting but this was something special. His station, the one he ran, would soon have a wonderful makeover with beauty for all. There was no reply.

He knocked again with still no reply. *Of course, he's out the back* thought George and headed through the garden.

'Hello,' cried a voice. George saw a woman by the side fence. 'Are you after Horace?'

'I am,' replied a worried George.

'It's Mr Miracle isn't it?'

'Yes,' replied George now definitely worried.

'Horace is poorly and has gone to the hospital in Attleborough. I'm looking after Melville and the old chap misses his master terribly. Can I help?'

George muttered his thanks but declined the kind offer as disappointment swamped his thinking. With a heavy heart he limped home. Whenever his spirits took a battering, his limp became pronounced.

His mother and sister noticed his mood.

'What's happened son?' asked Connie.

'Mr Gardiner, the man with the glorious garden, is in hospital.'

Both women reacted with concern.

'Will he be all right?' asked Emily.

'What will happen to the station garden?' asked Connie.

'Don't know,' said George not daring to think if the man he hoped would work wonders may now be unable to do anything.

'I don't mind if you leave the rehearsal early,' said his sister. George grimaced. 'Oh George, you've forgotten.' It was true, he had. 'A girl doesn't marry every week. Why can't you take my wedding seriously? Pa would never have let me down.'

Her remark hurt mainly because it was true. George tried to make amends. 'I'm sorry, Em. I'll be there and on time. A station master is never late.'

The meal was eaten in silence until Connie announced she was going to London this coming weekend. 'I'll be home in time to make your supper,' she said leaving her children, especially her daughter, more than curious to know why she was going and more so, why she wouldn't say so.

'Are you going by train, Ma?' asked George.

'Yes, Mr Beckwith is taking me to a choir concert in the Royal Albert Hall. He'll be singing in the Norfolk All Male Choir.'

Both Connie's children could see their future changing before their eyes. Apart from a few months working in Norwich, George had always lived at home, and Emily never left her mother's side. If their mother re-married, how would her new status impact their lives?

Emily's fiancée waited in the wings. George dreamt of his girl.

Next morning he received a phone call from the agent of the MP, Mr Edward Carruthers, with news about George's appointment next Saturday morning at the politician's surgery in Chelmsford. He studied the timetable and planned his day.

He rang the hospital where his favourite gardener was a patient asking about the old man's health.

'Are you family?' asked the nurse.

'No, I'm a friend from his village, and Mr Gardiner is helping me with a garden at our station.'

'Oh, are you Mr Miracle the station master? Mr Gardiner hasn't stopped talking about you.'

George gasped. 'Is the gentleman all right?'

'He suffered a dizzy spell and fell. A neighbour called an ambulance and I'm pleased to say he's resting peacefully.'

'I'm glad to hear your news,' said George feeling much better.

'But I think he'll be pretty much restricted in his future movements. His gardening days may well be over.'

Crash went George as his spirits collapsed. 'Will you please give him my kind regards and wish him a speedy recovery.'

'I'll do so, sir.'

'Oh but most important of all, please tell him the company has approved the station garden.'

'The station garden has been approved,' repeated the nurse making a note. 'I'll pass it on, sir. Good bye.'

George drifted in a kind of no-man's-land. *The proposal is approved, Horace is alive but incapacitated. What next?*

Come Saturday morning, George took the train to Chelmsford and his appointment with George Carruthers' uncle.

The MP shook the SM's hand. 'I was beginning to give up on you, young man,' said the politician.

'Good morning, sir, and thank you for agreeing to see me.'

'I haven't agreed to see you, Mr Miracle but to help you. Now there are others waiting so tell me what I can do.'

George liked this style of behaviour—cut unnecessary chatter and put your cards on the table. The SM explained the failing branch line and his plans to revive its fortunes with the Whittleton Station Day. 'My major problem, Mr Carruthers, is I know nothing about running such an event or advertising.'

'Easily fixed,' he said and George became excited when handed a business card. 'This chap's the man to see. Tell him I gave you his name and jolly good luck to you.'

He stood, they shook hands and George was ushered outside. The whole meeting was over in less than two minutes.

Boy, how efficient, thought George. *Why can't I make decisions and get things done like that?*

The name of the man recommended by the MP was Mr Oswald Fortune who happened to be a cousin of Mr Carruthers. His contact details were a business address, a company in the City.

George wanted, no needed to strike while the iron was hot. Writing to the gent could see a letter delayed, the man might be ill or on holiday in New Zealand. *I must knock on his door here and now.* George hopped on a train to Liverpool Street. Then it hit him.

Oscar Wilding! Of course, why not the lost son of Daisy from Norwich? Oscar is a broker for an advertising agency. He is perfect and he knows me, and he and his family love me for reuniting their family. Forget the MP's cousin, go straight to Oscar in Cricklewood. George's main problem was to avoid former workmates at Liverpool Street. He peered out the window as his train pulled in. The coast seemed clear. He waited until several passengers walked past his carriage then slipped out and mingled, heading towards the exit.

Near the barrier, a distinctive voice was heard. 'George Miracle.' A familiar face stared at George. 'As I live and breathe.'

The former ASM now SM at this station, Jack Rogers, spotted his former colleague. George stopped and returned the warm greeting.

'Station master George Miracle,' beamed Rogers. 'When I read of your promotion, young man, my only reaction was to ask why it took him so long.'

'You're too kind, sir. And I see congratulations are in order for you as well.'

'None of this sir business, George, we're equals now. Call me Jack. Now come and have a cup of tea and tell me the story of your life.'

George wanted to politely refuse but couldn't. This man helped him when George was a mere lad porter. He even saved George's career when accused of theft from Lost Property, and he knew George's Uncle Fred and for that reason alone, the young SM couldn't refuse.

In the SM's office where George experienced many a scary moment, they chatted a little about the now-forgotten war, Uncle Fred Carmody, the demise of the Great Eastern Railway and much more. When Rogers asked George if he faced any problems, he decided to unload his major concern.

'Somebody is trying to do me over.'

Rogers was instantly alert. 'Tell me,' he said and listened as George explained the inflated Crabbie reports.

'I have no proof but think it might be a jealous colleague, someone upset by my promotion at such a young age.'

Rogers stood. 'Leave it with me, George. I'll have a sniff around. There are a few nasty blokes on the rail. Now it's wonderful to see you again, but as you know, we SMs never have time to scratch ourselves.'

They laughed and George left feeling better than good. Jack Rogers was a true friend as was Oscar Wilding. Was there a chance the young SM might escape the mire?

At the Wilding home in Cricklewood, George was greeted with open arms. The three children knew their second Grannie was found thanks to this railwayman. After the whole family hugged him with enthusiasm, George was alone with Oscar.

'I don't wish to be a nuisance, Oscar, or take advantage of our friendship.'

Daisy's son snapped. 'Stop all that nonsense, George. Anything I can do to help you will never come within a bull's roar of repaying the gift you have given me and my family. Now, how can I help?'

George explained his idea for the Whittleton Station Day and mentioned the Druids' site, the wine-tasting at the manor house, the station garden and the local award-winning author.

'Is there anything else?' asked Oscar taking notes.

George's heart glowed. 'No and the garden is still only a plan, and the author may not wish to participate.'

'Then you must persuade him.'

'I can't thank you enough, Oscar.'

'I haven't done anything yet. So you need to win over your author and confirm if the garden is going ahead. Once I have your say-so, I'll write copy for the newspapers. Some photos would help.'

'I'll find someone.'

'Good man. Now come and have some lunch.'

It was a cracking meal in great company and on the train back to Whittleton, the young stationmaster purred.

He thought about the MP who gave him a tip but not for long. He thought about his mother and daughter and their respective romances. He thought about his own love life which didn't exist—yet. George Miracle now dwelt on his new hopes and dreams.

Chapter 9

George called a meeting of his porters, the Crabbie crew, signalman Monty and gatekeeper Desmond. 'Gentlemen, the next train is due in eight minutes so I'll be brief. Since the amalgamation of the railway companies, and my appointment as SM, a number of events have taken place.' The others were hooked. 'Business on the Crabbie has hit an all-time low. On current figures, our new employers must seriously think about closing the branch.'

'I knew it,' said Madge.

'Damn,' muttered Bobby.

'But something strange has happened. Head office believes the Crabbie is booming.'

'What?' exclaimed Monty. 'How do they figure that?'

George let rip. 'Because someone is sending reports to London with wildly inflated figures.' The others buzzed.

'It's that silly Welshman at Crabbtree trying to keep his job.'

'It's not Owen,' said George. 'I have someone investigating the mystery and while it continues, we are fighting back.'

'Tickets,' cried a voice from the platform and Eric departed.

'I'll wait till Eric returns,' said George. 'I want you all to hear this.'

A strange silence settled in the SM's office with the tension broken by a loud meow. Whitty the station cat fancied a feed and announced the fact. Lad porter Pip picked up the animal and nursed it as Eric returned. George continued.

'Gentlemen, there are three new proposals to boost the Crabbie and to give us all a new lease of life.' He paused and could see the expectation on their faces. 'We're going to have a station garden.'

The news didn't set the staff afire. *Is that all?* they thought.

George persevered. 'Ripley Hall is to revive its vineyard and open its cellar for wine tastings and sales.' A little interest peaked.

'Will they employ anyone?' asked Desmond. 'My missus would like a job.'

'Mr Fitzsimons tells me they definitely need a workforce and will advertise locally.'

Now there was a buzz in the room.

'And we have plans to establish a tourist spot near Pickling where people can inspect the historical site used by the ancient Druids.'

'A tourist spot at Pickling?' said Madge with a healthy dose of skepticism. 'There's nothing there, boss.'

'There will be soon, Madge,' said George, 'and to get the ball rolling, you and Bobby can upgrade the privy.'

A barrage of laughter reverberated around the office. A warning bell sounded announcing a train had entered their area, and the meeting broke up. George called.

'Keep all of this under your hat, gentlemen. Mum's the word.'

'Mum's the word, hey?' asked a voice outside the office. 'Sounds interesting.' Stephen Fitzsimons appeared grinning.

'Stephen,' said a delighted George. 'How are things? How is your father?' The mood dropped.

'He refuses to go to hospital and wants to die in his own bed.' George gave a solemn nod. What could he say? 'But I am also the bearer of good news, George. First, plans for the restoration of the vineyard are going ahead.'

'That's brilliant!'

'Our former vintner has agreed to return to work and I'll advertise for vine workers and cellar staff in the local newspaper.'

'That's wonderful!'

'And more to the point, Lord Carruthers and his family arrive next Friday and you, my friend, are invited to dinner. His Lordship has threatened to come and drag you from the station if you do not appear.'

'You leave me no choice,' said George grinning but with an accelerating heartbeat. *Will the lovely Louisa be there?*

'I'm told 7.30 for 8 is the instruction for guests.'

'Oh damn,' grimaced George. 'I don't own a dinner suit.'

Stephen pretended to be shocked. 'What! That's outrageous!' He grinned. 'Come as you are, George; you're among friends. Now how are you getting on with all your plans to turn Whittleton into the tourist hot spot of East Anglia?'

'Slowly,' said George. 'One problem is the creator and inspiration of the station garden is unwell and may not be able to work on his dream. He's produced some dazzling illustrations and it's such a shame to fall at the final hurdle.'

'Well please remember the Hall and its selection of fine wines is ready to be a part of whatever you do.'

'Thank you again,' said George.

A train approached and Stephen took his leave. 'Friday 7.30 for 8, George and don't be late,' he called heading home to Ripley Hall.

As George Miracle planned his tuppenny-ha'penny schemes at his tuppenny-ha'penny Whittleton station, and the impoverished and run-down Crabbtree branch line, his employer, the London and North Eastern Railway was thinking big; seriously so.

In 1923, when the LNER came into existence, the company appointed a talented mechanical engineer, Herbert Nigel Gresley CBE. He rose through the ranks at various railway companies but in terms of design, his best was yet to come.

Tucked away on his rural station, George and his staff couldn't even imagine the types of locomotives Nigel Gresley would design. With LNER rail lines running from London to Edinburgh, powerful locomotives were required. But as well as speed, the LNER wanted style and the Gresley designs sported glamour in spades.

In the LNER grand scheme of things, magnificent locomotives, luxury carriages and record speeds were its top priorities. There were no thoughts and certainly no plans for the moribund Crabbie branch.

Horace Gardiner recovered but it seemed he would never again bend or kneel to dig his flower beds or reach up to trim his beloved climbing roses. It wouldn't be until 1929 that the Local Government Act encouraged local councils to care for frail people in their homes.

So with home help from neighbours, friends and the church, he returned to his cottage to live out his days in relative comfort. But without his garden to work on, his heart suffered from the condition of sadness.

George followed the old man's progress and when he discovered Horace was home, called to see him.

The gardener opened his back door grasping a stick to steady his balance.

'Mr Miracle,' he beamed and urged the young man to enter.

George made the tea, and they sat and talked. 'I am so sorry, young man,' said Horace, 'but my heart and legs appear to have gone on strike.'

'Ah but your spirit is thriving, sir, and long may it do so.'

Horace appreciated George visiting him and being so positive. 'I still think the station garden is a good idea and would work but alas I must retire from the project.'

'It's not a good idea, Mr Gardiner, it's a grand idea and I've been thinking, sir. If the workers are available could you become the supervisor of the project?'

The idea hit Horace like a punch. He gasped dropping his cup in its saucer. 'Are you serious?'

'I am never more so, sir. You could have a wheelchair on the platform and staff to move you around enabling you to ensure the beds are dug where you want them, the pots positioned properly and the plants planted exactly as you would do yourself.'

George saw the old man's eyes glisten before a tear then another rolled onto his face.

'I would love such an opportunity, sir. You have made an old man very happy.'

'And me,' said George standing. 'I'll put together a group of station volunteers and when they're ready, we'll make a start. The station is quietest on a Sunday. Will such an arrangement suit you, sir?'

Horace's face screamed pain. 'On the Sabbath, Mr Miracle; you want to work on the Sabbath?'

George bit his tongue. 'I'm so sorry; forgive me for being ignorant and inconsiderate. Of course we'll find another day.'

'It's not a problem for me, but if you want community support, it's best to avoid upsetting those folk who are religious.'

Of course, of course, you idiot.

'Let's make it on Saturdays,' said George and Horace's face shouted "Yes!" 'I'll pop round as soon as we're ready to start.' He stopped at the door. 'You take care, sir, and we'll see your wonderful garden built in next to no time. Cheerio.'

Back in his office, George produced two copies of the same notice. It read as follows.

Whittleton Station Garden

The London and North Eastern Railway has approved the creation of a garden at Whittleton Station. Local resident, Mr Horace Gardiner, has designed a beautiful layout and will supervise its construction.

Volunteers who wish to help create the station garden are welcome to attend the first working-bee at the station on Saturday August the 12th from 2pm.

You can register your interest in the project at the Whittleton station at any time.

George Miracle
Station master

He headed into the village and placed one notice on the Public Notices board in the High Street then popped into the post office and asked the postmistress if she could display a copy. She read it, smiled and willingly agreed. Now all he needed was a response.

He glowed with pride. Running an efficient station would always be his top priority but why not run an efficient station boasting a stunning garden? Why not give the residents of the village something to enjoy and be proud of?

On a high, he remembered his unfinished task; of course—Septimus Oldmeadow. He was next on George's list and another of the ways to give his village and its trains a boost. These projects thrilled him and then he remembered. Next Friday he was dining at Ripley Hall with the families Fitzsimons and Carruthers and, hopefully and best of all, with the adorable Louisa.

His heart soared then experienced a sharp pain. A dagger loomed ready to plunge into his heart.

What if she's not there? Worse, what if she is and is already spoken for? Or worse than worse, what if she doesn't feel the same about me as I do about her? Ahhhh!

At home, life changed gears and took what he thought was a dangerous course. Emily wanted to talk wedding plans and did so constantly although now she faced competition.

Connie wanted to talk about the deacon, Mr Beckwith. Now she stopped calling him Mr Beckwith switching to John. Her children exchanged glances; they worried.

'John has been asked to be a lay representative at an important meeting of bishops next year. It's a great honour.' Her children gave a supportive endorsement.

'I'm sure he deserves such an honour, Ma,' said George speaking on behalf of his sister.'

'Where is the meeting held, Ma?' asked Emily not really wanting to know but wondering if her mother would attend.

'I think it's at Lambeth Palace in London.'

The silence spoke volumes. George chose to change course. 'I have some news. Mr Gardiner is out of hospital, back home and keen to supervise the building of his garden at the station.' Talk about underwhelming responses. 'I've displayed notices calling for volunteers. You and Bert could join us, Em.'

'I'm not a gardener and Bert's a farmer,' she retorted.

'Who has a tractor,' said George. 'We could do with some help shifting soil and pots and plants.'

He smiled but she showed little interest.

'Oh and next Friday, Ma, I'll be dining at Ripley Hall.'

That statement produced a response complete with face changes. 'I thought His Lordship was poorly,' said Connie, fishing for details.

'He is but his son is hosting Lord Carruthers and his family and they insisted the godfather be there.'

'Good for you,' said Connie and then reverted to her usual question. 'But what will you wear, George. Do they dress for dinner?'

'They do but Stephen told me not to worry. He said I'll be among friends.'

'You can't arrive wearing your work clothes, George. If you move in upper class circles, you must follow the rules and dress for dinner.'

'Ma, I'm not in their class and never will be. George and Valerie asked me to be the godfather of their son, not to wear a dinner suit.'

Connie gave up and the atmosphere cooled until Emily rocked the boat. 'Will your unnamed girlfriend be there?'

George's reaction gave him away. *How did she know that?*

'Aha,' said Emily pointing at her shocked brother. 'I believe I should come along and meet her.'

Connie snapped. 'Emily, don't be so childish.' A peace of sorts settled and Connie, true to form, put her sticky-beak oar in again. '*Will* she be there, George?'

The poor station master lost his temper and tossed his serviette on the table. 'Oh for pity's sake, there *is* no girlfriend.'

He stormed out leaving the women staring at one another.

George slept badly and in the morning left for the station before his mother and sister were out of bed. Spike became confused. Dogs like routines.

The SM potted in his office making notes of work he needed to do. He prepared another list of the activities he wanted for his Whittleton Station Day. The only outstanding item was Septimus Oldmeadow. If George could persuade the eccentric writer to reveal his true identity and give book readings and signings, people might come from far and wide to meet the award-winning novelist.

Come on, Septimus, let yourself go.

As the trains came and went, George was out and about supporting his staff and greeting passengers. He stared at the empty platforms trying to imagine them as the Garden of Eden, well, as a smaller version of Horace's glorious English country garden.

If he could solve the mystery of the branch line false reports, and win over Septimus, life might, just might be on the up.

The morning proved normal when the Crabbie came in after its first trip on the branch. George stepped onto the Up platform, looked across to the branch line hoping to see any passengers disembark at Whittleton. As usual he saw no-one; not a single passenger.

He expected it but eased his depression about the terrible results and false reports by thinking about the planned tourist site near Pickling. With Oscar's advertising expertise and knowledge of newspapers and writing copy, surely this might entice people to travel on the branch. Certainly, patronage couldn't be any worse.

He stopped his paperwork duties when Madge appeared.

'Morning boss,' he said with a glum face.

George developed a skill of reading faces. 'What's wrong?'

'We stopped at Pickling on the way home and took a look around.' George frowned. Madge spoke quickly to allay the SM's fears. 'Only for a couple of minutes because there was no-one on board.'

'And?'

'There's bad news about the site for the Druids.'

George steeled himself. 'Has the landowner fenced off the area?'

'Didn't see no fences but them rocks you reckon were used by the Druids have been painted.'

'What? Painted?'

'It's in big letters, boss. *DRUIDS ARE DUMB.*'

Chapter 10

Sherlock Holmes was the man for this job. Someone was writing false reports and sending them to the LNER in London pretending to be the SM at Whittleton. Someone defaced the proposed tourist site making it a laughing stock for visitors. Someone was out to destroy George Miracle. But who? And why? And how?

George planned a later trip on the Crabbie, and told Madge to say nothing about the vandalism.

Alone, a scary thought entered the SM's mind. He'd told his colleagues to keep the Pickling project under their hats. Did one of them blab to George's nemesis? Was one of the Whittleton employees a vandal? Who else knew about the plans for tourism at Pickling?

He studied his desk calendar. Next Friday seemed to be printed in a bright colour. It was the date of his dinner invitation at the manor house. It was his chance to be with friends and possibly one in particular. Thinking about the companion of Lady Carruthers stopped him concentrating.

'Parcels!' cried a guard and George 'awoke' and fled outside. His hip screamed. The guard on the Up was unloading parcels himself when a porter should have been by his side. George remembered he was filling in this morning but his romantic daydreaming prevented him from doing his job.

'Many apologies, Henry,' said George taking as many of the parcels as he could. 'It won't happen again, I assure you.'

'You're all right, George. And good to see you're no longer wearing short pants.'

Both men smiled as George waved the train on its way. Eric arrived early and George took advantage. 'I need to pop into the village for a few minutes, Eric. Do you want my station master cap?'

Eric would never want such a cap, knew his retirement drew ever closer and willingly provided cover for his boss. George walked as fast as his hip allowed heading to the home of the reluctant writer. People always said "Hello" or "Good Morning" in this village but now they stopped the SM.

'I'll be there on Saturday, Mr Miracle', and 'Looking forward to helping with the garden, sir', and 'I think the station garden is a wonderful idea. Good luck with it all.'

With a spring in his step, on his good leg, George knocked on the door of the man he desperately wanted onside. Would he again be miserable?

From the back of the cottage came a familiar sound.

There once was a prize-winning author
Whose novel was reckoned a snorter
But critics did sneer, with a jeer for a cheer
Spilling beer leading snobs to their slaughter.

George's heart caught fire and more so when Septimus opened the door and produced his magical smile.

'Good bell-ringing bicycles, it's the station master himself.'

'Good morning Mr Oldmeadow.'

'Come away in, young man and take a glass of my latest vintage.'

George entered in trepidation. If he kept up this practice of imbibing when in uniform, his walk on the slippery slope would only become worse. He managed to avoid accepting the home brew by raising the subject of making the real Septimus Oldmeadow famous. To George's surprise and delight, Septimus announced his news.

'You're too late Mr Miracle. My publisher and I have reached an agreement. P. J. Beaufoy is to come out of hiding. My true identity is about to be exposed.'

'How wonderful, sir. May I ask what brought you to this momentous decision?'

'You did.'

George gasped. 'Me? Surely you jest, sir.'

'You were the straw that broke the camel's back. I've long worried about my serious work being mocked once Beaufoy and Oldmeadow were revealed as one and the same, and the person who wrote award-winning novels as well as nonsense poetry. Literary critics will say I can't possibly be taken seriously.'

'But they've already given you a prestigious award.'

He grinned. 'I know and isn't it marvellous?'

George copied his grin. 'It is indeed.'

'What better way to poke a literary snob in the eye, hey? When you queried my stance the other day, it made me think. Be yourself, Septimus, I said. If anyone wants to condemn your work, good luck to them. Crack on with life, my son, and enjoy what you do.'

'Bravo,' said George applauding. 'I'm thrilled to my back teeth, sir, as my dear old gran used to say.'

'God bless your dear old Gran.' He turned to the cabinet. 'Now let us celebrate my new identity with a glass of …'

George hated speaking as he did. 'Mr Oldmeadow, please, I must decline your splendid hospitality.' The old man's face turned to shock, more at the emphatic way his visitor spoke. 'As station master I am required to follow strict rules. Consuming alcohol when at work is a sackable offence.'

Septimus seemed to slump. 'My dear fellow, how selfish and stupid am I? Please do forgive me.'

'Think nothing of it, sir,' said George trying to restore their previous happiness. 'I am here to ask for your help in saving the branch line to Crabbtree.'

'Of course, anything, but what can *I* do?'

'Give a public reading from your books.'

'Is that all? Of course I will. When and where should I be?'

George beamed. 'Mr Septimus Oldmeadow, you sir are a gentleman and a scholar, and it is a privilege and pleasure to know you.' Their smiles and handshake sealed the deal. 'I'll let you know the date and venue.'

'Excellent,' beamed the author, excited his cloak of anonymity was about to be lifted and his public reading would launch the new man.

George went to leave but on the wall noticed a photograph of the homeowner taken many moons ago.

'You cut a fine figure there, sir.'

He laughed. 'Ah, the days of dark hair and dark dinner suits,' he laughed. 'Both are long gone, thank goodness.'

'I'm attending a dinner at the manor house this Friday and my mother insists I wear a dinner suit which I do not possess. But I'm going to behave like you and defy my critics, the snobs of fashion.'

'Why? Whatever for?' George froze. 'Wait,' said Septimus, disappearing. 'I'm sure it's here somewhere.'

He's not, is he?

Septimus appeared holding a dinner suit. 'Needs a bit of a clean but I'm sure it'll do the trick and it will please your mother.'

'But sir, I can't.'

The suit was thrust at George. 'But sir, you can. Now clear off before I threaten you with another glass of my delicious poison.'

Clutching an ancient dinner-suit, George was bundled out the cottage door. Walking back to the station, he wondered if his new garb would impress a certain young lady. Arriving at an odd hour, he surprised his mother and more so flaunting his latest outfit.

'Here you are, Ma, Cinderella *shall* go to the ball.'

She stared in admiration of the garment. 'Where did you find it?'

'I think the question is, "Can you work your magic please, Mrs Miracle, and make your son look respectable"?'

'Try it on and let me see.'

George turned and left. 'Later please, Ma; right now I have a station to run.'

In the afternoon, he travelled on the Crabbie alighting at Pickling. With no-one on board or at the Halt, the footplate crew walked with the SM into the woods.

'Hell's bells,' said Madge, 'there's even more writing. Yesterday it was only one stone.'

George surveyed the vandalism. Someone was out to thwart his plan to save the branch. It would take a lot of work to restore the site.

At Crabbtree, the nervous Owen Griffith greeted his boss. 'You're doing us a great honour, sir, visiting our humble station.'

'This is business, Owen. Have you seen any strangers in the area in the last two days?'

'Strangers, you say? We're lucky to see any locals.'

'How could anyone reach Pickling without travelling by train?'

He shrugged. 'Well you could cut across country on foot and there's the road to Mallingham but you'd be two miles from the line.'

'In Crabbtree, who would know about any strangers in the area?'

'You want Joshua.'

'Joshua? What's his other name and where can I find him?'

'Don't think anyone knows his other name or even if he has one but ask at the pub. The whole village knows Joshua.'

'Thanks Owen. I'll be back.' He waved to the crew and walked into the village and in the pub was greeted by the landlord.

'Good day station master. Do you fancy a drink, sir?'

'Thank you, another time perhaps. I wish to find Joshua.'

The landlord nodded. George turned and saw an old chap sitting alone in the corner nursing a drink he ordered an hour ago. George approached. 'May I join you, sir?'

Joshua's nod was of the minimalist variety.

'I'm the station master at Whittleton and investigating some damage to property near the railway at Pickling. The porter at Crabbtree said you're the one to ask about strangers in the area.'

'Aye,' said Joshua.

George waited for more information. None came.

'Have you seen anyone suspicious in the last two days?'

'Aye.'

No further comment. *Well at least he's consistent.*

'Could you describe them please?'

'Aye.'

This became tricky forcing George to try another approach.

'Why did you think they were suspicious?'

Joshua took a sip on his drink. George took the hint.

'Might I buy you another drink, sir?'

'Aye,' said Joshua finishing his current beverage in two seconds.

George returned with another glass of beer. Joshua gave thanks with one of his close to imperceptible nods.

'Any advice you can give me, sir, will be much appreciated.'

'Two geezers come in a nice car, black with large headlamps and a runnin' board thingy. One took out a bag with stuff innit, couldn't see what, then they walked towards Crabbtree station. When they come back, there was no bag.'

George tingled. 'Can you describe these men? Were they young or old, tall or short or fat? Did they walk in a strange way?'

'They was normal.'

'And is there anything else you remember about them or their car, anything at all that might be helpful.'

He shook his head with barely any movement. 'Nothin' more except I can remember the number plate.'

George nearly fell off his chair, and walked away with what he hoped was a vital piece of information. *Who needs Sherlock Holmes?*

He reached Crabbtree, chatted with Owen then decided to walk. 'Tell the crew I'll meet them at Pickling on the Up.'

Instead of following the rail line, he walked to the river and followed it upstream. At the first bend he saw a natural weir where fallen branches slowed the flow forming a sort of dam.

He headed in the general direction of Pickling admiring the countryside thinking such glorious surrounds made a lovely backdrop to a minor railway. Reaching Pickling, he searched around the halt then wandered into the woods. The Druid site stood there, its stones wondering what they'd done to deserve being defaced.

He tried to think like the vandals. Where would they place, hide or dispose of their tools of trade? He saw nothing; no freshly dug soil, no broken branches, nothing to suggest the materials were still in the vicinity.

The Crabbie was not due for half an hour so he wandered away from the station towards Danny Wight's hotchpotch of a farm. He opened a farm gate and saw it. Paint, no, whitewash, yes, kalsomine on the ground, the same as the writing on the stones. It was only a small amount but a definite clue. This is the way they came. His heart rate accelerated.

There wasn't a trail of the liquid so he kept going. He was in a meadow knee-deep in grasses and weeds when the shotgun was fired. George's heart rate exploded. He froze, flattening himself in the grass.

'Get off my land or next time I'll aim straight.'

George recognized the unkempt farmer's voice, thought about opening a line of discussion, then opted for the turn-around-and-hobble-like-hell option. He didn't stop until he reached the shelter of the woods behind the halt where he slumped to the ground and spoke quietly to his hip.

'Sorry, old man, won't do that again, I promise.'

The Crabbie on the Down puffed past with George still in hiding. He was back on the miniature platform when the train returned. The crew expressed concern at his frazzled appearance.

'I'm fine. Just get me home.'

Madge made waving signs which confused the SM. He moved to the locomotive. 'Passengers,' whispered Madge pointing to the carriage.

Passengers? On the Crabbie? George boarded the carriage to be observed by no fewer than six human beings, all adult, who were more than surprised to see a man dressed as a station master and who seemed a bit worse for wear, boarding their train in the middle of nowhere. He smiled and said, 'Good afternoon.'

They all nodded and smiled, replied before whispering amongst themselves. Once the train departed, all six passengers—five males and a female—moved towards George.

'Hello,' said their spokesman. 'Are you the station master for this branch line?'

'I am and for the Whittleton station.'

'We're a part of the Railway Ramblers. We go on country walks which always includes a train journey.'

'Hello,' said George.

'We wondered why a station master was in so remote a place.'

'Ah,' said George, thinking on his feet. 'Do you know anything about the ancient Druids?'

A buzz of excitement exploded from the travellers. 'We do. Our rambles always try to include historical places.'

'Well you've come to the right branch line,' said George and off he went. He should have been a salesman. By the time the Crabbie sounded its whistle announcing its arrival at Whittleton, each of the Railway Ramblers was promising to tell all their friends about this place and return once the Druid site was up and running.

George shook hands with the passengers making the footplate crew scratch their heads.

'Did Owen check their tickets at Crabbtree?' asked George.

'Yes, boss,' said Madge and Bobby together.

'Well done. Carry on,' he said heading for his office.

Eric greeted him. 'All those passengers on the Crabbie, sir; you must be pleased.'

'Indeed, Eric and what's been happening here?'

'There are 11 expressions of interest so far.'

'How many?' gasped George. 'You mean for the station garden?'

'Some wanted to know if they needed to bring spades and trowels, and are you all right for bulbs, seedlings and mature plants?'

'Blimey,' replied the shocked SM. 'Ah, please tell anyone else who asks, tools are fine but not plants as those decisions will be made by Mr Gardiner. What a response.'

'You've started something here, sir. Your uncle would be proud.'

That comment hit hard as George knew Uncle Fred would be tickled pink to see his nephew making a real go of his first SM posting.

Chapter 11

'George?' called Connie as her son came home for his supper. 'Who were you expecting, Ma, the Prime Minister?' He entered the kitchen, stopped and stared at the dinner suit hanging by the back door. It looked immaculate.

'You need to try it on so I can make any changes if they're needed.'

'It looks magnificent, Ma. How do you do it?'

'Asking me how I clean a garment is a bit like me asking you how to blow a whistle or wave a flag.'

He removed his cap, coat and jacket. Connie held the dinner suit jacket and George slipped into it. It was close to a perfect fit. She fussed pinching the back and tugging the sleeves.

'Now the trousers,' she said. The shiny black satin stripe down each leg matched the wide, shiny lapels on the jacket. It was classy.

George removed his shoes and dropped his trousers as his sister entered. She acted as if her world was about to end.

'George!' she shrieked, 'I'm about to eat my supper.' The dog found the scene amusing and barked his delight.

George laughed at his sister's mock outrage, and she laughed at his attempt to pull on his new trousers.

'Take off the jacket,' said Connie, and Emily stepped in to help.

'They're a bit loose, Ma,' said George waggling the trousers to show their size. His mother pinched them at his back.

'I'll take them in here. Now your plain white shirt won't do so I've asked John and he's going to let you borrow his formal dress shirt with a bib. I'll starch it for you. He'll have a tie and cufflinks too.'

George felt overwhelmed. 'Please thank Mr Beckwith, Ma.'

Not that George's family knew as much, but all this effort was to help him impress the young woman of his dreams. The one he refused to name. He couldn't explain why he was so excited because his plan might fail, his affection might not be returned. How embarrassing, how deflating it would be to report that his proposal to walk out with Louisa was turned down. About the young lady, he kept schtum.

Over supper, George told his family of the encouraging response to find volunteers for the station garden. 'On the first day after the notices were displayed, we have 11 people keen to participate.'

'You'd better make it 14,' said Emily not interrupting her dining.

George stared at her. '14?' he asked confused.

'Bert and I will be there.'

'You mean 13,' said Connie. 'Have you forgotten your arithmetic?'

'No Ma, Bert's bringing his tractor and I reckon it counts for another person.'

George wanted to kiss his sister. 'You're a champion, Em, and please tell Bert I will definitely allow him to marry a Miracle.'

She poked out her tongue at her brother as a seriously happy mood settled in the station house.

Next morning, the day before the dinner, pressure was on in earnest. George had obtained evidence about the vandals who attacked the Druids' stones including a car number plate. His suspicions, although without evidence, suggested a work colleague was trying to blight his career. He needed to contact Jack Rogers at Liverpool Street with this new information. But who wanted to wreck the young SM's career?

He needed to tell Oscar Wilding that the author, Septimus Oldmeadow, was on board for the promotion of Whittleton.

The good news continued with even more people calling at the station offering to help with the new station garden.

But all this activity faded compared to his dinner engagement tomorrow night. Now he could arrive in stunning evening wear, his mingling with the aristocracy seemed perfect. He would look the part and hope and pray the night became a romantic success.

On the issue of being set up, even ruined in his job as SM, he decided to set a trap. If it was one of his station staff passing information to his enemy, or actually *was* the enemy, this might be a way to expose the turncoat.

He called a meeting of his staff and seriously doubted if the lad porter, Pip, was a suspect. He couldn't be; he was an ailurophile and anyone who loved cats is automatically a decent person.

'Gentlemen,' said George, 'I have a new idea to promote the branch line. The river at Crabbtree is to have a fishing competition.' No reaction from the listeners. 'There's a small natural weir near the bridge and the plan is to build it up making a pool ideal for fish to gather. The banks either side are perfect for folk to cast a line.' He stared at them with a serious face. 'Please don't tell anyone about this project until we have permission from the authority that controls the waterways. Understood?'

The men murmured their agreement then returned to work.

George rang SM Jack Rogers at Liverpool Street. 'Hello Jack, it's George Miracle, how are things?'

'I'm well, young man and was about to telephone you. I have a possible suspect, George. This chap, who's pushing 50 and is still a porter, has been bad-mouthing you in some angry tirades.'

'Why?' asked George wanting to understand the hatred against him and not knowing the meaning of *tirades*.

'Not sure but he was granted an exemption from conscription and reckons the GER and now the LNER have always held it against him. You're half his age and already an SM. That could be his motivation. Anyway, at this stage it's no names, no pack drill but I'll try one or two other sources. Have you any news your end?'

'I have a car number plate of two suspicious characters seen in the area but don't know what to do with the information.'

'My pal at Scotland Yard could help. We were in the same unit in France. Give me the number and I'll ask him to investigate.'

George relayed the details growing more positive and even more determined. He wrote a letter to Oscar Wilding about all the confirmed activities but with no mention of a fishing competition.

In the evening, his mother handed him his freshly starched formal dress shirt. 'Pop this and the formal trousers on but not the dinner jacket,' she said. George stood there in his trousers, black shoes and socks and crisp formal white shirt.

Connie opened a brown paper parcel and handed her son a tie, white waistcoat and black cuff links. Try these on as well.' He did.

'Oh my, who's the movie star?' asked Emily entering the kitchen.

'Can you tie the tie?' asked his mother.

'Ma, I can manage shoelaces, socks and a Windsor knot for my work tie but this bow tie with the starched shirt, waistcoat and cufflinks is like a foreign language to me.'

'I'll do it,' said Emily, stepping forward. Up close and in his face she struggled. 'The sooner you get your true love to tie this the better.'

He went to say something rude but hesitated as he thought of an answer. 'Oh I forgot to tell you, I've remembered her name. You know, my mystery girlfriend from London, the one I was thinking of inviting to your wedding.' He grabbed the women's attention, then paused milking the moment. 'It's Henrietta Clackendacken.'

Emily failed to finish the tie as she doubled up with an attack of laughter. Her mother too caught the giggles.

George feigned shock, becoming aghast. 'What?' he asked, staring at one and then the other. '*What?* What's wrong with Henrietta?'

The day of the dinner dawned. George spent the previous night tossing and turning. If a flower had been to hand, he might have pulled out one petal at a time. "She loves me; she loves me not."

Having the dinner suit gave his confidence a boost. In his uncle's hand-me-down day suit he would have stood out like a sore thumb. He imagined the others, sitting and standing, dressed in formal attire, the ladies with jewellery on show, and there would be George, dressed like an undertaker's clerk on a Bank Holiday.

'You're lucky with that dinner suit, George,' said his mother at breakfast. 'It's a quality garment and would have cost a pretty sum. And remember to stand straight and don't fiddle with your bow tie.'

'Yes Ma. But what if I notice it's gone crooked?'

'Upper class people ignore such things. They break the rules and conventions ignoring criticism. Pretend you don't care.'

'Yes Ma.' *But I do care and especially about Henrietta.*

That morning, with the Crabbie about to start its first run, George slipped across to the other side of the island platform.

'Morning boss,' said Bobby checking the fire.

'Gentlemen, I have a small favour to ask.' Both men moved to the SM. 'At Crabbtree, either or both of you are to walk to the river, head north about a hundred yards and tell me the condition of the small dam wall made by fallen branches and other driftwood.'

They studied him, confused. 'The dam wall?' asked Madge.

'Yes, the venue I suggested for the fishing competition. Is it in good condition? It'll take you all of three minutes. Don't make a fuss and don't tell anyone about it. Are we clear, gentlemen, not a word?'

The driver and fireman nodded and when George departed they glanced at one another and shrugged.

More people dropped in to register their interest in working on the garden project. George thanked them, gave simple instructions and couldn't wait to tell Horace about the response.

A busy weekend lay ahead involving the dinner at Ripley Hall tonight and the start of the station garden project tomorrow.

In a decent break between trains, George hurried into the village to tell Horace the good news. The old man fell silent. Not only did this project mean he could continue his love of gardening, but the villagers were keen to work with him. He choked with emotion.

'I'll send someone to collect you at 1:45, Mr Gardiner.' The elderly gardener smiled and didn't stop until long after George left.

The Crabbie returned with George planning how to make the garden working-bee proceed without interfering with trains and passengers. Madge tapped on his open door. George beckoned him inside.

'Well?' asked the SM.

Madge shook his head. 'There's no weir or dam on the river, boss.'

'Are you sure?'

'There's just a smooth stream flowing all the way to the bridge.'

'Thanks,' said George. 'Say nothing about this to anyone.'

The afternoon dragged. George kept glancing at the clock in his office. The words, "7.30 for 8" keep sounding in his head. He'd rostered both adult porters on this evening and they knew their SM was only a short distance away. The telephone number of the manor house was deposited in Eric's top pocket as well as being listed on the office wall.

After the penultimate Up at 19:24, he headed home.

'You're cutting it fine,' said his mother. She and Emily were already eating.

'I bet you have five courses, you lucky so-and-so' said Emily.

George went to his room to change. It took him longer than he thought because he was shaking. Not uncontrollable movements but when he held out a hand, there was a small but steady tremble.

'Come on, George,' called Connie. 'Upper class dinners are like trains. You have to be on time.'

He stepped into the kitchen and both women gasped. Who was this dashing young man in the smartest dinner suit in town?

It was a beautifully styled and tailored garment with the tips of the side pockets lined with satin. When he undid the jacket button, the silk bib and waistcoat gave him a real sense of style. He managed to tie the bow-tie badly and his mother stood.

'Let me fix your tie.' She did and patted his shoulders to flatten a quarter inch of material. 'You'll do, son,' she said and kissed him.

Emily came around and took hold of his hands. She kissed his cheek then whispered. 'Don't forget to give my love to Henrietta.'

'Ha, ha,' he said. 'Don't wait up and I'll see you in the morning.'

He headed for the front door with his relatives straining to see him from behind. He stepped outside, closed the door and took the first steps on what he hoped would be an exciting and rewarding journey.

A clear sky saved him. He kept telling himself to not be nervous. He knew some of the other guests including his young namesake, his godson. All the subjects his mother told him were acceptable to discuss bounced around inside his head.

He wished she hadn't told him the topics to avoid because they kept popping into his brain as well.

He crossed the tracks with no trains in sight. Ripley Hall stood well back from the road on its grand estate, meaning prying eyes could see nothing until they were well along the driveway.

George thought it silly he was walking to the large home as even tradespeople would certainly drive. He avoided soggy ground and the freshly mown lawn. Fancy traipsing through the corridors and rooms leaving a trail of muddy and messy footprints.

There were lights on in several rooms. He climbed the wide concrete steps and reached the tiled floor surrounds. The front door towered overhead. He told his heart to relax, brushed his hair and stepped forward to ring the bell.

Chapter 12

Aservant opened the door and his mouth opened as if surprised. George recognized him as a passenger, a Mr Fortesque.

'Good evening Mr Miracle,' said the servant stepping back so as to welcome the guest.

'Good evening, Mr Fortesque,' replied George, nervous already and now more so because of the reaction of the servant.

Is my tie crooked? Why does he look surprised? Is he surprised?

'This way, sir,' said the servant and headed inside.

As George walked through the house he could hear voices and the occasional burst of laughter. He thought he knew one or two voices. His nerves ramped up knowing he was the odd man out. I'm working class or lower middle at a pinch. These people have titles and wealth and property. I make a modest wage and live in a humble cottage which I'll never own.

In a corridor along which a coach and horses might travel, they stopped at a pair of doors. The servant opened both, stepped inside and made an announcement.

'My Lady, Mr George Miracle.'

The room fell silent. A grandfather clock worth at least a hundred times George's annual salary refused to stop ticking and seemed to George to be a harbinger of doom. Why?

He stepped inside and froze. The others stared at him in his magnificent dinner suit. Was it even more expensive than their quality garments? They stared because they all wore day wear. In deference to the working-class chap, the dress-for-dinner dictum had been abandoned. Alas, poor George didn't receive the memo. Damn.

The day before, the group decided they didn't want to make him feel inferior and stand out in his basic suit. They dressed down. They were not to know the generous Septimus Oldmeadow and John Beckwith would help dress the SM to the nines. Oh dear.

The word *embarrassment* seemed to flash in lights above the heads of the guests, on the walls, on the ceiling, everywhere. George wanted to say a word or words his mother would find shocking.

The characters of George Carruthers and Stephen Fitzsimons shone as, without batting an eyelid, they strode or limped towards George with smiles as broad as could be.

'George,' they both chorused and pumped his hand.

'Welcome,' said Stephen, 'thank you so much for coming.'

George Carruthers juggled his crutches expertly and managed to hug his former fellow soldier. 'It's grand to see you again, old man.'

As George tried to recover from his fashion faux pas, he realized none of the people in the room made any mention of his clothing. They behaved as if he was the guest they wanted to meet and there was an end to it. He might have been the Emperor in new clothes but at least he actually wore clothes and fabulous ones at that.

Is this how the well-to-do behave? They don't mention, highlight or react to an embarrassing situation.

Stephen took control. 'Now, George, you've met my mother, and Lady Carruthers of course, and this is my cousin Rupert and his wife Virginia and ...'

George was introduced to people whose names and faces he failed to remember such was his outfit disaster. He wanted to return their smiles but found his face muscles had frozen in a reaction to his choice of finery.

He was under strict instructions not to bow but did nod as he spoke. 'Good evening,' he said leaving out names mainly because he wasn't sure which went with which person.

'Now I hope I'm not stealing your thunder, George,' said Stephen, 'but I'm sure the others would love to hear about your plans for our village and the railway in particular.'

Lady Fitzsimons remained seated but calmly put in her oar. 'Stephen, Mr Miracle may be bound by some railway regulation which prevents him revealing company secrets.'

She sparked a response. *Blimey*, thought George, *someone else has a mother who keeps their son in line.*

George wanted to save Stephen from any embarrassment. 'Please do not worry, my Lady. I'm happy to tell you about our plans to create a garden on the station at Whittleton.'

The gathering added another polite response.

'So my son's godfather is not only a station master but a horticulturist,' said Lady Carruthers.

People laughed and George relaxed being fairly confident he knew the meaning of the word *horticulturist*.

Drinks were served with George skipping the sherry in favour of a fruit juice. Stephen led George to his mother who remembered the railway man's kindness in the past when George was a mere porter.

'When I heard you were the godfather to the little Carruthers baby, I was so delighted.' She indicated a chair. 'Please sit, Mr Miracle.'

'Thank you, my Lady.' He sat.

'I was saddened to hear about your uncle. People spoke so highly of his work as the station master. He was much respected in the village. And now I hear good things of his replacement. You have made your mark in the village, sir, and I congratulate you.'

George struggled with the status of the person speaking to him, her words of praise and genuine interest. He stuck to the basics. 'You are most kind, my Lady.'

'How are things now the Great Eastern is no more?'

Goodness, she knows about railway events.

'Life goes on, my Lady, and we do have plans to help the station and the railway.'

'Oh,' she replied, 'do tell. Is it anything to do with the Crabbie?'

A feather would have floored the SM. 'I'm delighted you have such an interest in our branch line, my Lady.'

'Am I right in saying it's in trouble? My spies tell me the patronage has never been so low.' She pulled back. 'Oh dear, now *I* am intruding on railway regulations.'

George smiled. 'Not at all, my Lady and rest assured, no matter what happens, we will fight hard to keep the line open.'

This discussion and every other was interrupted when Stephen made an announcement. 'My Lords, Ladies and Gentlemen, pray silence for the guest of honour.'

An inner door opened and George's wee godson arrived in style. His garments were bespoke and as the lad was paraded, people made appropriate sounds of admiration and delight.

A tremor of pleasure shot through George's heart, not because he was about to see his godson, which gave him pleasure, but because the carrier of said child was the woman constantly in his mind.

"His" Louisa came ever closer holding the precious cargo. She stopped in front of George and held the baby towards him.

'Good evening, Mr Miracle. As soon as your godson heard of your arrival, he awoke and demanded to see you.'

Others smiled, some laughed and teased the godfather. He was struck dumb and while pretending to care about the babe, was desperate to stare at and speak to Valerie's companion.

'Good evening,' he said then added, 'young man.'

Stephen broke the ice. 'There are too many Georges in this room.'

Spontaneous laughter was interrupted by a dinner gong, and the guests headed for the dining-room. To George's dismay, his godson was removed elsewhere in the hands of the lovely Louisa.

What is her family name?

George Miracle played the role of the humble guest. His knowledge of scripture was limited, but he took advice from the Gospel of Luke.

"But when thou art bidden, go and sit down in the lowest room; that when he that bade thee cometh, he may say unto thee, Friend, go up higher: then shalt thou have worship in the presence of them that sit at meat with thee."

'You're here, Mr Stationmaster,' said Stephen, and Fortesque the family retainer stepped forward to withdraw George's chair. He was between two females he didn't know. They smiled, he smiled, and his stomach made a rumbling sound.

Be quiet, shouted George in his mind and the next disaster lurked ready to strike. Cutlery! His mother gave him a lesson on what was what and how starting from the outside and working in was the correct and only way to behave. It was a bit like the wedding of George and Valerie in London during war time.

The number of diners was small enough for all to be heard by one speaker but large enough, seated at a round table, for conversations to be held between neighbours.

Emily was right about the number of courses. *When will they end?* George's immediate neighbours were not remotely interested in railways or any form of manual labour—they had staff for such tasks—and so George tried hard to follow another of his Ma's instructions and select what she called the safe topics. But for how long can one discuss the weather and the royal family?

Both women, either side of the guest in the wrong attire, wondered why Lord Carruthers chose a railwayman as the godfather, and the only godfather of his son. *He is what, a station master? Really?*

But there he was dining in the home of Lord and Lady Fitzsimons, sans the patriarch, dressed to the nines when the dress down order was observed by everyone else. Please George, do *not* mention the dying Lord of the manor.

Finally, finally the dining ceased and the women stood to leave. All the men stood and George wondered if he should draw back the chairs of his female neighbours. It's not your job, sir. "His" two ladies were as glad to leave as he was to be free of their stifling company.

The men sat and Stephen spoke. 'Now George of Whittleton, I gather you are not fond of a drink.'

The SM went all biblical. 'I do take a little wine for my stomach's sake, sir, but generally I drink tea and, if I'm lucky, some coffee.'

On cue the servant placed a pot of coffee on the table.

'Help yourself, sir,' said Stephen while he passed the port to the other George.

With the women long gone, Carruthers raised the dress code issue. 'George, Stephen told me you were worried about dressing for dinner so we, and by we, I mean Lady Fitzsimons and my dear wife decided we'd not dress for dinner to save you being the odd one out.'

'Please gentlemen,' said George wanting to drop the matter.

But the other George persisted. 'Then you, you cunning old devil, upstaged us all by arriving in full battle dress.'

The guests laughed and George's embarrassment began to fade.

'And a damn fine suit it is,' said Stephen; 'you dandy, you!'

The SM knew an explanation was required and gave it. His companions laughed loud and long and even took to slapping the crisp tablecloth so great was their amusement.

George relaxed in this house with these men. One was a Lord and the other soon might be one. The other men were from ancient families and old money. Yet here was a man from the Wood Green Estate in North London, a Level 3 house, breaking bread and swapping yarns with men of substance treating him as an equal.

It worked the other way too. George's heroism and humility appealed to these aristocrats not to mention his lack of pretence.

Their bonhomie stopped when a gentle tap was heard.

'Come in,' called Stephen, and Valerie appeared. All the men stood which of course included the father with one leg.

'My dear,' he said, 'are we behaving as brutes? Please accept our apologies.'

'I believe Mr Miracle would never know how to be brutish and he it is I wish to poach.' The other males made a stirring sound. 'Your godson refuses to sleep until he can say goodnight, George. Please will you come?'

Trying not to scramble, George nodded to his companions and followed Lady Carruthers from the room.

Once in the corridor, she leant in and kissed his cheek. 'Please forgive me, dear George.' He was surprised and shocked. 'I was the one who suggested we not dress for dinner so as to make you feel comfortable. Will you ever forgive me?'

'There's nothing to forgive. When your husband explains the story of my sudden rise to the status of Beau Brummel, you'll understand.'

She smiled and squeezed his hand. 'You're a darling. Now why don't you trot along and see your godson.' She pointed. 'Down this corridor and it's the door on your left opposite the painting of Stephen's great-grandfather, the man with the magnificent whiskers. I'll see you soon.'

She left and alone, George stood wondering what was happening. He set off, reached the room then tapped gently.

'Come in,' said a female voice.

It's her, he thought. *Well don't just stand there, man. Get inside.*

He opened the door. A bassinet stood in the middle of the room and on the settee beside it, with a book in her hand, sat the lovely Louisa. She put down her book and moved to the bassinet.

'George,' she cooed to the baby. 'Look who's come to see you.'

Godfather George approached and stood on the opposite side of the bassinet. He studied his sleeping godson then turned to Louisa.

'Hello again,' he said and went a bit wobbly when she smiled.

'Hello again to you. How was your dinner engagement?'

George didn't seem to be able to think straight. 'Why were you not there?' he blurted then knew he was wrong. 'I'm sorry, but I would have liked the chance to get to know you better.'

'Well you can now. Come and sit beside me and tell me everything about the life of a station master.'

George thought all his Christmases were arriving at once. 'Thank you,' he said sitting not too close.' And I see you are well and looking even more beautiful since last we met.'

George bit his tongue. He'd told himself not to be so personal, so over the top, so … enthusiastic. Mind you it was difficult and who could coach him in the fine and delicate art of seduction?

'How convenient it is that Lord Carruthers and Lord Fitzsimon's son are friends and little George's godfather lives in the nearby village.'

'I agree,' he replied unsure of what to add.

'When your godson is older, he can visit the manor house where his godfather can show him the trains and allow him to ride on one.'

'What a wonderful idea. Of course you'd be welcome to come too,' said George still stuck in the enthusiastic, tongue-hanging-out mode. 'You know, ever since we met at the christening, I've been trying to remember your surname but for the life of me I can't.'

'Perhaps that's because I never told you. It's …'

She said her name as wee George let out a loud cry. George didn't catch what Louisa said but thought he heard something horrendous.

Did she say Clackendacken? Oh no. Emily will tease me forever.

'I'm sorry, my noisy godson interrupted our conversation.'

She smiled. 'My surname is McClaren,' and George breathed a huge but silent sigh of relief.

'How are things in Hampstead? Are you happy?'

She considered him, admiring his boyish face and thinking his appearance and manners suited him well.

'I'm very happy, thank you.'

'Are you staying long in Whittleton? If you are, I would love to show you the station and the village.'

'We're here for a few days and I think visiting your station and the village sounds wonderful. When do you suggest?'

'Sunday would be good. Tomorrow there is a working-bee at the station but if you are free, we could go for a walk the day after.'

'How lovely,' she said and stood to check on the baby.

There was a gentle tapping sound, and Valerie popped her head around the door. 'May I come in?'

'Of course,' said George standing and on cloud nine.'

'The station master has invited me to visit the station and the village on Sunday,' said Louisa. 'Will that be satisfactory, my lady?'

'More than satisfactory,' replied Valerie. Baby George complained. 'I do believe your godson is hungry, George. Would you excuse us?'

'Of course,' he said, 'and it was lovely to see you both.' To Louisa he smiled and said. 'Shall we say 10.30 for 11 on Sunday?'

'Perfect,' she replied and George bowed and left.

The women exchanged glances. 'It's obvious the station master is a keen admirer, Miss McClaren,' said Valerie taking her son from his bassinet. 'Don't forget the soon-to-be Lord Fitzsimons is single.'

Louisa looked at her friend, smiled but said nothing.

Chapter 13

When George arrived home, his mother and sister were waiting in their night attire. There was no way he would escape without answering their many questions. 'Well?' demanded Connie. 'Did they appreciate your splendid dinner suit?'

Walking home, apart from thinking about the girl who made his heart beat fast, George thought about the social disaster of the dinner suit. He knew his mother would die of embarrassment after all her efforts to then discover her son wore the wrong outfit. He lied.

'It was fine, Ma, nobody paid much attention.'

Emily demanded her turn. 'Was I right about the number of courses? Did they have loads of dishes?'

'You were right, Em. Now ladies, I have a station to run in the morning, and later the supervision of many enthusiastic gardeners.'

'Bert said he'll park his tractor outside at about half one.'

George remembered. 'Great, Em, and you've reminded me. Could you and Bert collect Mr Gardiner and bring him to the station?'

'Yes but there's only one seat on the tractor.'

'He can sit next to you on the tray. Remember how you travelled as a little girl on the rag and bone cart back in London?'

Emily remembered and smiled. 'I do. We gave Mrs Entwhistle a lift around to Grannie's place on ...'

She stopped, remembering it was the day their father died. To change the subject, George thanked his sister for her offer to help but stopped when his mother told him her news.

'George, the ladies from the knitting club will be operating a tea urn for the working-bee people at the crossing end of the Up platform. As soon as I mentioned it, they all volunteered.'

'Ma, that is absolutely marvellous, thank you so much.'

'Many hands make light work,' said the mother who was quietly so very proud of her son.

'Well it's a big day tomorrow, so come on, ladies, time for bed.'

Next morning he heard a nearby rooster crowing as he made a cup of tea for himself and his mother. He reached his office 40 minutes before the first train. This was a unique occasion for the SM. Here he was dealing with trains to and from London, albeit a reduced service being a Saturday, while later supervising a tribe of enthusiastic volunteers all keen to beautify the station, *his* station in their village.

Staff arrived with Monty carrying a tray of petunias. 'Potted 'em last night, boss,' he said. 'Where do you want 'em?'

George beamed. 'Ah, in my office till Mr Gardiner arrives. Good upon you, Monty. I forgot you're a green fingered signalman.'

The morning passed as expected although a few locals wandered in to enquire about the working-bee. 'Come back at 2,' said George. 'You'll be more than welcome.'

Well before 2, the Up platform started to acquire people. A few were passengers but most arrived keen to work on the new garden.

Eric approached the SM. 'They're not passengers, sir, and having them standing around and even sitting on the platform seating might cause confusion.

George agreed. 'Ask them to move to the London end and to stand well back from the front of the platform otherwise we'll have guards holding trains thinking there are passengers yet to board.'

'Very good, sir,' said Eric leaving to shepherd his flock.

The Crabbie gave a toot on its desperate-to-please whistle and departed on its first run of the afternoon.

George rostered everyone on in case Operation New Garden ran off the rails. He studied his full complement of porters and now reckoned he knew the enemy within, the rat in the ranks. The only people he told about the small weir on the river near Crabbtree were his colleagues. Within 24 hours of telling only them, the natural dam was dismantled. Monty and Desmond loved Whittleton as did the Crabbie footplate crew. Their job was their life. Eric likewise, and young Pip was still a child. Only porter Gordon Littleton remained.

It has to be him and if so, why? What is his motive? And if I accuse him without evidence, I'll be sunk. I need a smarter way to discover the truth.

Volunteers arrived early and obviously weren't getting paid. Digging, lifting and planting meant hard work. The sun was out. But Whittleton's community spirit came alive. Chatting spread like wildfire.

Emily weaved her way through the crowd guiding Horace the hero. 'George, we're here. Bert's minding the tractor awaiting orders.'

'Good afternoon, Mr Miracle,' said Horace who seemed to have a permanent smile on his face; Melville tried to grin. Horace lent on his walking stick thrilled at the growing bunch of budding gardeners. 'Are all these folk here for the garden?'

'They are indeed, sir.' George beckoned to Pip who appeared carrying a sturdy chair which normally lived in the SM's office.

'Mr Gardiner, this is Pip and his job is to follow you carrying your chair. Whenever you wish to rest or need to sit to deliver instructions, the lad porter with your chair will be by your side at all times.'

'How kind,' said Horace looking overwhelmed. 'I still can't believe all these people are here for the garden.'

'They are and please ensure you have the wording correct.' Horace lost his smile. 'It's not *the* garden but The *Horace Gardiner Garden*. I hope we are clear.'

The smile returned to Horace's face but a lump in his throat prevented him from speaking.

'Now, if you're ready, sir, I'll call the volunteers to order and then the floor, or rather the platform is yours.'

An even bigger smile from Horace and the curtain rose.

'Ladies and gentlemen,' called George. 'Oh and girls and boys,' he added seeing the good contingent of young gardeners. 'Please gather round.' They did with George moving away from the station entrance.

'Good afternoon, welcome and thank you from the bottom of my heart for coming along to help beautify our station. Before we start, may I ask one favour of you all? This is a working station. When trains arrive, please make sure you stand well back and allow passengers to come and go.' He paused. 'Thank you. Now this entire project is the idea and dream of our own and much-admired resident, Mr Horace Gardiner.' George indicated the beaming chap. 'He has the vision and the plan to make the Whittleton station beautiful; I apologize, *more* beautiful.' People smiled. 'I'll ask Mr Gardiner to say a few words and then we can form groups with a job for everyone. But first, please welcome Whittleton's own, Mr Horace Gardiner.'

The crowd applauded instantly and with feeling. Everyone knew him and about his recent bereavement. The old chap was overcome before he'd said a word. He recovered, spoke beautifully and kept it short. Pip held up each relevant drawing on command and people strained to see his handiwork.

Horace finished and didn't know what to do. George stepped forward. 'Ladies and gentlemen, there are many jobs. Let's form three groups to suit your talents.' He pointed to different areas; lifting and carrying over there please, digging and planting there, and watering and tidying here.'

People chatted, called, moved and formed groups. George approached each group asking them to select a leader who went to speak to Horace.

Bert approached George. 'My tractor's ready, George. What do you want collecting?'

They chatted to Horace, received instructions, then with three strong helpers the heavy moving brigade disappeared.

George was surprised when his mother's friend, John Beckwith, approached. 'Good afternoon, George. I see Barney Grieve, the retired builder is here. He will never push his talents but the man would be ideal as a site manager.'

George adored this spirit of co-operation. Barney was invited to meet Horace and the SM and, in his usual humble style, the former builder quietly agreed to become site manager. Now things moved.

The organized chaos became planned activity. Using Horace's illustrations, parts of the platform were marked where beds were to go. Benches and seats were placed in new positions to suit the new layout. Spots were selected for hanging baskets. People went home to collect tools, and plants they wanted to donate. Such moves were easy as most folk lived only minutes from the station.

Trains on the Up and Down came and went. The Crabbie performed its Saturday timetable. George watched as the gardening community swung into action. Between trains, George crossed to the Down and waited for the next arrival. People hopped on and off and Gordon, as porter, worked hand in glove with the guard on each train.

The Down departed and George approached Gordon from behind. He turned and spoke.

'Good afternoon, sir. All going well with the garden project I see.'

'Yes, and I'm delighted but listen Gordon, I have a problem. I need a person I can trust to perform a special job.'

The porter reacted with pleasure. 'I'll do my best, sir.'

'There's been a spot of bother with vandals out by the Pickling Halt.' Gordon's happiness vanished as a chill crept up his spine.

'I'll be honest with you, Gordon, the branch is in dire trouble and could be closed at any time.'

'I didn't realize it was that bad,' lied the guilty-looking porter.

'As you know we have plans to save the line and I need a reliable chap I can trust to help me pull the Crabbie out of the fire. Some vandals have defaced the Druid rocks, and I need them cleaned of all the kalsomine daubed on them. Can I ask you, please, to bring them back to their original condition?'

What could the porter say?

'Of course, sir.'

'Good man. Simple tools will do the trick. Use a blade to scrape off any loose material then plenty of soapy water and hard scrubbing. Give them a final rinse with water. There are materials in the store.'

'When do you want me to go, sir?'

'Now please, on the next Crabbie.'

Gordon set off but stopped when George called. 'And stay clear of the farmer who owns the nearby land. He's keen on using his shotgun.'

Gordon left with fear and trembling running behind him. He was between the Pickling rocks and a hard place. 'Sir,' was his only offering as he hurried to collect the materials.

The SM crossed to the Up platform asking Eric to work the Down. 'The lad and I will take care of things here.'

Eric nodded leaving George to ponder the dozens of busy bees buzzing about making flower beds and more. At the crossing gate end of the Up platform, George spied his mother and several women serving tea and scones to hungry volunteers.

'Good afternoon, ladies,' he said. They responded in kind. 'Is Mrs Miracle keeping you in order?' They laughed although Connie made a face while feeling tremendous pride to see the community supporting the local station master who just happened to be her son.

'Mr Miracle,' called a voice and George saw Godfrey Grantley-Smythe, the chairman of the parish council heading his way. A man, unknown to George, walked with the Chairman who held a dog leash on the end of which was a delightful black and white dog once discovered thanks to extraordinary good fortune by the SM. The pooch was being minded by its grandparents for the weekend.

'Mr Chairman, good afternoon.'

'Good afternoon, Mr Miracle. This is Mr Rupert Green ...'

'Browne,' corrected the man, 'Rupert Browne with an *e*.'

'How do you do, sir?' said George.

'Mr Browne is from the *Echo* and would like to write a piece about the new station garden. He would like to take a photo of the parish council chairman and the station master to go with the article.'

'Thank you, Mr Chairman and to you, Mr Browne but I'm merely a humble helper. The man you need to interview is over there resting on his walking stick. Mr Horace Gardiner is the inspiration and designer of the entire project. Please,' said George indicating, 'Mr Gardiner knows everything.'

Humble Horace agreed to the interview although wanting the garden to be the star attraction. Godfrey never liked his suggestions being rejected but still saw a chance to maintain his reputation as the most successful parish council chairman for getting his name and photograph in *any* newspaper. As the two gents headed to Horace, the dog turned back at George thinking, *Do I know you?*

Horace bubbled with pride and happiness. Before his eyes his vision became a reality. It was a double win for George with his station beautified and his community pitching in on a railway project.

By four o'clock, people stared to drift away. As they left, most went to George to thank him for the chance to take part.

George asked Emily and Bert to take Horace home. Of course he wanted to stay but George insisted.

'We'll have another working-bee next week to help finish things sir, and then we'll draw up a roster for people who want to take care of your beautiful masterpiece. The old man grasped George's hand and only managed a brief response.

'Thank you, Mr Miracle, thank you, thank you.'

Pip returned the chair to the office, and Eric came back to the Up platform to mention his absent colleague.

'I haven't seen Gordon for a while, sir.'

The Crabbie whistled as it returned from its final run. George watched the island platform and saw the Crabbie's only passenger disembark. Carrying a bag with what George knew contained cleaning material, Gordon looked out on his feet.

'He's been on assignment helping the Branch,' said the SM.

Gordon was sent home and George crossed the tracks to talk to Madge and Bobby. 'Did you have a look, gentlemen?'

You wouldn't know they'd been painted, boss,' said Madge.

'It's like a new canvas, boss,' said Bobby. 'And now they're as clean as a whistle, I could paint flowers on them rocks if you like.'

George was tempted. 'Thanks Bobby. Let's give the Druids a chance first, and if that plan fails we could turn the space into an outdoor art exhibition. Good night, gentlemen.'

'Good night, boss' they said as one. 'Garden is great,' called Madge.

'And I've painted many of them flowers,' called Bobby pointing.

Admiring the brand new garden, George's insides glowed. His small country station now boasted beds of flowers and shrubs with hanging baskets and pots happy to live in their new location.

He looked at the Whittleton station sign and thought.

Some of Bobby's art at either end would look great too.

Chapter 14

That night, all the talk in the station house was about the garden. Both Connie and Emily were there serving tea or helping plant flowers and told George of the many comments they heard about the new-look station. He glowed, revelling in the success of the project although his mind was often elsewhere.

Tomorrow he was to "walk out" with the lovely Louisa. He'd told her 10:30 for 11 and needed to stick to that time. His mother and sister would be in church from 11 until noon so to avoid been seen by the Miracle clan, he needed to be out of the village and back to the station before the vicar finished his sermon. His mind buzzed.

Why am I hiding Louisa from my family? Surely I can't be ashamed of courting such a stunning and friendly young woman? Am I courting her? Is she being polite because I'm the godfather of her charge? Ah, I know. It's fear of rejection. I believe if I'm not up to snuff in the suitor stakes or if another chap wins her hand, how will I explain I've been dumped? It's the shame aspect; the fear of failure.

Sometimes he wished he didn't have to wear his uniform. In a small village with a small station, the SM almost always wore his uniform except when in his bed or bath. Today, a Sunday, was the one day when the timetable displayed the longest gaps between trains. George could steal an hour from his station duties and made sure even the traitor Gordon was on duty.

He headed to Ripley Hall, sans dinner suit, with his SM uniform in splendid nick. Standing at the front door, he checked his pocket-watch, noted it ticked over to 10:30 hours so rang the bell.

Expecting the same elderly, faithful retainer again, George was surprised to see the ever smiling Valerie.

'Good-morning station master Miracle, right on time I see.'

'Good morning your Ladyship.'

'Now George, we're not out in public here; Valerie will do nicely, thank you.' He smiled. 'And here comes your party.'

George's heart beat quicker then exploded when Louisa came from inside pushing an expensive perambulator. He gasped at her beauty in a gorgeous floral dress with matching hat. It was a few moments before he acknowledged she was in charge of his godson.

'Good morning, Mr Miracle,' said Louisa negotiating the small step onto the tiled surrounds. George stepped forward to help and finished up beside his lady friend.

Valerie surveyed the group. 'You make such a lovely picture. Now enjoy yourselves you three and be back in time for luncheon.'

She closed the door and George peered into the pram to greet his godson. 'I've told him to be on his best behaviour,' said Louisa, 'now, shall we begin?'

George knew nothing about the etiquette of perambulating with a perambulator but offered to be the driver. Louisa walked free and down the long drive they went with George in control of the vehicle but not his emotions.

They were being watched by Lady Carruthers. 'Come and see this, George,' said Valerie. Her husband picked up his crutches and crossed to the window. He joined his wife in watching the SM and his lady friend steering their son towards the village.

'What a fine couple,' said Carruthers. 'Is there something I should know?' Valerie gave her husband a certain smile, and returned to her letter writing.

Once the godson and the caring couple in charge of his conveyance reached the end of the drive, Louisa gave George a serious problem.

'We heard wonderful comments about the new station garden, George. Might we make a brief inspection?'

What could he say? The village first was the plan, his plan.

'The villagers in Whittleton are lucky to have such an imaginative station master who not only runs an efficient station, but turns it into the Kew Gardens of the English countryside.'

Flattery will get you anywhere. George could hardly say, "We'll go to the village first and there's an end to it."

Forcing a smile, he pushed his godson's perambulator into the station and onto the Up platform with not a passenger in sight. Pip and Eric were on duty and both did a double take seeing their SM with a woman and what presumably was a baby.

'Good morning, sir,' said Eric. He nodded to Louisa, 'Madam.'

George acknowledged them but failed to introduce his staff to his guest and godson. He wanted the village trip to begin yesterday.

Louisa wandered towards the soon to be blooming garden. 'George, this is wonderful. Daffodils always make me smile, and wait till those shrubs come into flower.' She indicated the hanging baskets. 'And in Spring, your station will be a riot of colour.'

He delighted in her happiness but died when Monty hurried down the steps of the signal box and crossed the lines.

'Oh my lordy lord,' said the man with more gaps in his teeth than a honeycomb. 'Here am I in my eyrie, never keeping up with the real world and never knowing you was a married man with a bairn.'

George sought a spot in the new garden in which he might bury himself. Eric and Pip remained at a distance but stared, gawped and eavesdropped for all their worth.

George froze. *Help me, someone, please!*

Louisa intervened and spoke to Monty. 'Good day to you, sir but I'm afraid you have the incorrect family tree details. I am the companion lady to the mother of the baby, and Mr Miracle is the child's godfather.'

Monty took a few seconds to comprehend and the two porters filed away the details for future reference. 'Oh I'm begging your pardon, I'm sure,' said Monty and went all Uriah Heep before disappearing.

George was desperate to enter the village. He couldn't bring himself to say, "Can we go now, please, Miss McClaren?"

Louisa gazed across the tracks and, in a terrible case of timing, for the SM, the Crabbie huffed and puffed her way back home. 'Oh my, it's the lovely little train. Can we show George?'

No! No! No! The staff now know the baby's even named after me.

Louisa went to the perambulator and lifted the baby enabling him to see the old GER 0-6-0 tank engine as it hissed to a stop. Was this the making of a future rail enthusiast? Would this cause wee George to grow up collecting engine numbers?

Putting the bairn back in his conveyance took time but finally George guided his godson off the platform. They were away when Louisa stopped. 'Would this happen to be the domain of the station master?' she asked with a glint in her eye. 'May one take a tiny peek inside?'

Pip pounced. 'I can show the lady, sir, and introduce her to Whitty, the station cat. Do you like cats, Miss?'

'I adore them.'

'This way, Miss,' said Pip becoming the station tour guide.

George smiled at his namesake. 'Sorry about this, old chap. We need to pray there are no unexpected visitors once we reach the village—if we ever do.'

Finally Louisa emerged full of praise for the office, the cat and the large clock on the wall in George's office. She seemed genuinely impressed. George relaxed a tad thinking his station might boost his credentials in his quest to win a certain fair maiden's hand.

They pushed the perambulator to the village. George planned the route wanting to encounter as few gossipy residents as possible.

'It's a lovely village, George,' she said. 'How lucky you are to live here. Are you happy?'

Her question threw him and before he could answer, who should spot him on the other side of the High Street than the garrulous author, poet and dinner-suit supplier, Septimus Oldmeadow.

'Mr Miracle,' he called heading across the street. George tried not to cringe. 'How wonderful to see you and, to my surprise and delight, your beautiful wife and darling child. Boy or girl?'

George wanted to explain then wanted to about turn and flee. Louisa spoke first. 'It's a boy called George,' she said.

'Of course,' rejoiced the poet, 'and named after his dashing pater.'

True, yes, but confusing because father and godfather shared the same moniker. Godfather George gave up and planned their escape.

'Now tell me, kind sir,' said Septimus, 'how did your spiffing dinner suit shape up the other night. Were you a hit?'

If George thought it fair to groan aloud, he would have done so. He knew he could not be more embarrassed. He went to speak but his lady friend, not his wife or the mother of his godson, spoke first.

'He was the hit of the party, sir. Every other guest was left in awe at his fashionable finery.'

'Splendid,' said Septimus who waved goodbye and headed home.

'You tell a tall tale, Miss McClaren,' said the SM whose emotions bounced from despair to elation.

'Miss McClaren?' she replied in mock shock. 'I'm sure I asked you to call me Louisa, *Mr* Miracle.'

He loved her sense of humour. They headed along the High Street where locals wished him "Good morning" while taking in his new status as a married man with a family.

'When did that happen?' whispered one.

'I didn't even know he was married,' gasped another.

George purred. He didn't try to give himself any kind of status. The response from the villagers was natural and genuine.

This might work out well. Then he crashed. But not if they wonder why my wife and child have suddenly vanished.

To return to the station he planned a circuitous route to avoid as many of the locals as possible. He headed along a quiet street and was close to its end when four locals turned the corner coming straight towards George and his party. The group was twenty yards away and closing fast. His mind exploded.

Oh my sainted aunt, hell's bells and buckets of blood, and what have I done to deserve this?

If George was in turmoil, those in the approaching quartet were having kittens. Mrs and Miss Miracle were accompanied by would-be beau, Mr John Beckwith and fiancé Bertram Culpepper.

Cross the road, George and pretend you live on another planet.

Connie's face was indescribable. The two groups were about to collide so came to a stop.

'Good morning,' said George. 'Did the vicar cut short his sermon?'

He did actually but George's question and its relevance vanished. An explanation with full, even intimate details was required and now.

George turned to his slightly confused walking companion. 'Louisa, may I present my mother, my sister and these gentlemen are Mr Beckwith and Mr Culpepper. Ladies and gentlemen, may I introduce Miss Louisa McClaren, companion to Lady Carruthers, and this wee chap is my godson, Master George Carruthers.'

'The *Honourable* Master George Carruthers,' corrected Louisa in the most gentle of ways.

'Of course,' added George nodding to his friend.

Connie recovered from serious shock and now wanted to see the baby. Bert destroyed the moment with his awkward remark.

'Blimey, George, for a minute there I thought you'd beaten us to the wedding service and to starting a family.'

Emily only heard part of the remark and gave Bert a glare which included daggers. Connie peered into the pram. 'He's such a beautiful baby.' She looked at Louisa. 'Please make sure my son doesn't start telling the lad all about railways.'

'Oh we've already begun,' said Louisa. 'This morning, on the station, little George got his first taste of a small locomotive.'

The others, especially Connie, were shocked.

'I think it's called the Crabbie,' said Louisa seeking George's backing. He nodded with meekness, his new characteristic.

Connie looked horrified. 'All that steam and smoke, George, you need to *protect* your godson,' admonished his mother, and right on cue, wee George supported his godfather's mater and commenced to cry. It was a miserable howl rich with discomfort.

Louisa leant in to the little chap and made a discovery. 'Oh dear, the poor wee mite needs a change. We must go back, Mr Miracle.'

Connie took over. 'It's too far for the baby. Come to the station house and we can change him there.'

'How kind,' said Louisa and George wondered if his life, which was spiraling out of control, would now derail?

The group headed to the station house. The beaus were anticipating a free luncheon but due to the infant's condition now felt uneasy and superfluous. Mr Beckwith suggested he might excuse himself but the lady of the station house swiftly and firmly told him his invitation had been accepted. Bert looked at his fiancée whose eyes told him he was not backing out under any circumstances.

Accompanied by the baby's crying, all seven arrived at the cottage. George maneuvered the pram inside then suggested Mr Beckwith and Bert might like to inspect their handiwork from yesterday with the new garden. Both men jumped at the chance.

This left the Honourable George Carruthers having three females to attend to his needs with the only mother in the trio proving she well remembered the art of wiping and powdering a baby's bottom.

Chapter 15

The young and the Honourable George Carruthers left the Whittleton station house with the cleanest bottom in East Anglia. His godfather's mother believed strongly in cleanliness being next to godliness and her son, the station master, enjoyed an enormous sense of relief when escorting Louisa and their passenger back to Ripley Hall.

The fear or worry he faced about his family meeting Louisa was based entirely on two issues. He was madly in love with the Lady's companion, and he dreaded being rejected. If his family discovered his affection for Louisa, and he failed to win her hand, his sadness and embarrassment would be multiplied many times over. He would go from distress to despair. If his family never met Louisa, there would be no need for any explanation. Now he lived in hope.

Back at Ripley Hall he was invited to stay for luncheon. He could have arranged for his colleagues to operate the station and branch on the quietest day of the week but chose to decline the invitation.

Lord and Lady Carruthers thanked him profusely for all he did for their child. He said goodbye to them, the sleeping baby, Lady Fitzsimons and her son, Stephen. There was no mention of the gravely ill Lord Fitzsimons.

Stephen walked him to the massive front door. 'I have good news, Mr Miracle,' he said with a sparkle in his eye. 'My mother thinks the idea of the vineyard being reborn is exactly what the estate needs, and selling the wine which has been slumbering for years is long overdue.'

'Sounds wonderful, Stephen.' He paused. 'May I ask about your father?'

Stephen grimaced. 'No change I'm afraid. I hoped the vineyard news would buck him up but alas, no.'

'I have my publicity agent ready to produce ...'

'Your publicity agent?' exclaimed the newly restored heir to Ripley Hall. 'What happened to George Miracle the humble station master?'

'This chap is the son of my housekeeper when I lived and worked in Norwich. He works for a major London advertising company and has offered to help promote the station free of charge.'

'You are a dark horse, station master Miracle. I'm keen to hear the next instalment of your latest news.'

They both grinned and shook hands with the firmest of grips.

George headed off disappointed at not being able to farewell the woman who gave his heart a start. Setting off down the driveway, his heart caught fire when a voice floated across the lawn.

'Goodbye, Mr Miracle.'

Instantly he knew the voice, looked to his right and saw Louisa sitting on a garden bench beneath a magnificent oak tree. She held a small umbrella as protection against the sun. George's only thought was, "pretty as a picture". He moved across the lawn and sat beside her although not too close. From a second floor window in the manor house, Valerie Carruthers watched and smiled.

'I was afraid I'd missed you,' he said.

'I was afraid you'd leave by another path.'

He smiled and became excited, in fact overawed.

'It's been a wonderful morning, Louisa. I've loved showing you the station and the village.'

'And the branch line,' she said. 'We mustn't forget the Crabbie.'

Now his smile became a laugh. 'Indeed not and there are plans to help the station and the branch line grow and become prosperous.'

'I'm fascinated, please do tell.'

'Ah, for now, dear lady they must remain a trade secret.'

'A trade secret?' she reacted with a gentle mocking.

'But once things are up and running I shall count it an honour to give you a guided tour of the new Whittleton station and surrounds.'

The distinctive sound of the Crabbie's whistle floated across the fields. He reached forward and took her free hand in his, raised it, kissed her gloved hand then stood.

'But for now, Miss McClaren, duty calls and I must depart.'

'Goodbye Mr Miracle,' she said, her eyes sending messages he took to mean love, 'and thank you again for a lovely excursion.'

He bowed his head as if to a titled woman, turned and walked away. The twinge of pain in his hip as he stepped from the lawn to the path vanished. What pain?

Skipping would ping his hip but still he moved with joy. He knew he was in love and even more exciting, he was sure the young woman's affections were returned. What could be better? He wanted to go home right now to hear what his family thought of the young woman who captured his heart. How could they not fall in love with Louisa?

He walked through the station gate and onto the Up platform and stared. Horace Gardiner used his walking stick to point as he instructed three villagers in making changes to the new garden.

Eric approached his boss. 'They've been here some time, sir, and asked if it would be all right to make changes and I said you'd approve.'

'Of course,' said George. 'Mr Gardiner is welcome at any time. But how did he get here?'

'I believe he walked.'

George's eyes widened as he gasped. 'He walked?'

George was spotted by the gardening expert. 'Mr Miracle,' cried Horace and set off. Melville looked peeved feeling obliged to move so soon after he'd settled. George stood still being so impressed by the gardener's gait.'

'Mr Gardiner, it's lovely to see you and moving so freely.'

'I've decided to ignore my doctor's advice, sir. I believe exercise is the best cure for loneliness, boredom and stiff joints.'

'Even on the Sabbath?'

'*Especially* on the Sabbath.'

They smiled with George struggling to believe the situation. 'You walked from your cottage to the station?'

'And will do so again, with your permission sir.'

'Mr Gardiner, I hereby present you with the key to the Whittleton Station.' He mimed handing over an imaginary key. 'This key entitles you to access the station on any day at any time.'

Horace beamed. Thoughts of his dear departed wife lingered in the background and would do so for the rest of his life but he could hear her speaking to him. "Don't sit around feeling miserable, Horace. Get out in your garden and keep busy."

'Now tell me,' said George, 'what are your plans for the garden?'

'This garden is well on its way, sir,' he said turning to face the Down. 'But over there on the island platform, I think we could create a certain bit of magic; simple but striking. The little locomotive with its single carriage would be beautiful against a backdrop of evergreen shrubs in pots. Do you agree?'

George, already in seventh heaven thanks to his favourite girl, found himself climbing higher. *Is there an eighth heaven?*

'Your vision is inspiring, sir. Of course I agree and insist you begin work next Saturday. What should I say in the public notice?'

Horace lost his sparkle. 'I'm afraid my garden cannot supply all I would like to use but I am willing to pay for the pots and plants.'

'You'll do no such thing. Kindly furnish me with a list of all you require and I will take responsibility for the pots and plants.'

George instantly regretted his comment thinking money may be required. The conditions outlined by the LNER pinged in his brain. "The company to not incur any costs including maintenance."

Not for the first time, the old man couldn't speak. He lived for his garden and to be able to extend it, and have the public share and enjoy same gave him a deep and lasting pleasure.

George had been absent for some time and now needed to visit his office. 'Please excuse me, sir,' he said, 'and I await your list.'

In his office on his desk were the usual items of mail. The railways may lack certain abilities the haulage companies and post office have but in-house mail delivery is a strength of the railways.

Amongst the mail was a hand-addressed envelope from a person whose writing he recognized.

Oscar Wilding, true to his word, sent George copy for newspapers promoting the new garden, the award-winning Whittleton author, the new tourist attraction at Pickling, and the wine tastings and sales at the local manor house.

"It's over to you now, George," wrote Oscar. "Change the details if necessary and take the photographs. Then tell the world. Here is a list of local newspapers and good luck!"

George exhaled. His excitement levels couldn't climb higher.

If all these ideas, these projects take off, what will happen? Will passenger numbers take off? Will the Crabbie survive?

He needed to obtain Stephen's approval for the wording of the notice about wine tastings and sales at Ripley Hall, and would have loved to return to see him in person. Another rendezvous with the lovely Louisa filled him with joy. But returning so soon might embarrass Louisa and be seen as inappropriate behaviour within the upper class. He wrote a note to Stephen and included a copy of the copy written by Oscar about the winery, seeking Stephen's approval. He popped the letter and document inside an envelope addressed to Stephen, and gave the lad porter the role of postman.

'Always show respect, Pip,' he said, and sent the boy on his way.

He thought about his unfinished tasks. Arrange the time and venue for Septimus to perform a book reading. Find someone who could take and develop photographs without charging the Earth or preferably nothing. And beg, borrow or steal the pots and plants required by Horace for the island platform. Phew!

Oh, and discover who is sending those ridiculous false reports about the Crabbie.

As George sent the next Up on its way, a worried Pip returned. 'What's happened?' asked the concerned SM.

'I wasn't able to speak to Mr Stephen, sir,' said Pip. 'A servant opened the door, took the envelope and told me there has been a death in the family. I hope I did the right thing, sir.'

George nodded. 'Thank you, lad and yes, you did. There was no name mentioned I assume?'

'No sir.'

Pip was dismissed and George stewed over his next move. He couldn't send a condolence message without knowing who was deceased. It most likely was Lord Fitzsimons but what if it was his wife or, incredibly, his son?

George made sure station duties were covered, and between trains, popped into the village and knocked on the soon to be well-known writer's door. No limerick was heard, instead footsteps and happy singing came from within. It sounded like the tune to a popular song about a man who "did over" a bank in Monte Carlo. The singing stopped, the door opened with a sweeping gesture and there stood Septimus Oldmeadow imitating an overdressed Beau Brummel.

'My dear boy,' effused the writer who wore a bright blue jacket with lapels sporting sparkling trim. His white silk shirt was brunched at his throat. His white trousers had razor-sharp creases and the white patent leather shoes made it tricky for George to know where to start. Try his head, George, as there perched a rakish hat sporting an ostrich feather.

'Good day to you, sir.' George couldn't help himself. 'Are you going anywhere special?'

'Come in, come in,' commanded Septimus and once inside George received the news.

'I'm rehearsing for my coming-out-in-public as the award-winning-novelist-who-loves-limericks role.' He made a stylish stance. 'What do you think of my appearance? Is it too timid?'

George failed to stop a huge grin from tickling his ears. As he had arrived to make sure Mr Oldmeadow was definitely "going public", George's mission was irrelevant. Joy flooded his heart and mind.

'I would regard it as totally perfect, my good sir. I cannot decide which I prefer more; your superb attire or your witty and memorable limericks.'

Goodness, his remarks went down a treat and George faced a dickens of a job to escape without imbibing. He used his cap as a sort of shield to avoid drinking on the job.

'Once we have the venue, date and time, sir, I'll let you know.'

Septimus changed his expression and spoke softly. 'Might there be more than one appearance?' politely enquired the author.

'Most definitely,' said George who hurried back to the station and again wanted to skip but couldn't because of his darn hip.

The last Sunday train departed, George said good night to fellow railwaymen but sat alone in his office. His supper waited in the station house as did his mother and sister. Each had prepared over a hundred questions for the SM about his friends in the manor house and, more importantly, the young woman with the baby.

He too wanted answers. *Who has died at Ripley Hall? Will this help or hinder the plans to promote the station and the branch? Will the death see the visiting family Carruthers and the Lady's lovely companion return to Hampstead sooner than planned?*

Delving deep into romantic love was a new experience for the station master. Confusion reigned. The experience of yearning he understood but being afraid of not being accepted became a new type of fear. Surely a beautiful young woman would attract another suitor, *many* other suitors. She mixes with the rich and powerful, even the titled. Why the interest in a country SM with a limp?

Who am I? I'm a lowly SM on a rural railway with a battered and bruised branch line for company.

You have no status, Miracle and little money. You'll never be rich. What can you offer? You're a miniscule fish in a massive pond stretching almost the length of the country. You are lower middle class at best. Stop trying to live above your station. Settle for a person of your own class.

But I think she likes me. She smiles, even laughs at my so-called jokes. She even teases me. She wouldn't do so if in love with another.

And why was she waiting in the garden after I left to return to the station? She must have wanted to be there.

He went home and didn't face a hundred questions about Louisa and godson, George. He faced two hundred.

But George was pleasantly surprised at the respect his family showed to him regarding Louisa. 'You certainly know how to pick them, George,' said Emily. 'Do you think being a station master is the key to attracting such a beautiful girl?'

For a moment he thought his sister was teasing him but he saw she was serious. He dodged the question.

'You're both putting the cart before the horse. We're only friends.'

Connie wanted answers. 'Will you be walking out with her before she leaves?'

'No,' was the definitive answer. Both women were shocked and were about to ask why when George told them. 'There's been a death at Ripley Hall.' He raised a hand. 'And please don't ask as I don't know who but Lord Fitzsimons has been poorly for a long time.'

They watched him eat his supper. Trixie watched from the next chair and Spike lay on the floor beside George hoping for scraps from the table. Connie forbade the animals being fed with humans' food. She knew her children disobeyed but did nothing to stop them.

Connie reckoned a change of topic was called for. 'The vicar is reading the final banns on Sunday, George.' He glanced at his mother knowing next to nothing about canon law. She knew he was ignorant. 'It means Emily and Bert are free to wed and the date and time can be set. Please make sure you are free.'

Emily pressed the point. 'It'll be a Saturday, George and you need to be off work all day, and be available for a rehearsal in the church in the week before the wedding.'

In-between mouthfuls, he smiled. 'Received and understood, Ma'am.'

'And you are most welcome to bring Louisa,' added Connie with Emily's face beaming her approval.

'We'll see,' he said still eating. His reply didn't please the women. Far from teasing him about having a lady friend, they were thrilled at his choice. He hoped their enthusiasm might help support his case.

Chapter 16

As the Whittleton station garden took shape, in London a gentleman, although many would question such a description, the aristocrat Richard Carrington, the Earl of Fakenham, went about his hedonistic life. He possessed rank but no estate, a moniker but no wealth. Rugged good looks helped the young Earl swim in social circles. His father was a second son and Dickie's uncle scored the wealth and sired three sons.

This turned the Earl's mind to finding a rich middle-aged widow, and the richer the better. Of course a ravishing virgin with a loaded pater would do just as nicely, thank you very much.

Richard associated with the Hamilton-Weir family who, unlike him, was loaded. The two Hamilton-Weir siblings, the twins Sophronia and Enoch, were both in love or lust or both with Dickie who was happy to bowl fast or spin. He would spend weekends at the Hamilton-Weir country seat where the trio caroused until becoming bored when they retired to prepare for more of the same on the morrow; much later on the morrow.

The patriarch of the Hamilton-Weir family, the philanthropist Sir Jerome, struggled with a secret. Many moons ago, he sired a third child following an adulterous relationship with a single woman. The birth was hushed up with the child raised by its mother who, when the child grew older, told the youngster the father was deceased.

Years later, Sir Jerome's wife and mother of the twins became seriously ill, and as she lay dying, called her adult children to her bedside. 'You need to be warned, my darlings,' she said, and told them of their illegitimate half sibling. No details and no names were known but their father had definitely sired three offspring, not two.

Their mother died leaving the twins to ponder how they could discover the identity of their unknown family member. Asking their father seemed far too risky. If he wanted it kept a secret and they told him they knew, he might disinherit them altogether. No, the twins chose the softly, softly, catchee monkey approach.

One day at the Cheltenham races, a clerk for the solicitor who handled Sir Jerome's affairs, sidled up to Enoch in the betting ring.

'I have a tip for you, Master Enoch,' he said.

The wealthy punter sneered. 'Don't tell me; your cousin knows the neighbour of the stable boy's girlfriend.'

'Not 'orses, sir. Your pater's been in to change 'is will.'

You could have knocked Enoch down with a betting slip. He gasped. 'What? When? Changed to what? How?' Now he threatened. 'Tell me.'

The clerk paused, Enoch twigged, gave the man a fiver and waited, desperate for the answer.

The clerk protested. 'Oh come now, sir, it's more than me job's worth, but at least now you and your sister know.'

He was right. Enoch knew he'd been conned but knowing there was a new will was worth a lot more than a Lady Godiva. He couldn't wait to tell his sister the news. She exploded.

'It's his damn love-child. The lucky bastard's come of age and is now to be rewarded.'

'It's our money,' fumed Enoch.

'Knowing the old man, he'll give half to the brat and leave us to split the remainder.'

'You do realize the brat is about our age.'

Sophronia leaked hatred.

The twins were desperate to learn the contents of the old man's new will. Sophronia would kill for such information; literally as it was no coincidence, behind her back of course, her brother called her Lucrezia.

The siblings raged. How dare their pater share what was rightfully theirs with anyone. This rage proved incendiary and became the catalyst of the quest to discover the identity of their step-sibling, and to see if he or she was now a beneficiary of their father's new will.

The twins were hopeless as detectives. They needed help and their intimate acquaintance, the Earl of Fakenham, needed and craved wealth. The stars aligned. The twins discussed engaging the Earl in their plan to help rid them of their troublesome half-sibling.

'Would he do it?' asked Sophronia.

'Of course,' said Enoch. 'Offer him money and he'll do anything.'

'But is he clever? He's cunning but is he discreet?'

'Let's keep him in reserve and bring him on board when the target is identified.' She agreed.

Could those in the upper class stoop to such wickedness as murder? Bloody oath they could.

The next morning George needed to know who had died in the nearby estate. He waited till late morning, told Eric he would be gone for a short time, and headed to the manor house.

The estate seemed in mourning. He saw no workers in the garden or surrounding fields. Cattle grazed in deathly silence. His chest tightened. He planned a brief visit to express his condolences and then be gone. If fortune favoured the brave and he caught a glimpse from afar of a particular young lady, he'd count it a bonus.

He knocked gently on the huge front door; ringing the bell seemed bad manners. No-one responded and he thought he should go. Knocking a second time didn't enter his head. He turned to leave when the door opened.

'Good day, Mr Miracle,' said the family retainer dressed in a black suit with a black tie. The only white items were his shirt and his hair.

'Good day, Mr Fortesque,' replied George. 'I'm here to convey my condolences to the family but please, I don't wish to disturb anyone.'

'Will you wait, sir while I fetch his Lordship?' He disappeared leaving the door ajar.

George died. *It's Lady Fitzsimons. It couldn't be Stephen.* He twigged. *Stephen is now Lord Fitzsimons.* The seconds ticked by. They became minutes. Then he heard footsteps and squeezed his SM cap firmly as the door opened.

'George,' exclaimed Stephen. 'How kind you are to call. Please come in.'

'I won't, sir, if you don't mind.'

'Of course, you're a busy man.'

'Please accept my deepest sympathy and convey my condolences to her Ladyship.'

'I will indeed and there is a silver lining, George. On his deathbed, my father and I were reunited. I can tell you there was a significant shedding of tears from both of us but forgiveness reigned supreme and my mother is a new woman.'

'I'm so glad to hear that news, but I'll be away and leave you to your grieving.'

'Before you go, my friend,' said Stephen. George stopped. 'Now I've inherited my father's title, I want you to know I am never more keen to push on with the changes we discussed. And your words about the winery for the newspapers are spot on. Please go ahead and make Ripley Hall a part of your Whittleton Station Day.'

'Excellent news; thank you my Lord.'

'That's enough of the title stuff, and certainly when we're alone. Oh and because of my father's passing, the Carruthers have left but asked me to say goodbye and they hope to see you again soon.'

Stephen offered his hand which George shook with feeling. He turned and walked down the steps. Stephen went to close the door then opened it and called. 'Oh and Valerie's lady companion asked me to thank you for the powdered bottom, whatever that means!' He laughed and waved.

George waved and thought his heart would burst. Once again the damn German shrapnel stopped him skipping back to Whittleton.

He walked to the station to be greeted by Eric. 'I've just hung up from a chap from Head Office who wanted to tell you when the inspection team is coming to Whittleton.'

Eric knew nothing of this but could see from George's face, a serious matter was in the wind.

'Did he give a date?'

'The 24th,' said Eric.'

'This month?' asked George with fear in his voice.

'It's Thursday fortnight.' He paused. 'May I ask what this is about?'

'Yes, your survival and my sacking,' replied George going to his desk and leaving the senior porter with an open mouth.

George circled the 19th, the Saturday before the LNER inspection. He referred to it as WSD; Whittleton Station Day. He had the events and the publicity copy. Now with a date fixed, he wrote to newspapers about the Druid tourist spot, the award-winning author in the little village, the garden transformation of the station, and the wine tastings at the manor house, Ripley Hall. He told the world about his Whittleton Station Day.

Photos were important and he had none. But time was more important and publicity was vital. He used a few of the garden illustrations designed by Horace Gardiner hoping they would appeal to the editors.

He prepared notices about the need for pots and plants to decorate the Crabbtree branch line platform, and a separate notice promoting the Druid meeting place being a perfect spot to discover the history of the area. Access to the site was easy from the Pickling Halt reached via the Crabbie. All this was happening on Whittleton Station Day on Saturday week.

He went into the village and posted the letters to local newspapers at the post office, and placed notices in the post office and on the noticeboard in the High Street.

He popped into Mr Oldmeadow's cottage and advised him of the date of his first book reading.

'But what about my limericks?' he asked, worried they would be forgotten or dismissed as unimportant.

'They are essential, sir,' replied George and the grin on the poet's face lit up his front room.

The chairman of the parish council was minding his own business when the SM knocked on his cottage door. Hearing about all these events on the Whittleton Station Day shocked the councillor. 'Why didn't I know about these events?' he demanded.

George didn't realize he possessed political expertise but became a natural by turning a tricky situation into a win. 'Because Mr Chairman, we can't seek your approval until all the basics are in place, and now they are we seek your approval and beg you to provide your great ability in dealing with the strong interest from newspapers all over the county.' "All over the county" was a major exaggeration but the chairman spoke fluent baloney so why not embellish?

Oh my, did George turn trouble into a triumph. Godfrey Grantley-Smythe enthused with glee. He seemed to be gurgling. Publicity for his good self could only enhance his chances of being successful in winning pre-selection for the Conservative Party in his local electorate. Godfrey was on board. Was he ever!

What remained? What did George fail to do? If head office received any more reports about the branch with greatly inflated figures, his career was over unless by Saturday week, he could conjure some sort of miracle; a miracle courtesy of Miracle.

A few days earlier, Septimus enjoyed paying a visit to his literary agent to declare his days of anonymity were over.

'Are you sure?' asked the veteran power-behind-the-throne expert.

'Before I die, I want the world to know who I am, what I did, and how my first love is and always will be writing nonsense poetry.'

The agent made no comment about the nonsense rhymes but set in train the announcement of his client's wishes.

When the news broke and the literati discovered the identity of T. J. Beaufoy, many were stunned. Most were sure the novelist was female. 'She has to be a woman to write such deep and meaningful female characters,' they said.

The most common response went as follows: 'He's an elderly eccentric buried in a village in the back of beyond.'

Bookworms craved more details. 'He's giving a reading from his latest novel in a village hall on Saturday week.'

Few people knew anything about Septimus and especially not about his passion for limericks.

All of a sudden critics, journalists, and excited readers studied the railway timetable. Where on Earth is Whittleton? How does one get there? I've never heard of it. Which train will get me there in time for the reading?

Stephen, now Lord Fitzsimons, trod carefully. His father's funeral was strictly a private affair. Obviously Stephen wanted to support his mother at this time and do nothing to upset her. But his plans to revive the family estate were primed and ready to go. With the SM's hand being forced by the LNER inspection, it was time to launch.

'How are you, Mother?' he asked as she sat at the desk in her late husband's study.

She put down her pen. 'There are so many letters to write, so many people who need to be told about your father.'

'Can I find you some help, a person with secretarial skills?'

'My darling boy, telling family and dear friends about your father and his broken heart is not easy. Sharing such news with an outsider would never do. I'll take my time but thank you anyway.'

He paused wondering how he might raise the subject of business and commerce when his mother was still in mourning. He decided to leave it until days, even weeks would pass.

'I'll leave you to your work, Mother,' he said, kissed her head and set off for the door.

'Stephen,' she spoke softly but with conviction. He stopped. 'I think the best thing you can do now your father has left us is to crack on with those plans you have for the revival of the estate.'

He froze, struck dumb. 'Are you sure, Mother?'

'Never more so. Let's lift the gloom which has settled on the Hall for the last umpteen years. Let's make it prosperous again, let's be open and sociable. I hear the station has a new garden. Why can't we bring a bit of colour back into the Hall? Let's have a day when the villagers can come and enjoy pony rides and lucky dips and celebrate the rebirth of our estate.'

Stephen couldn't stop the tears. He hurried back to his mother and they enjoyed the strongest of hugs.

He left immediately for the station and surprised George. 'I have good news, Stationmaster Miracle, no, great news. My mother wants the plans to revive the estate to start now.'

'Now?' gasped George, 'before your father's funeral?'

'Well not exactly this afternoon but certainly in the next few days or weeks. We can plan now and be ready to move by next week.'

George told Stephen the Whittleton Station Day date and the new Lord was as keen as mustard.

'Include us in your plans, George. My mother suggested an Open Day in the future where the locals picnic in the grounds. But your Station Day on the 19th sounds perfect.'

George's smile became contagious. 'You have made my day, my Lord.' They shook on it.

'We are ready to go with the wine tastings and sales from our cellar, and we can plan for an Open Day on the estate in a month or two.'

George purred with excitement. 'That sounds wonderful.'

'Please include us in all your publicity. Tourists, wine lovers, gardeners and book lovers; invite them all, the more the merrier.'

Stephen caught fire. His face lit up as he thanked George and promised to do all he could to make the day a great success.

When the Crabbie returned on its final run, George came out and watched the tank engine arrive with not a living soul disembarking. George waited until eventually a distressed porter, Gordon, stepped from the carriage, a broken man. With his "bucket and spade", his cleaning material, he slinked off to the storage shed before returning to the Up platform. This was his second Pickling secondment. George refused to challenge him about his betrayal instead telling Gordon he knew what he'd done without telling the porter. George's plan worked. Gordon swam in guilt, terrified he'd be sacked. George worked away not acknowledging the man who knocked on his door.

'I'm back, sir,' said the exhausted porter.

George looked up. 'Well done, Gordon. How did you go? Is the Halt and its facilities ready for masses of curious tourists?'

'It is, sir. The ablutions area is clean, the station sign has been repainted, and the pathway to the Druid rocks is clear.'

'Thank you so much, Gordon. I'll put in a good report for all your work and mention you in dispatches when the inspection takes place in a couple of weeks.'

Gordon stood there stunned. As the rat in the ranks, being bombarded with kindness took its toll on his mind. He worried on several fronts. *Why hasn't he asked me to name those who engaged me to help destroy him? And what's this "inspection?*

'Now you cut along, Gordon,' said George. 'I'll lock up.'

The porter couldn't find the words for anything and left for his digs, boarding as he was with Monty and his missus. If they found out he was a traitor to the cause, his next meal might well contain arsenic.

George completed his list of things to do. There were so many. One thing he needed but couldn't control was publicity. Without the newspapers coming to the party, all his projects were doomed to fail.

Chapter 17

People have used prosthetic limbs for thousands of years. In the 19th century, as medicine realized the importance of cleanliness in treating patients, amputations became more successful, or perhaps less disastrous. Fewer patients died and the operation took into account the prospect of having prosthetics added later.

George Carruthers saw other limbless ex-soldiers getting on with life having received an "added-on" limb. He consulted an expert and, after measurements were taken and explanations given, he ordered a bespoke half-leg and, when made, George "legged up".

Valerie was by his side in the consulting room. The prosthetic fitted well. 'How does it feel my Lord?' asked the technician.

'Feels fine,' said Carruthers. He sat on the edge of the narrow bed. Two assistants in white coats stood either side of him.

'Right,' said the surgeon, 'let's see you stand and become an honorary homo erectus.'

George blew air. This was the real test. Valerie's stomach tied itself in knots. The assistants took one of George's arms apiece and helped him become upright. He didn't feel pain, but certainly a strange sensation. The men studied him and then their supervisor. He gave an imperceptible nod and George was flying solo.

He wanted to take a step but couldn't. Figuratively he lurched towards despair.

'I don't know what to do,' he whispered.

'Yes you do, your brain wasn't wounded. Think about the instructions. Repeat them aloud.'

George remembered and acted as he spoke. 'Push down on your, *my* right. Swing your, *my* left hip. Land my left foot and pause.' He did as instructed.

Everyone in the room clapped, cried "Bravo" or similar, and Valerie cried a bucket of tears.

The transformation was spectacular. The patient wanted to use his crutches as kindling but was persuaded not to. 'You can use them for short journeys. If it's 2am and you fancy a pee, by the time you've added your new leg, you'll definitely be caught short.' They laughed.

'Thank you, Doctor, thank you from the bottom of my heart but one other thing.' Everyone, particularly the medical man, stared at him. What now? 'How soon before I can drive a car?'

The laughter was long and loud. With his wife slightly terrified by his side, and using a fancy walking stick, George managed to make it to the end of the corridor.

The telephone rang in the SM's office at Whittleton.

'Whittleton station, station master Miracle speaking,' said the other George.

'Carruthers here,' announced the titled George.

'George,' exclaimed George, delighted to hear from the father of his godson who was often cared for by a certain fair lady.

'I wanted you to be one of the first to know I've grown a new leg.'

The SM failed to understand. 'You've what?'

'Prosthetics, squire; I'm back on two legs.'

Now the SM understood. 'Oh George, you're fantastic. If anyone can overcome adversity, it's Carruthers, DSO, father of the century.'

The caller laughed. 'I'm working on learning to drive and finding a horseless carriage with special controls. We'll put your godson in the back and nip down to the country for a slap-up lunch. What say ye?'

'I've only one thing to say, my Lord; when?'

They continued to joke and when their call ended, George Miracle was buzzing, the phone call being a happy distraction from his current hectic lifestyle. Running the station and the branch was a fulltime job. The LNER kept sending what many call bumpf, and each item needed to be digested and, if necessary, acted upon.

But the steam train roaring down the track at present was the inspection of his station and, more particularly, the dear old Crabbie.

Reports, false reports told head office the branch at Whittleton was booming when in truth it was dying, if not dead.

To save the branch and his reputation, George cobbled together a series of activities to put his stations on the map. Each new day brought new offers of help or materials such as plants in pots. The Crabbie now arrived against a swathe of potted annuals. One kind villager offered an ancient wheelbarrow which soon contained small pots with plants. It sat proudly on the island platform. Whittleton exuded character.

George's list of items-to-do would be reduced during the day then new items would appear and the list grew longer by late afternoon. People called at the station offering their services for the Whittleton Station Day. If George wasn't at work, they'd walk to the cottage nearby and knock on his front door.

On the Wednesday morning, ten days before the LNER inspection, Freda arrived on the Crabbie as usual for the weekly visit to her sister in Whittleton. George tried just about everything to avoid being kissed on the lips by Freda and especially by Rufus. This Wednesday, Freda was less amorous because of something she wanted to do.

'I've got a great idea, George.' George worried. 'I could be the guide for the Druid site,' she said oozing enthusiasm.

George saw immediate problems. 'But you can't sit at the Halt all day hoping a tourist might arrive,' he said.

'Of course not but when I hear the Crabbie on the Down, I'll trot over to Pickling and be ready to work.'

'I can't pay you, Freda.'

'No, but I can have a stall with a collection of my jams and pickles and even a small tin for tips. Tourists like to tip the good guides.'

George wanted to encourage everyone but would have no control over a lone operator far from Whittleton.

'Here's a better idea,' she said. 'I'll have Madge give a special signal on the whistle if there are any passengers for Pickling. If the train's empty, I'll stop home and keep working. It can't fail.'

She grinned at George. What could he say? 'It sounds wonderful, Freda,' he said and instantly regretted those words.

She and Rufus now must say "Thank you" and did so the only way they knew. Oh, Gawd!

His morning exploded when a couple arrived asking for Mr Miracle.

'I'm station master Miracle,' he said and met a female journalist and a male photographer from the *Gazette,* a prominent county newspaper.

'We're here to write about the plans to revolutionize your station, sir,' said Miss Rankin.

'George's heart hit a roadblock. He remembered his experience in London when a female journalist tricked him. She conned him into describing his involvement with the Carruthers family in Hampstead and the murder of Lord Carruthers, father of George.

The SM needed publicity but the wrong sort could backfire and hurt rather than help.

'It's not a revolution, Miss but interesting new activities which people from surrounding districts are welcome to enjoy.'

That didn't sound exciting. The journalist sensed a wasted journey. George needed to make the day sing. *She needs excitement.*

'Did you know our humble village is home to the award-winning novelist, P. J. Beaufoy alias Mr Septimus Oldmeadow?' Miss Rankin looked interested. George pushed on. 'And Ripley Hall, our local manor house, has produced some of the best vintages in England with free tastings on offer. I'm sure many of your refined readers would be lovers of good literature and fine wine, Miss Rankin. From Whittleton station, the Hall is a mere five minute stroll away.'

Steady George.

He pointed across to the Crabbie. 'And a few stops along our branch line is a rarely visited historical site where once Druids came to worship. We even have a local expert acting as free guide. You've only just missed her.'

Miss Rankin sighed with disappointment. Then George gestured along the Up platform. 'And this is part of the beautiful Whittleton station garden designed by a local resident and built by many members of the village. It makes catching your train a delight, don't you think?'

His begging the question prodded her positive response. He was in for a penny and in for a pound.

'You would photograph superbly, Miss Rankin, beneath those baskets.' He gestured to the mute photographer. 'Sir?' The man moved as if instructed. Miss Rankin knew her editor disliked staff in photographs—"Readers want to see themselves or their neighbours, not journalists"—he would say but Miss Rankin wore a brand new hat and rather fancied it and her in a picture.

Photos were taken and the couple went into the village to interview Septimus. He went "Over the Top" and plied them with his homemade brew. They loved it, and him and were struck by his

Currer Bell Medal. Their article and picture gave his talk in the village hall next week a huge promotion.

The *Gazette* was a thrice weekly so when the article appeared complete with a magnificent shot of the station garden including Miss Rankin and her new hat, other papers which were dragging their feet, sent scribes to cover the saga.

George was swamped by the press. He gave Freda permission to become the Druid guide not knowing what she would say or do. He asked his mother's friend, Mr Beckwith, to compere the village hall meeting in which Septimus would reveal himself to the literary world. In the manor house, Stephen was raring to go and as his father had been laid to rest in the family cemetery beneath the pines in the far meadow, life moved up a gear.

Stephen employed two locals to work on days when the cellar was open. His gamekeeper erected signs directing visitors to the venue.

George arrived home at night exhausted. His mother and sister became genuinely worried.

'You're no good to anyone, George, if you have to take to your bed,' said Connie.

'I'll be fine, Ma. I have a lot on my plate.'

She placed a plate in front of him. 'Is this too much on your plate?'

He smiled and tucked in.

'In all your plans and schemes as you save the world, George Miracle,' said his sister, 'don't you dare neglect my wedding. Our Da will never forgive you if you're late or missing.'

'She's right,' said their mother.

'And if you *are* late, I'll never speak to you again, ever.'

George looked at Emily and his mother. He wondered if this was what was meant by the expression, tough love.

Chapter 18

Sophronia Hamilton-Weir and her brother Enoch were up in town in the family's Belgravia townhouse. They had arranged an appointment with a private detective renowned for his discretion, success and outrageous fees.

Meet Carlos Riff, a cunning so-and-so. His eyes proved it; they glowed even in daylight. He once dabbled in petty crime until he discovered the British aristocracy hid more skeletons in their wardrobes than you could poke a tibia at. Many rich Brits wished to retain their wealth but hide their issues. Carlos thrived in this niche market.

Within well-heeled circles, if you needed a problem solved without any legal hiccups, hire Riff. The Hamilton-Weir twins intended to do just that. Carlos was shown into the second drawing-room and given the facts with Enoch leading the way.

'Our father, bless his braces, was a naughty boy twenty odd years ago and fathered a child, our half sibling.

'Male or female?' asked Carlos.

'Let him finish,' snapped Sophronia allowing Carlos to quickly learn who wore the pants in the Hamilton-Weir family.

'Not sure,' said Enoch. 'But we strongly believe our dearest Papa, whilst refusing to publically acknowledge the bastard, still wants to include him or her ...'

'It,' snapped his sister.

'*It* in his will. More fool him. What we require, sir, is the identity of our half-sibling and a way whereby he/she/it can be excluded from said pater's largesse. For us, fifty per cent each is a hell of a lot better than a third. Oh and of course it's the principle of the matter.'

Carlos reckoned both twins couldn't even spell *principle*.

'We wish to make a deal, sir,' snarled Sophronia. 'You will receive an agreed fee when you identify this creature, and double the amount if you have a fool-proof method, legal or otherwise, which permanently excludes the interloper from the will. What say ye, sir?'

'It depends on the fee, madam,' said clever clogs Carlos.

She wasn't finished. 'Oh and you receive nothing if you are unable to correctly identify the target.'

Carlos didn't flinch. He held all the cards. If they didn't agree to his fee, he'd walk. If he found the task too difficult, and he regarded that possibility as unthinkable, he would quit while ahead.

'I agree to your terms although my fee is not negotiable.' He fixed a rock-solid gaze on them, and although their faces showed bravado even contempt, both knew they were over a barrel. A pin dropped, crashing on the hand-woven carpet.

Breaking the silence, Enoch asked, 'And what is your fee?'

Carlos named his price, and the twins refused to flinch. They were expecting an outrageous amount and furious they underestimated his greed. Greedy folk are alike; they hate being bested by someone more greedy than them. But as they needed him more than he needed them, they agreed to his eye-watering quotation.

He was given the name of the legal firm which handled their father's affairs, and the solicitor's clerk who informed them about Daddy's will being recently changed. He left promising to keep them informed of any developments.

George's phone rang. 'Station master Miracle, this is station master Rogers. How are you managing, George?'

'Good day to you, Jack. I'm glad to hear your voice but worried you may have bad news.' He moved to close the SM's office door.

'Worry not my friend. Scotland Yard identified your car parked in Crabbtree and to no-one's surprise, it's linked to a nasty chap who, as they say, is known to the police.'

'But he's not a railwayman?'

'No but I'd give you odds he's been instructed and paid by someone in the LNER who hates your guts.'

George breathed easier. 'I've got news too. I've found the traitor in the ranks here at Whittleton. He's one of my porters.'

'What?' cried SM Rogers. 'Why didn't you tell me?'

George explained his life of late, how busy he was with preparing for the Whittleton Station Day and the LNER inspection, and how he was sure Gordon wasn't directly responsible for sending the false reports or the vandalism.

'He's the spy telling some jealous railwayman what we're doing.'

'What's your porter's name?' asked Rogers.

'Gordon Littleton.'

'Right, I'll lay money a bloke called Ralph Topliss is involved. He's based at Chatham, and has been running you down for a while now claiming you won promotion thanks to your uncle.'

'They're cousins,' said George.

'What?'

'When Gordon first arrived, he told me he had a cousin in the service at Chatham, a porter called Ralph something.'

'Topliss,' added Rogers. 'You've cracked it George; well done. Now what can I do?'

'I've hit on a way to punish my double-crossing porter. I've pretended I don't know he's the snitch and instead given him the job repairing the vandalism and upgrading the tourist site. Then I've praised him to the heavens. He's exhausted and confused.'

The London SM laughed. 'What a brilliant ploy, young man. Your uncle would be mighty proud of your clever thinking.'

'But I'm in a real mess here, Jack. Head office is inspecting me and the branch the week after next. Those false reports will bring me undone unless I can work a sort of miracle.'

More laughter sounded from London. 'A miracle from Miracle.'

George explained his plans and the London SM wished him every success. 'Thanks for your support, Jack. I'll keep you posted.'

The call ended and George leant back in his chair. He thought of his wild schemes, the tactics he planned to save his skin, and then he thought of a young woman called Louisa.

Would his plans work? Would he be able to save the branch line and his career? And would he be able to persuade that certain young lady to accept his invitation of marriage?

Carlos worked hard. He needed access to the latest Hamilton-Weir will. A break-in was risky. His tactic was simple. Discover a weak link within the solicitor's office then convince this weak link they needed to help Carlos by providing him with the information for which he would collect a king's ransom. Of course his real motivation and goal would never be revealed. He needed a stooge and a story.

He discovered the weak link by watching the solicitor's building. Two young females left at 5.30 every afternoon. They walked together to the Underground but separated, one heading north, one south.

Carlos chose the female he reckoned more gullible and followed. Being a sleuth came naturally to him, stalking became his strength. He discovered the simple suburban home of his mark.

He researched public records and chatted with neighbours while in disguise. He discovered who lived in the property, and confirmed the young woman he followed worked for the appropriate solicitor.

He was a week into the case when he made contact with the mother of his weak link. He ingratiated himself into the invalided woman's life reckoning if Mummy bought his story, her daughter would too. That night, the mother had great news.

'He's our long lost cousin on your father's side, Gabrielle,' said her widowed mother, 'and he's calling tonight to meet you.'

Carlos arrived. 'I'm delighted to meet my beautiful young cousin,' he oozed, his perfectly rounded English accent stating his name as Edward Fairhaven. You would never guess he was born in Moscow.

Two days later, Carlos "accidentally" bumped into Gabriella and took her to afternoon tea at Claridge's. With the full silver service and a waitress treating Gabrielle like a "proper" lady dominating, Carlos told a vague tale about helping his best friends—no names at this stage—who were being cheated out of their rightful inheritance by a wicked step-mother and her evil daughter. Gabrielle was hooked.

When the self-appointed cousin by marriage delivered Gabrielle home, she regaled her mother with the social event.

'It was wonderful, Mummy,' babbled Gabrielle. 'The sandwiches were tiny but perfect and the cakes divine.'

Mrs Laidlaw seemed to suffer a fit of the vapors.

The set-up continued apace and soon the trap would be sprung.

The amount of press coverage worried George. An article or two would be ideal. Tell the locals and others about the wine tasting and the Druid rocks and, of course, about the local literary hero, but now the snowball gathered size and speed. People discovered Whittleton and asked questions.

How old is the vintage in the Whittleton manor house?

Eric came into George's office with news of a lost parcel. 'Mrs Carlyle from the village says her sister posted it from London ten days ago and has been here twice with no sign of her wool.'

'Is it still on the sheep's back?' asked the SM. He would not normally be so flippant but pressure from various sources changed his personality. At home, his mother noticed.

'What's happened, George?' she asked. 'You're being short with your own family, and being short with anyone is not you.'

'I'm sorry, Ma. I'm under pressure at the station.'

'Has it got anything to do with Louisa?'

He stared at his mother and scratched his chin not wanting to answer the question.

'I think I'll go for a walk, Ma, and have a chat with your friend, the Big Man in the sky.' George didn't usually opt for such a cop out.

George Carruthers loved his new leg. Any challenge suited the young Lord and the more difficult the better. He refused any help in attaching the prosthetic leg and then when standing. 'I can do it, I'm all right,' he announced whenever Valerie or his manservant stepped forward to help. He kept pestering people about finding him an automobile with special controls for a driver sporting a false leg.

Over breakfast he tapped an item in his newspaper, *The Times*. 'We're going my darling,' he said grinning at his wife. Wee George sat in his high chair being fed expertly by his mother. More of the high-class gruel landed on his bib than in the little mite's mouth.

'Going where?' she asked then changed her expression. 'Oh George darling, please open wide for Mummy.'

'Buckingham Palace Garden Party,' said his Lordship. 'We're hardly ever seen in public and never at any society social events. Our wedding was the smallest in the British Isles so now it's time Lord and Lady Carruthers stood up and greeted the world.'

Valerie thought the use of "stood up" was risky given her husband's recent acquisition of half a leg but another issue troubled her and she hesitated to raise it. He babbled away.

'You shall have a new hat, my darling and a new dress. In fact you shall have a complete new outfit. No longer will my stunning bride remain hidden. To the ball you shall go, Cinderella, via Harrods of course.'

'Thank you, George,' she said without excitement and about to raise the controversial topic.

'You don't seem so keen, my wife.'

'Darling, do you not think the tragedy of your father's death may still be important to some people?'

He reflected on the scandal of his father's murder and the convictions of his mother and her lover. If you wanted gossip fodder, there it lay in spades.

George spoke with a calm conviction. 'We have done nothing wrong. If the King and Queen will accept us at the Palace, the rest of London can be damned. We're going.'

His decision stood and Valerie acquired a new and stunning outfit. When the couple retired, in bed, Valerie asked her husband if her lady companion, Louisa might attend the garden party.

'Of course my dear but surely it's unnecessary to have two women help a gentleman even if he has only one fully functioning leg?'

'Louisa will not be there for you, my dear.'

Silence filled the darkened bed chamber. After a lengthy pause, Lord Carruthers hopped out of bed and switched on a bedside lamp. The size of the bed and the location of its bedside table forced such a move. He stared at his wife. 'Am I missing something?'

She smiled. 'I do believe your son is to have a playmate.'

His cry of delight was heard as far away as the kitchen.

In Belgravia, the Hamilton-Weir twins discussed the very same topic, i.e. the Buckingham Palace Garden Party. Their house guest, Dickie Carrington, grew nervous. As an Earl, Richard should and could be invited to the Palace, but his copybook, able to be viewed by those of a certain class, sported a variety of black splotches; his escutcheon bore blots, plural. Adultery was a sin for religious believers but a way of life, even a trophy for the Earl.

Mind you, being a friend of the offspring of the well-known philanthropist, Sir Jerome Hamilton-Weir, made Dickie a walk-up start at the Buck House bash.

And so the planning was complete.

Chapter 19

George couldn't sleep. Tomorrow was the Saturday before the LNER inspection, the Whittleton Station Day with the new garden blooming, the wine tastings, the author's reading and the Druid meeting place reveal. He'd been sleeping badly for about a week and Friday night was a tortuous toss and turn routine.

He arrived at the station early every day but today he was earlier still. Even the birds were still asleep. A sparrow peeked above his nest and said to his wife. 'He's *very* early today.'

The SM opened his office and double-checked everything he and his staff needed for the day train-wise. With all the other items he needed for the special events, he shuddered just thinking about them.

'Good morning, boss,' said a voice and frightened George.

He studied Gordon, the rat in the ranks and the one person who accidentally and indirectly caused this special day to happen.

'Good morning, Gordon, you're early.'

'Well I know this means a lot to you, sir, so I want to do whatever I can to make your big day a success.'

George struggled to contain his shock, gave Gordon a few tasks and cracked on with other work.

'Hello,' called a voice. George came out of his office.

'Good morning,' he said to a tall, thin gent holding a bicycle.

'I've come for the Druids, the wine tasting and the author's talk. Am I in the right place?'

George wanted to hug the visitor. 'You are, sir, albeit a tad early. 'I'm the station master, George Miracle.'

'Trevor Ravensglass,' he said, 'and I'm starving. Where can a fellow find a decent breakfast around here?'

'Well I suggest you board your sturdy machine and ride a hundred yards into the village. The bakery in the High Street has a splendid reputation for its homemade cakes, pies and sausage rolls. But rumour has it their bacon sandwiches are little short of heavenly. You'll never go hungry in Whittleton.'

In response, one of Trevor's stove-pipe pegs, complete with trouser-leg and bicycle-clip, swung over his seat, and George's first customer of the day disappeared to spend his hard earned in the local village. *That's what it's all about.*

The SM glowed with pleasure as something brushed against his leg. There stood Whitty the station cat requesting an early breakfast.

He bent to pick up the feline when Pip bounced onto the platform.

'Good morning, sir. I'll take her ladyship if you like.'

Her ladyship? George handed over the cat thinking, since the feline arrived, she was a he.

What haven't I done? he thought. The Crabbie being coaled and watered made him look across the tracks. 'Good morning, gentlemen,' he called and Madge and Bobby waved back.

'Of course,' said George, trying not to panic as he spoke to himself. 'I have no-one to keep an eye on Freda.' Every other venue or activity was either under his control or with a person he trusted. The Halt at Pickling was all on its own, miles from civilization and George's control. *I can't go out there or spare anyone.* Then it hit him. He went home, entered the cottage, calling.

'Emily!'

His mother and sister were in the kitchen eating breakfast.

'What's happened?' asked Connie worried.

'I need a favour, Em,' said George and explained the situation.

'You want me to go to Pickling to watch Freda be a tourist guide?'

He nodded. She hesitated. 'I'll come to two wedding rehearsals instead of one.'

His sister laughed. 'All right. But what do I do if she goes a bit silly? You know Freda can be like that.' He knew.

'She'll be fine but I'll feel better if she has someone to help her if necessary.' Emily nodded, copped a kiss from the SM who took off calling, 'Be on the Crabbie platform before 08:29.'

The first Down brought no-one to Whittleton. George's heart ached. He wondered if his scheme would flop. But then it was early. Who goes to a wine tasting before breakfast?

The first Up usually only accepted passengers en route to London and this Saturday there were half a dozen waiting to board. But wait. They couldn't gain easy access. Carriage doors opened and people alighted; alighted at Whittleton. They were dressed in casual clothes. Many carried a picnic basket. There were 16 passengers. Sixteen on a Saturday morning arriving in this village from further down the line. That was a first. George's heart rate quickened. The Up departed.

He greeted people and explained the Crabbie, the village and location of the manor house. People explored the station garden, sat on a bench and opened their thermos, or walked across to the branch.

The bell clanged and Desmond popped out to operate the gates. The next Down was due.

George watched from the Up. The carriages were well populated. But this wasn't the end of the line. So where were these people going on a Saturday morning? They weren't going any further, they were at their destination. Twenty-nine passengers stepped out at Whittleton. Twenty-nine on a Saturday morning! Eric was flabbergasted and struggled to give the guard the all clear.

The train left and George hurried across the tracks to give Eric a hand. Several passengers left for the village, a few to the manor house, and others lined up on the island platform with their return ticket to Pickling.

To where? Pickling? Why? What's at Pickling? It's only a Halt!

George's excitement was overshadowed by panic. Madge found him and stated the bleeding obvious.

'We're full, boss. One carriage has always been all we ever needed. What'll we do if more passengers turn up?'

Emily arrived wearing a sun hat and summer coat and carrying a small picnic basket containing a thermos and sandwiches.

'Make sure my sister is aboard,' said George who squeezed her arm and took off back to the Up.

The young Lord Fitzsimons copied the nearby SM. Up at the crack of dawn, he went to the driveway to again check the signs made and erected by the gamekeeper, whose grandfather worked on this estate when Queen Victoria was a youthful monarch.

The word *Cellar* and an arrow would direct wine connoisseurs and others who wanted a sticky-beak around the grounds. Then back to the cellar, he unlocked the doors, swept the already swept floor and dusted the already dusted chairs and tables.

He worried the newly-employed locals might be late but deep breathing helped him relax. They were early. His plan to start to revive the family fortunes was about to be put to the test.

The morning wore on and every train, Up and Down, arriving at Whittleton contained people wanting to visit. The biggest problem was getting the Crabbie away. She was never late but people struggled to board the single carriage. George told the crew and Eric to suggest people go into the village or to the manor house and catch a later branch line train.

A few took his advice but weren't happy when they returned to find an even bigger crowd waiting to travel to Pickling. It's a nice problem to have when a roaring success produces complaints.

Life was as mad as a bag of ferrets with people sitting on family members' knees and even standing in the "deluxe" Crabbie carriage.

At the Ripley Hall cellar, wine lovers studied the blackboard listing vintages for sale. Tasting was all the go. The plates of cheese and dry biscuits disappeared at a rapid rate but the sales of fine wine kept staff busy throughout. Stephen found himself buttonholed by people who remembered the vineyard in its early days, and by those who wanted to discuss what made their favourite vintage so special.

He smiled when his mother popped out to see what was happening. He moved to her and, in her eyes, saw a new happiness, something she'd lost these last few years.

'Lots of interested wine lovers, Mother.'

She smiled and gave a tiny nod. 'It's lovely to see a bit of life around the house again. What have you done about the Open Day?'

'We're making plans. It will be an event for the entire village.'

She smiled and went back inside. Life for both of them changed and for the better.

When the Crabbie came back, George crossed the tracks to speak to the crew. They were hard to locate due to the number of people arriving back from Pickling, mixing with those wanting to go there. People came from London and elsewhere to travel to Pickling. There were lovers and supporters of small branch lines, with historians keen on Druid sites. A few simply wanted a day out.

'What's happening at the Halt?' asked George.

'Pandemonium,' said Bobby, and George panicked.

Madge told the truth. 'It's fine, boss. Never seen so many people but everyone wandered around like they owned the place.'

'And Freda?'

'Oh she's having a grand old time running a farm produce stall and I think Rufus was collecting the money.'

George didn't know if they were serious. He couldn't stop for a chat because of the non-stop action at Whittleton.

What is happening?

He wanted to hear Septimus and his book reading so making sure all three porters knew their roles, hurried to the village. The meeting was underway when he crept into the rear of the hall. Dead silence from a packed audience. On the undressed stage stood the overdressed Septimus, reading beautifully from his award-winning novel. Spellbound best described the audience. George purred.

The literary toffs and bookworms who came to see what he looked like were clustered together while the locals who knew him from the High Street shops, the pub or the Most Rude Vegetable competition at the village fete, stared openmouthed as their fellow villager announced himself to the world with "all them fancy words".

Septimus finished the excerpt to strong applause, and Connie's close friend, Mr Beckwith, who was chairing the gathering, invited questions. These came from critics who mentioned subjects such as stream of consciousness, irony, metaphor, imagery and symbolism. George understood little if anything of these subjects. Septimus dismissed most as twaddle which infuriated several critics but excited others. Apparently the literati are an odd lot.

When someone asked Septimus to name his favourite genre of literature, he set tongues wagging by answering, 'Nonsense verse and especially limericks.' The audience buzz bounced around the hall.

'Give us a limerick,' yelled a local and the writer obliged.

> *'A literary critic, Ned Nibble*
> *Would frequently cavil and quibble*
> *His opinions were farce*
> *Coming straight from his ... bottom*
> *And rendered his statements as dribble.'*

The hall erupted. Septimus struck gold. His tag, with the pause before *bottom*, produced a raucous laugh being chased by thunderous applause. The author grinned. He was off the lead and loving it. A few literary critics up and left. A penny-dreadful writer would describe them as having "a face like thunder". Cries of "more" filled the hall, and as the critics headed for the Whittleton station aiming to flee this laughable village with its buffoon of a poet, the laughter of the audience ran after the departing visitors teasing them, cat-calling and tongue-poking.

George departed delighted with the entire event. Good old Septimus; puppy finder, dinner-suit provider, comic and pricker of pomposity.

The SM reached the station as the Crabbie pulled in on her final run of the day. Passengers piled out of the carriage which heaved a sigh of relief, its seats having never supported so many bottoms.

People moved to other platforms for their journey home. Emily hopped off, picked her way through strangers and reached the Up. She spotted her brother and bowled up to him, grinning.

'Well?' was all he said. She kept smiling. 'Was it a disaster?'

She held up two jars. 'Two bob for two jars of homemade blackberry jam. It was a brilliant day, George. Everyone loved Freda. Mind you, I told her she has to put her prices up.'

George struggled. 'Hang on, hang on, what about the Druid rocks?'

Emily scoffed. 'They were okay and Freda told 'em stuff which I knew she made up but I think most fell for it hook, line and sinker.'

He thought this too good to be true. 'But what did she do? How did she get people to move about?'

'She used a megaphone, a homemade one.'

'A what?'

'You know, one of those thingamabobs the captain of a ship uses. She welcomed everyone, told them where they were and how her family had lived in the area for hundreds of years.'

'She didn't!'

'Oh and her dog was the hero of the day. George, if Freda was a hit, her dog was a star.'

'Rufus the dog?'

'Did you know he can put his front paws on a person's shoulders and give them a kiss?' George knew. 'And he's not choosy, he'll kiss anyone. I told Freda she should charge a penny a pucker.'

Apparently the one venue George dreaded turned up trumps. All he needed to know about now was the activity at the manor house. Emily wanted to leave.

'Bert's coming over for supper, George, and don't forget you have *two* wedding rehearsals to come to.' She slipped through the crowd.

Eric and Gordon approached him. 'Congratulations, sir,' said Eric and Gordon supported him. 'I've been at Whittleton for nearly 30 years and there's never been anything like this. If we continue like today, the Crabbie will need to attach a second carriage.'

The next Up arrived and dozens of passengers on the Whittleton station clambered aboard. Excited, tired people with smiling faces were set to depart a village, until today, most never knew existed.

George studied the platform for any stragglers and even closed two carriage doors himself. He gave the guard the all clear and as the train headed back to London, the guard called, 'Great day, George; the big boys in London won't believe this!'

George gazed along the now empty platform, empty except for one person seated on a Whittleton platform bench. He recognized the individual and moved to him. Even Melville nodded.

'May I join you, Mr Gardiner?'

'Of course, Mr Miracle, and congratulations on the splendid success of your Whittleton Station Day.'

'And we've received many compliments on your beautiful garden.'

The old man couldn't speak. George patted his knee seeing Horace's emotions. They paused. The old man turned to George. 'You have changed my life, sir. You have given me a new reason to go on living and now I will forever be in your debt.'

Horace grasped George's hand and squeezed it as hard as he could. George said nothing but stood and helped him to stand.

George spoke directly. 'Now please remember, sir, this station garden is yours to visit and maintain at any time.'

Again Horace was speechless but with Melville his trusty beagle by his side, walked away en route to his humble cottage in the now much better known village of Whittleton.

Chapter 20

There was a downside to the success of the Whittleton Station Day. Owen Griffiths, the pretend SM at Crabbtree, would see the little loco arrive with one or two passengers who told him of the mass evacuation at Pickling. 'Pickling? Passengers got off at Pickling?'

The footplate crew reinforced his disappointment. Owen protested. 'But why wouldn't they come to the end of the line? I can show them the engine shed.' He pointed. 'There it is, empty I grant you but what an architectural gem it is, boyo.' It was a brick lean-to as ugly as tin. 'And my waiting-room is far better than theirs and I even have an office. There's a proper desk in there and Crabbtree is such a lovely village.'

'Never mind, Taffy; look on the bright side,' said Madge. 'The Pickling triumph might well have saved your bacon.'

The porter added confusion to his disappointment.

George walked to Ripley Hall as the afternoon drifted towards dusk. He followed the signs to the rear of the great house and found Stephen stacking chairs.

'Now there's a sight; the Lord of the manor putting his back into manual labour.' Stephen turned to greet the SM.

'It's the man himself. I hear your events were a triumph.'

'They were and I hope the same can be said of your wine tasting.'

'Dozens of people, George, I'm not sure of exact numbers unlike you railway chaps, but plenty of sales. I know you're too polite to ask for figures but rest assured we have made a handsome beginning.'

'Congratulations.'

'Once we have the vineyard back up and growing, Ripley Hall will be back on the map supporting Whittleton and its railways.'

George couldn't stop smiling. Both men came from a background of misery in a world war as well as recent family sadness. Both faced a challenge in their lives and both gambled on making a success of their careers. To achieve so much success meant the world to both men.

'Now before you go, my friend,' said Stephen, 'what are we going to do about this Open Day? Forget the rest of the world. Let's put on a show exclusively for our local friends and neighbours. Agreed?'

Grinning, they shook hands and agreed on a date six weeks in advance, choosing to make detailed plans next week. George departed feeling everything was right with the world.

He arrived home to find his future brother-in-law sitting in the kitchen while his sister and mother fussed preparing the meal.

'Ah,' cried Bert, 'the hero is home.'

George enjoyed the praise and especially from his mother who he knew was a tough nut to crack when it came to giving compliments.

'Well done, son' said Connie. 'You should be proud of yourself.'

'Thanks Ma. I hope it means a brighter future for our village.'

'And for your crappy Crabbie,' said Emily to her mother's horror.

Bert laughed. 'So what's your next project, George?'

The SM took his question in all seriousness and made a grand announcement. 'We are going to have a special event, an Open Day at the Hall for the whole village and we've set the date, Saturday September the 21st.'

The room exploded.

All three listeners were up in arms, Spike barked and Trixie woke annoyed at not getting her full 16 hours of kip.

'George,' snarled Emily, 'that's my wedding day!'

'Mine too,' shouted Bert joining the chorus and being doubly upset his fiancée said "my" and not "our".

'I'm sorry,' protested the SM. 'I forgot.'

'I hope this is one of your terrible jokes, George,' said his mother.

'No, I *did* forget,' cried George. 'It's not definite and we can easily change it. Forget what I said.'

'Make it after and not before,' threatened Emily.

George thought about saying she'd miss *his* big day but said nowt.

The anger eased. George couldn't believe he made such a stupid mistake especially after such a successful, triumphant day. He tried to cover his mistake with humour.

'On your wedding day, I'll have all the locos sound their whistles to go with the church bells,' he said, grinning.

The others knew he'd never do anything to spoil the wedding.

'Supper's ready, George,' said Connie and a serve of normality settled in the station master's cottage.

The day of the LNER inspection arrived. George told his team to leave all the talking to him. The unnamed inspector was due on the 10:03 Down. It came through the cutting and George and Eric heard it long before it appeared. It was dead on time.

The Whittleton railwaymen stood halfway along the platform ready to move up or down when the heavies arrived. Inspector Rasmussen and his lackey stepped out of the last carriage. George knew they were from head office simply because the only other passengers were two elderly women with three small children.

'Good morning, gentlemen,' said George, 'Stationmaster Miracle at your service. This is head porter, Mr Eric Forsyth.'

'Rasmussen,' said the inspector with no reference to his colleague.

Here we go, thought George. *He's got rudeness to burn.*

'Where would you like to start, sir?' asked George.

The Down departed and the inspector stared at the plants behind him on the island platform and then across the tracks at the glorious horticultural display on the Up.

'What's all this?' he said pointing. 'Who pays for this lot?'

'It's a community garden, sir. We have an outstanding gardener in the village and he and other village volunteers created and maintain the garden. There is no cost to the LNER.'

Rasmussen's fault-finding copped a blow. He snorted. 'I'll see your books first,' he said and George led his visitor across the tracks. As they travelled, the underling whispered to Eric. 'His bark's worse than his bite.' Eric's miniscule smile appeared.

George was nothing if not meticulous. His Uncle set the standard. All paperwork was up to date, and George followed the traditional practice of everything in its place and a place for everything.

Rasmussen flicked pages, ran a finger up and down a column or across a line, and George stood there trying to remain calm. His pulse refused to obey any reasonable request.

'Now about this branch line,' said the inspector fixing his gaze on the SM. 'Barclay from *Forward Planning* tells me you've produced spectacular success with passenger numbers. How did that happen?'

Okay, thought George, *let's cut straight to the business.*

'There may have been confusion with some previous reports, sir,' said George sending goosebumps racing up the inspector's body. 'But our recent return does show what can be done.'

'What are you talking about?'

George produced a ledger. 'This is from a recent weekend. Here are the arrivals in Whittleton from both Up and Down trains.' He pointed again. 'And here are the return passengers who travelled on the branch line.'

The figures were seriously impressive and especially for a weekend. The inspector struggled to accept the data. 'Are you sure these are correct?'

'Positive, sir,' said George, holding his breath. 'We're most particular when it comes to accurate reporting.'

'Why were there so many travelling on the branch?'

'We're running a campaign to boost the line, sir.' George described the various activities and events which brought out the locals and others from as far away as London. Rasmussen pursed his lips. 'It's a project other LNER stations might care to copy.'

Goodness, was George holding up Whittleton as a model station?

Rasmussen made no comment other than, 'I'll inspect the branch.'

George nearly bowed and led the two visitors back across the tracks to the island platform with the young SM now seriously worried. The Crabbie was due in a few minutes, four to be exact.

The whistle of the tank engine cut through the country morning air. Rasmussen watched for the train as George watched him. The footplate crew, in fact everyone at Whitty knew the station was to be inspected meaning their uniforms were sparkling, well, less sooty. The loco's arrival was perfect, and even the steam hissed softly. The single carriage sat still with not a door being opened.

'So we have an empty train,' said Rasmussen making a note.

'With the branch, sir, weekends are our popular services.'

The inspector sniffed, appeared ready to speak harshly before walking away when George indicated a man approaching along the platform.

'Mr Rasmussen, may I present Lord Fitzsimons, owner of Ripley Hall, the manor house and estate adjacent to the village.'

You can often fool a snob. Rasmussen lost his superiority. It often happened when a bumptious know-all bumped into nobility.

'How do you do, sir,' said Stephen, whose pre-arranged arrival landed right on cue as requested by his friend, the station master.

'Mr Rasmussen is from the London office of the LNER,' said George telling the would-be vintner what he already knew.

'Jolly decent of you to come out to our tiny village, sir,' said Stephen going full bore on the softening up routine. 'I must say running a large estate as I do, having a reliable railway, main and branch lines, makes my life so much easier. We have plans to send the estate's wine all over the country using your company's trains. Anyway, must let you get on.' To George he said, 'Everything's set for the village Open Day, Mr Miracle. Let me know when you want my team to give you a hand.'

George smiled and was tempted to wink. 'Very good, m'Lord.'

Stephen addressed the visitor. 'It was so nice to meet you, sir, and thank you for providing such a wonderful service. Cheerio,' he smiled then departed.

Rasmussen sneered at George. 'What's this village Open Day?' he asked. 'This is a railway not a seaside entertainment.'

George spoke enthusiastically giving the impression it was an old custom in Whittleton. 'Yes sir, we have the whole village involved in activities held on the estate. Locals here have a wonderful community spirit. There are stalls with local produce, games and donkey rides in the manor house grounds, and we allow children to travel free on the branch—always accompanied by a paying adult of course. Can I send you the details?'

'If you must,' he said. 'I've seen enough. When's the next train?'

'To London, sir?'

'Yes,' said the inspector angry at not being specific.

'It's due in six minutes, Mr Rasmussen; this way, sir.'

They returned to the Up and George stood beside the visitors as the train arrived on time. He watched to see which carriage they chose and then stepped forward to open the door.

'Good day, gentlemen,' said George. The Londoners said nothing. George nodded at the guard as the train left.

His heart sighed as he murmured, 'Thank goodness that's over.'

Eric summed up the inspection. 'You've missed your calling, sir. You should have been a salesman.'

Chapter 21

There have been fraudsters and con-merchants for millennia. Carlos Riff was good, in fact better than most hence the size of his bank balance and the bespoke clothing reclining upon his back. Research was the foundation of his duplicitous schemes as he used voting roles, the telephone directory and the latest census to gather information.

Having picked a gullible young clerk employed in the firm which handled the legal affairs of Sir Jerome Hamilton-Weir, Carlos played the long game. Gabrielle believed in her long lost cousin and her mother more so.

Mrs Laidlaw's life changed for good. Besides, she now had something to discuss other than her bunion, the weather and Mrs Cruikshank's new hat.

Carlos paying compliments was new and fabulous. He became a trusted member of the family and now it was time to move through the gears. He was in London on a mission. Two of his dearest friends were being cheated out of their rightful place in their father's estate.

Some fiend claimed to be the love child of their father and this wretched so-and-so, together with a wicked stepmother, were threatening the father of his friends with blackmail. There was not a shred of truth in the claim but imagine the disgrace for a highly-respected and noteworthy family if the threat was carried out.

'Can you not go to the police?' asked Mrs Laidlaw.

'Of course but who is the criminal? These people are pure evil, and until I can identify them, my friend's unblemished family name is in mortal danger.'

Carlos added storytelling to his list of skills. Mrs and Miss Laidlaw were desperate to help in any way they could. The affairs of the fraudster's unnamed friends were handled by a particular legal firm.

'But I work there,' whispered Gabrielle. Her mother's jaw dropped.

Carlos froze. 'Really?' he gasped, his stunned expression coming straight from an acting class at the Royal Academy of Dramatic Art.

No request or begging was needed as Gabrielle willingly offered to help. The will would be examined inside the legal chambers, the information obtained meaning Carlos would soon be in the money.

He succeeded by eliminating the chances to fail. Having persuaded Gabrielle of the moral and righteous nature of the cause, he trained her in the art of stealing without stealing. She was never to remove anything belonging to her employer from the premises. Such an action would be illegal. The law must not be broken. This case is about justice, and preventing a noble family name from being ruined.

Until the day of action, there were no names. Carlos even requested a dummy run. Gabrielle uncovered vital details from a file the contents of which were of no interest to Finn. The girl done good.

The night before the real thing, he delivered a magnificent bouquet of flowers to the Laidlaw home. The women would admire them for days. Carlos kissed a hand of both women and wished them good evening. His plan, now set to begin, could see a good chunk of the terrible twins' inheritance move from their accounts to his.

The Buckingham Palace Garden Party was the place to be seen. If you weren't there, you weren't anywhere, and invitations to weekends at country houses, and balls in stunning ballrooms for the well-off and titled, evaporated before your very eyes.

George Carruthers wanted to attend the Palace because of his family scandal. It blighted his family name which to him was so unfair. Would his wee son be blackballed because of the lad's grandparents? Lord Carruthers, DSO and war hero, was no party-goer or social climber but wanted to show his face in public with pride, if not for him then certainly for his wife and child, children.

George was a proud man with no wish to hide because of the scandal in his family. If people wished to gossip about him and his family, let them, but nothing would stop him and his family from doing what they wanted to do and going where they wanted to go.

George and Valerie were off to the Palace.

As Lady Carruthers recently announced her confinement, her companion, Louisa **McClaren**, would accompany the mother-to-be. Jolly good then, we're all done and dusted.

Cracking weather gave the party a huge lift. Parasols popped up like daffodils with many being the same colour as the flowers. Milliners found their fingers ached for days after the event as only Ascot created a greater demand for headgear. It was all right for the chaps who could dust off the same old topper they'd been wearing for ages.

Valerie avoided anything slim and figure-hugging due to her condition. Louisa helped her dress. 'What do you think, my dear?' she asked her companion.

Louisa could speak openly as the two women had been friends since childhood. Their mothers went to the same boarding school decades ago, and when Valerie met George and they married, it was easy for the new bride to engage her childhood friend as her companion.

'It's lovely, Valerie, and the fashion is to have the waist line heading south this season.'

'If that trend continues, women will be wearing belts around their knees. Now what are you to wear, Louisa?'

'What I always wear to any occasion, my trustworthy day dress.'

'That won't do. We are to mingle with royalty and high society.'

'We and thousands of others,' added Louisa.

'I have a brand new outfit which you can wear.'

'No, Valerie, I can't.'

'It's far too fitting for me in my condition and it'll be an age before I'll wear it. There it is at the end of the wardrobe. Try it on.'

Louisa was reluctant but did so and looked startlingly beautiful.

'It's stunning, my dear. You'll have the King wanting to be introduced.'

The dress was of cream silk, shorter than the normal hem length at the time which worried Louisa. Valerie told her friend her perfect legs were shown off in the outfit which was true. It came with a matching light woollen cream coat with a white fur collar. As she added a double strand of pearls, matching earrings, cream shoes, matching stockings and an elegant hat which hugged her head, Louisa was fetching, no, enchanting. Everyone would describe her and her outfit as eye-catching.

'Fix your eye makeup,' said Valerie and admired the end result.

Being naturally shy, Louisa worried she would be "on show".

When the ladies came down, George's mouth opened. 'I say, am I the luckiest chap in London. You girls look absolutely smashing. With one on each arm I'll be the envy of every man at the Palace.'

'We'll be one on each arm to stop you falling over,' teased Valerie.

'Well it's a good job we chaps don't have to curtsy,' he joked and the trio climbed into their chauffeur-driven 1922 Morris.

The Hamilton-Weir twins were invited to the same Garden Party thanks to their father. At their request, Sir Jerome reluctantly acquired an invitation for their lecherous chum, the Earl of Fakenham. The trio knew most of London's affluent society and certainly were aware of the family Carruthers thanks to George's parents and their murderous scandal. They knew nothing of Valerie or her companion, few did. With thousands of guests in the many acres of gardens, bumping into friends or acquaintances was more by chance than design.

George and his girls, as he liked to call them, arrived and headed into the Palace grounds. With his new leg, George used his walking stick but pretended it was only there for show. Valerie took his arm, not so much as his wife but more as a crutch. Louisa tagged along, nervous at being in such august company. Her widowed mother, in a small cottage near the Epping Forest, would be thrilled to know her daughter was rubbing shoulders with members of the royal family and their guests.

On this sunny afternoon, the Palace grounds were a picture and the placement of marquees meant the dainty sandwiches and scrumptious cakes cried out for partygoers to help themselves. The fact everything was gratis only added to its appeal. Tea anyone?

George gave off bravado but inside was worried sick. What if people ignored him? *There's that chap whose mother conspired to have his father murdered. Avoid Carruthers like the plague.*

Some people are inclined to think like so. They avoid those with even a whiff of scandal lest they too become tainted.

After circulating for a few minutes, George was spotted by a former soldier with whom he once served. In the army, Major Phillip Greystone outranked George but the two became great pals. He knew how brave George fought in France and the horrific price he paid.

George introduced his two ladies and the conversation bubbled away. Louisa became uncomfortable as she thought the other guest paid too much attention to her. He offered to collect refreshments for the others and, at the last moment, invited Louisa to join him. What could she say?

They jostled through the crowd in the marquee. It became the next best thing to a bun fight; literally fighting over royal slices of cake. Greystone told Louisa to wait away from the throng while he volunteered to go "over the top".

Trying to remain inconspicuous, she failed as a hand gently took hold of her arm. 'Allow me, dear lady,' said a silky-smooth gent doffing his topper and leading her far from the milling crowd. Again, what could she say? "Unhand me you brute," would not a good impression make, and creating a scene at a Buckingham Palace garden party would seriously hurt Lord and Lady Carruthers.

'Carrington,' he said, 'Earl of Fakenham. 'And to whom have I the greatest pleasure to address?'

'Miss Louisa **McClaren**,' she replied trying to find the Major in the melee. *I need to be rescued.*

Before Dickie could continue, two young women, each wearing a marquee as a hat, approached hoping to impress the Earl. 'Good day, my Lord,' they spoke in unison each giving a refined curtsy.

He recognized them, knew they were from a filthy rich family but right now preferred sex with his latest discovery. He gave a polite smile then turned and guided Louisa away. She could hardly pull her arm free and ask him to leave her be.

'Have you been residing in a nunnery, Miss **McClaren**?' was his opening line. Apparently it worked for certain fellows. Before Louisa could reply, he continued. 'How else could I have only now discovered a woman of so rare and unmatched beauty?'

His charm was charming, some might say oleaginous, and Louisa sensed serious unease. An Earl, a member of the aristocracy, flattering her was impressive but still she became uncomfortable. If she knew Carrington's history with his "love 'em and leave 'em" routine, uncomfortable wouldn't come close to describing her doubts.

She thanked him for his kindness in keeping her safe from the stampede but now wished to re-join her friends.

'Your lucky friends,' he remarked fishing for details. 'Who are these lucky people, may one ask?'

Louisa hesitated. Would George and Valerie be upset if she answered a curious member of the nobility? He kept smiling, pressing for details.

'I'm staying with Lord and Lady Carruthers,' she said and left it there but believed she could see his mind working.

'Oh, you mean the Carruthers from Belgravia?' he asked knowing of no such family.

'No, my Lord,' is all she wanted to say but to not explain would appear rude. 'They reside in Hampstead.'

'Of course,' smiled Carrington, still not knowing who she meant but becoming determined to find out. His thinking was simple. If I know where the beauty lives, my end goal of seduction will be easier and achieved much quicker.

Before he could continue his charm offensive, Greystone appeared with refreshments. 'I thought I'd lost you,' he smiled at Louisa intending to give Johnny-cum-lately the old heave-ho.

Carrington didn't mind. He'd laid the groundwork. He'd discovered the name and location of this divine young woman. He ignored the "butler", kissed Louisa's hand and disappeared.

'I believe that gentleman is the Earl of Fakenham,' explained Louisa and Greystone didn't give a damn. He claimed the inside running and intended to make the most of it.

George Miracle expected a letter from head office. It never arrived. The inspector came and went and nothing happened. Did his report heap praise or scorn on Whittleton and its SM? Is there a report?

His bitter enemy, a jealous colleague, tried to destroy George by sending false reports boasting of great passenger numbers on the Crabbie when in fact the branch was dying.

George found the rat in his own ranks and the police discovered the identity of the criminals who came to Pickling as vandals. Pinning the crime on them proved tricky. But fortune favoured the brave and the luck ran his way when Lord Fitzsimons Senior and Mr Gardiner's dear wife both died, although you could hardly call such events lucky.

The new Lord Fitzsimons revolutionized the estate, and Horace, wanting a project to overcome his loneliness, designed a glorious station garden. Both visions gave Whittleton a serious boost.

Freda knowing the history of the Druid site, and Septimus the anonymous author coming out of hiding, meant the local railway line and branch enjoyed a super Saturday. Did those figures fool the inspector and Head Office? So far, no news was good news.

People kept coming on weekends to enjoy wine tastings or the Druid site although not in great numbers. The false reports stopped with Gordon refusing to continue his cousin's bidding. George worked hard at running his station and its branch.

'First wedding rehearsal is next Tuesday, George,' said Emily when he came home. 'You promised you'd come to two.'

He grinned. 'Make it three. I want this to be the wedding of the century.'

His mother worried. 'What's happened, George? Why are you in such good spirits?'

Emily knew. 'It's because Louisa is coming to the wedding.'

Bullseye! George's heart caught fire. Louisa was never far from his thoughts but of late, just surviving in the job took up so much of his time. Now a recent lack of contact with the girl of his dreams whacked him around the chops. The women saw him try to hide his mood change.

'Sorry, I have no news on that front. I imagine the young lady is busy with her social superiors in London.' He smiled and they didn't. 'She's probably been swanning around a garden party in the grounds of Buckingham Palace.'

If only he knew. His despair at false reports damaging his career was replaced by his despair at not being able to see and talk to Louisa.

The one saving grace, the one thing to give him hope was the village fair, the Open Day at Ripley Hall. Tomorrow he would make plans in earnest with his friend, Lord Fitzsimons.

Chapter 22

George Carruthers sat in his study writing a letter. The door received a knock and the butler, Francis, who'd been a part of the furniture in this house for forty odd years, entered to say a gentleman has called asking to see Miss Louisa.

'Miss Louisa?' queried a curious George.

'His card, my Lord,' said Francis.

George read it. 'What's the Earl of Fakenham want with Louisa?'

Francis, despite his lowly status, always spoke his mind. 'I should imagine it might be related to sex, my Lord.'

George sighed. 'Am I now my wife's companion's keeper?'

'Rather you than me, my Lord,' said Francis. 'The gentleman's in the front drawing-room.' Francis paused. 'Good luck, my Lord.'

George entered the drawing-room—the largest of the three on the ground floor—and found Carrington pretending to admire a fine painting of George's great-grandfather.

'Ah, Carruthers, damn fine painting you have here. Those arty chaps certainly knew their business.'

'My Lord,' said George wanting rid of the visitor with a minimum of fuss and in the shortest possible time. 'How may I help?'

'I come bearing gifts, sir, in the form of an invitation for Miss Louisa McClaren. It's to attend a luncheon given by Sir Jerome Hamilton-Weir at his home in Belgravia. It will be my pleasure to escort the young lady to the exclusive soiree and to return her safely to your residence, and naturally I wish to extend the invitation in person.'

It wasn't a request, there was no "May I" in his discourse.

George hesitated. Rumours concerning his visitor's reputation were well-known but, as he remarked, he was not his wife's companion's keeper.

'Please wait, my Lord and I shall make enquiries.'

Carrington nodded but said nothing. He'd laid down the marker, meaning let the others come to him. George went upstairs and told his wife everything.

'Louisa told me she met him at the Garden Party. Do you want me to speak to her?'

'Silly question,' said George who kissed his wife and left.

Louisa was given the news. 'What should I do?' she asked Valerie.

'Make a decision and tell him in person.'

'What do you advise me to do?'

'He's a powerful man, my dear and I'm sure persistent. A luncheon in Belgravia is not a weekend in the country. You may find it better to accept now so you will know later how to politely refuse.'

Louisa wasn't keen but trusted her friend. 'Will you come with me?' she asked then saw the expression on Valerie's face.

'George will be with you. Try and keep an open mind on life. Look at me.' Louisa stared at her friend. 'I married a man with one leg and am soon to have his second child. You never know what might happen until you engage with life and its opportunities.'

Louisa decided and with her friend's words swimming in her brain, walked downstairs to be met by George.

'I'm happy to remain in the room if you wish,' he said.

'Thank you,' whispered Louisa, as they reached the doors, 'I feel confident I can handle the Earl on my own, my Lord.'

George was surprised but naturally acquiesced. Louisa paused, took a deep breath and stepped into the room.

Carrington smiled with unctuous delight. Louisa bobbed and spoke quietly. 'Good day, my Lord.'

'Good day indeed, my dear young lady. Come, come, and let me see you in a better light.' Carrington knew he was so controlling and didn't care. It was part of his nature, doing what he wanted and expecting anyone, everyone to accede to his wishes. Louisa moved to him but stopped a good yard or more short of his grasp.

'Even more beautiful than when we last met. I trust you are well, Miss McClaren.'

'Thank you, I am, my Lord.'

He indicated the nearest settee. 'Please, be seated.' She sat. He remained standing, towering over her, his height exceeding six feet.

'Tell me your background. Who is your father? What does he do?'

Like George Carruthers, Louisa wanted the conversation ended and soon. 'You wish to enquire about my family, my Lord? You have come from the city to ask about my father? Surely a man of your class and standing has better things to do with his time.'

The subtle but stinging rebuke from a woman of a lower class didn't annoy or offend the Earl but rather spurred him on to win the battle. He loved a challenge and turned up the charm foray.

'When I discover a woman of such superlative beauty, I immediately wish to become acquainted with her family and her father in particular. I am a gentleman, Miss McClaren and assure you my intentions are honourable.' He lied often did Dickie. 'Are you ashamed of your pater, Miss McLaren?'

'Not ashamed, my Lord but concerned you should seek to pry into my affairs when we are barely acquainted.'

He loved this game and lusted after the woman. 'Then let us become better acquainted. Allow me to escort you to the home of Sir Jerome Hamilton-Weir in Belgravia to enjoy a luncheon attended by members of London's finest families. It's Tuesday next at midday. I shall call for you at noon. It's fashionable to be late and the others will be in attendance when we make our grand entrance.'

He stepped forward, took hold of her hand and kissed it.

'I suggest you wear that dazzling outfit you wore to the Palace.' He stood back and smiled. 'No need to ring for your man. I'll show myself out. Till Tuesday at noon.'

He departed without a backward glance. She sat dumbfounded wondering why she didn't decline his invitation.

George entered apace. 'Louisa, what happened?'

'I'm not sure.'

Her answer confused him. 'Did he extend an invitation to you?'

She nodded. 'He did. Will Valerie need me next Tuesday?'

George and Stephen met at the station to plan the Ripley Hall Open Day. They made a list of the events to be staged and what each event would require in terms of equipment and personnel. There would be a range of activities for the whole family in the grounds of the manor house and rides for children on the Crabbie.

'I considered rides on the footplate,' said George, 'then thought of the possibility of accidents. We'll keep all passengers in the carriage.'

'Could you decorate the little loco and give it a name?' asked Stephen.' George sparkled.

'Brilliant idea,' he replied.

'And what about a village Queen of the Fair? We could have a young local woman open the event.'

'I'm not sure the parish council chairman will support your idea.'

'Could we put *him* in a dress?' They laughed. George was on a high. The more he could involve the villagers in the railway, especially the branch, the better the chance everyone could prosper. But his elation copped a torpedo when Stephen made his next remark.

'I say, George, can I ask about that gorgeous young woman, Louisa, who travels with George and Valerie? She's a beautie.'

George froze. Words failed him. He studied his friend wondering what either of them would say. Stephen didn't spot George's alarm.

'I'm thinking of inviting George and Valerie for another weekend with the hope they'll bring their beautiful companion, only I'd step back if I thought I'd be treading on anyone's toes; and especially those of a certain station master.'

Stephen grinned as George died inside. His friend's comments came out of the blue. He knew his immediate response should have been, "Well actually, my Lord, Miss McClaren and I have an understanding".

But instead his spine turned to jelly. 'Good luck,' said George feeling sick. He couldn't compete with a titled gent who owned a large chunk of the county.

'We need to agree on a date for the Open Day,' said George changing the subject.

'We do,' said Stephen studying a railway calendar on the wall. 'What about the third Saturday of next month?' he said pointing to the date.

Reeling inside from Stephen's interest in Louisa, George agreed without thinking and they parted noting the need for more meetings.

George worked in his office popping out when trains arrived, but struggling to concentrate. The man who had become one of his closest friends was now a rival for the woman who stole his heart.

Carlos gave Gabrielle her final instructions. The dummy run on the wrong subject worked perfectly. Now it was time to investigate the real file. The master fraudster succeeded because of his meticulous preparation.

Gabrielle's target was the latest will or, if it existed, a codicil to Sir Jerome's will. Despite doing mundane clerical work in her role at the firm, now thanks to "cousin" Carlos, she became educated in matters legal. She knew what to look for. Her instructions were clear.

Nothing was to be removed from the office. If on the remote chance she was searched, nothing would be found. The time drew nigh; cometh the hour, cometh the devoted disciple.

As rehearsed, when free to do so, and tackling a relevant task near the Hamilton-Weir file, she discovered the full name of the half sibling of the twins, noting Sir Jerome's will was now to be shared three equal ways.

She provided Carlos, a.k.a. Edward Fairhaven, with the details and the man could even smell the money.

Over supper, George appeared in one of his quiet moods. If he knew the Earl of Fakenham had also dipped his toe in the waters of Lake Seduction, the poor SM would have been devastated.

Connie worried her son was finding being a station master at such a young age all too much for him. She saw how the job took its toll on her brother, Fred. Now her son seemed ready to crack.

'A penny for your thoughts, George,' she said.

'Nothing Ma, all is good at the station and the inspection seems to have gone off without a hitch.'

'Are you worried?'

'No, I'm fine. Oh and Lord Fitzsimons and I have set a date for the Open Day.'

'Do station masters normally tackle such non-railway events?'

'No, Ma but you know the branch is struggling and anything which brings the locals together to help the line is worth a try.'

Emily said little as they ate their meal. George sensed the silence was about to end. 'Now about the wedding, George,' she said. He knew what was coming. 'Have you decided if Louisa will attend?'

Connie added to his discomfort. 'She'd be most welcome, son.'

The killer blow saw George struggle to control his feelings. He pushed his plate away, stood and made an impolite exit. 'I've work at the station,' he snapped and left.

'I guess that means no,' said Emily.

Connie collected his plate. 'Pity, but let's not talk about Louisa again unless he brings up the subject.'

Louisa worried about her entrance into the aristocracy on an intimate scale. A dining-room in Belgravia was not a Garden Party at Buck House. She and Valerie spent time discussing the event.

'If he suggested the same outfit, Lou, then you should wear it.'

Louisa studied her nails. 'Are you saying a woman must obey a man even as to the clothes she wears?'

'Of course not but it seems a reasonable request.'

Louisa suffered doubts. 'Why am I so uncertain?'

'There could be many reasons. You're not from their class. You're worried about what to say and when to say it. You could even be secretly excited and wonder if this man is going to change your life.'

Louisa spoke plainly. 'And what if I wish to reject his advances?'

'Then do so but with your looks, my dear, suitors will be lining up to take his place.' Louisa stood to leave. 'George received an invitation this morning from Lord Fitzsimons in Whittleton.'

Louisa perked up. 'Oh?'

'His Lordship insisted Miss Louisa would be most welcome.' Her heart became busy, especially when Valerie continued. 'So the station master appears to have a rival. You are spoilt for choice, my dear.'

The day of the luncheon arrived and Louisa appeared radiant in Valerie's expensive outfit. She fretted as Valerie examined her.

'Remember you are their equal. If people look down on you, ignore them. Enjoy yourself and accept nothing or agree to anything unless you want to. Be in charge of your own destiny.'

They heard the doorbell. Valerie kissed her friend wishing her well. George came out of his study as Louisa came down the stairs.

'Stunning, Miss McClaren, and please be home by midnight.'

He too kissed her as the servant announced the visitor.

Carrington, acting the toff, flaunted his stature and status to greet Louisa, kissed her hand and ignored the others as he led her to the vehicle. They weren't travelling by omnibus or train.

They arrived late on purpose in Belgrave Square where servants opened doors. The Earl offered his arm. He wanted to enter flaunting his spectacular trophy and succeeded as their arrival drew all eyes to the latecomers, and especially to the gorgeous young woman in the remarkably impressive but borrowed outfit.

The twins studied Louisa thinking about how she could be of use or pleasure to them. Their chum, the Earl, owed them plenty, and share and share alike became an unwritten bond between the trio.

There were 18 for luncheon with a twin at either end and 8 on either side of the expensive French polished table. Sir Jerome, patriarch of the family, was nowhere to be seen.

Louisa remembered warnings from Valerie as to the consumption of alcohol. Carrington accepted his glass being re-filled on a constant basis. By taking tiny sips infrequently, she kept her wits about her.

The Earl seemed incapable of speaking quietly to anyone and his loud retorts and comments were heard by all. The gent sitting on the other side of Louisa struck up the perfect form of polite conversation. The weather, the season and the new fashions were non-threatening.

The food was exceptional. Louisa relaxed. She wasn't embarrassed or overawed or threatened and so far so good. It went well. The luncheon ended and the guests retired, mingling and drinking coffee.

Enoch moved to Louisa introducing himself. He gushed and like his pal, wanted to know about Louisa's background. 'Where are you from? What does your father do? Why have we not met?'

Remembering Valerie's advice, Louisa batted away the curious aristocrats. To many, she became an enigma and worth investigating.

When it was time to leave, she graciously thanked the twins and smiled when told they hoped to see more of her in the future. Carrington wanted to see more of her that evening.

He escorted her through the glorious home when a door opened and a gentleman appeared.

Carrington and Louisa stopped. 'Sir Jerome,' said Carrington offering his hand to the homeowner then indicated the young woman.

'Sir Jerome, may I present Miss Louisa McClaren.' She bobbed with head bowed then stood to find Sir Jerome admiring her. He smiled and retired whence he came.

Carrington was keen to get going. Seduction was all. The groundwork had been laid and a return on his investment was now due.

Chapter 23

Carrington took Louisa home. They drove into the Hampstead property and pulled up in the circular driveway outside the front portico. The Earl popped the question inviting the young woman to a weekend house party in the country. Confident his seductive charms would do the trick, he waited for her gushing acceptance but never in a month of Sundays did he expect her response.

'Thank you, my Lord, but I am unable to accept your kind invitation as I have another engagement.'

He sat stunned, his mind a mess. *Nobody refuses the Earl of Fakenham. Nobody. With my looks and title, women fall at my feet.*

His battered pride stung. Louisa said nothing more and waited.

Francis took an age to arrive. Carrington bristled. Finally the car door was opened and Louisa alighted. She studied her escort. He stared straight ahead, the blood draining from his face. It imitated the colour of a sugar beet in one of the nearby Norfolk freight trains.

'Thank you for a delightful luncheon, my Lord. Good afternoon.'

It was a goodbye slap wrapped in velvet. She mounted the portico steps, George opened the front door wider, she entered and the Earl ordered his driver to leave using ungentlemanly language.

Louisa was confronted by Lady Carruthers who spoke one word.

'Well?'

The trio settled in the smallest sitting-room with the married couple desperate for news.

'It was most enjoyable,' said Louisa. 'The food was superb and I met several charming people including the patriarch, Sir Jerome.'

'Louisa,' snapped Valerie, 'stop playing games. What happened with the Earl of Fakenham? When will you next see him?'

'Hopefully never,' she spoke with assurance. 'He is obnoxious and when he invited me to a weekend house party, I said I was unable to accept his kind invitation as I have another engagement.'

'What!?' exclaimed the married couple in unison. It was a double shock. The fact she rebuffed a powerful man was surprising, and equally so using the excuse of another engagement.

'What did he say?' asked George.'

'What other engagement?' enquired Valerie.

A coy Louisa complained of being tired and wanting to change out of her employer's beautiful clothes lest they be spoiled. She retired and her friends discussed her comments with Valerie educating her husband about the SM connection being serious. He shook his head when told of the couple's strong affection.

'Why are men always the last to know?' he muttered.

As Louisa changed, elsewhere in London, the man employed by the siblings, Carlos Finn Esquire, arrived to collect his fee.

The twins weren't expecting him which is how Carlos liked to operate. Turn up and catch them off guard was his modus operandi. The trio settled in a slightly smaller sitting-room.

The twins longed for details but, at the same time, dreaded discovering their half-sibling lived in Peru or Timbuctoo or worse, was a person of wealth and power.

'I have the details you asked for regarding your father's recently-changed and latest will. It is true he has included the illegitimate child and they will receive the same amount as each of you.'

Enoch swore, stood and threatened to break a knick-knack. There was nothing remotely cheap in this room, this house.

Sophronia swore longer and more crudely than her brother. 'What is the name?' she demanded.

Carlos remained calm, taking his time. 'All in good time, dear lady; first we attend to business.'

'Oh for God's sake, Finn, you know we're good for the cash. What's the bastard's name and where does he live?'

The fraudster said nothing. Talk about holding all the cards. Sophronia snapped at her brother. 'Write him a cheque.'

Enoch hated being told what to do by anyone and especially by his sister. He went to fetch a cheque-book.

'Please,' said Carlos, 'our agreement is strictly cash.'

Enoch fumed. 'We don't have a pile of cash lying around. We'll take you to the bank in the morning; you have my word on it.'

Carlos stood. 'Fine, we'll go to the bank, put the cash in my account and then I'll give you what you paid me for. Shall we say Coutts in the Strand at 11?'

Enoch exploded. 'How do you know where we bank?'

'Please, I'm a professional,' he sighed, didn't wait for their acceptance and walked out. The twins fumed.

They were not surprised when the Earl of Fakenham was announced. He stormed in, poured himself a drink and skulled it before pouring another and sat.

'Woman problems, my Lord?' asked Sophronia. 'Don't tell me your shapely virgin rejected the dashing knight in his shining armour?'

'The little minx,' he snapped. 'I introduce her to society, even to your pater, and when I offer her a weekend in the country, she declines my invitation; the bitch.'

The twins laughed. 'Oh, Dickie,' said Enoch. 'I'm staggered your superb seduction skills have finally failed.' The Earl seethed.

'What reason did she give to turn you down?' asked Sophronia.

Carrington mocked Louisa. 'Thank you, my Lord but I am unable to accept your kind invitation as I have another engagement.'

Enoch laughed and his sister roared. 'Oh, that hoary old excuse.'

'What do you mean?' demanded Carrington.

'Dickie, when a woman fancies someone other than the man she's with, she says she's busy, has another engagement. It means she's got a fancy man, Dickie and it sure ain't you.'

'Shut up,' spat Carrington.

'Forget her,' said Sophronia acting serious, 'how would you like to earn a large amount of cash?'

The Earl's thinking switched in an instant. Louisa who?

Enoch stared at his sister. 'Are you sure about this?'

She ignored him. 'We have a problem, Dickie. Our darling pater has recently changed his will and reduced our inheritance share.'

Carrington tried to be funny. 'He's giving *me* money?'

'We have a half-sibling,' explained Sophronia.

'What?' blurted the shocked Earl.

'We don't know his name or where he lives but if this bastard is due a slice of our inheritance, we need the will changed or the newcomer removed.'

The males paused. The word *removed* floated in the air.

'If this fake family member sadly dies, we will receive what is rightfully ours.'

Carrington sniffed. 'You want a beneficiary to disappear?'

'For a fee, of course,' added Enoch.

Dickie didn't hesitate. He raised his glass and toasted, 'To the most deserving twins in the world.'

They laughed repeating the toast.

After Carrington departed, the siblings discussed the possibility of extracting the details from Carlos without paying him, there being no honour amongst thieves, aristocratic or otherwise.

'He won't have the name and address on a piece of paper tucked in his jacket pocket,' said Sophronia. 'It'll be stored inside his brain.'

Enoch wondered aloud. 'Could we blackmail or torture him?'

'Sure and why not recommend him for a knighthood? Listen, brother dear, Carlos is miles smarter than both of us put together. We pay him, we discover the name, and then we let Dickie loose.'

Next morning, both twins went to the city. They would need money from both their accounts to make up the fee demanded by Carlos Finn. He appeared from nowhere as they stood in the Strand outside Coutts, the bank for the seriously rich.

'Good morning,' he said and smiled. Warmth in expression and language never occurred when Carlos appeared.

They went inside with bank staff keen to help. Carlos too was a customer here and, in a small private chamber, the twins signed the necessary paperwork. Their business partner waited until he noted his new balance. It was now much healthier than yesterday. From inside his coat pocket he produced an envelope and placed it on the table. It *was* on a piece of paper in his jacket pocket.

'It's been a pleasure doing business,' he said and stood to leave.

'Hey, hey, hey, hey,' said Enoch also standing. 'You wait till we check the details.'

Carlos shrugged. Sophronia grabbed the envelope and struggled to open it. The two men watched her, one with desperation on his face.

'No!' she screamed. Outside, bank staff believed something criminal or dangerous was happening. A silent alarm sounded and security staff came running. Enoch hurried to his sister's side, snatched the piece of paper and read the details.

'It's a trick. You're a damn liar!'

Carlos stood firm. 'My reputation for perfection is long established. Do you think I would throw it away on a couple of moronic, upper-class shits like you two?'

Enraged, Enoch launched himself at Carlos as the door opened and two security guards rushed in. Enoch was tackled, Carlos stepped back and the bank officials, restraining Enoch, turned to Sophronia.

She indicated Carlos. 'He can go.'

Displaying a creepy smile, the fraudster left. His "cousins", Mrs and Miss Laidlaw, never saw him again.

The twins pre-arranged a rendezvous with their partner in crime, the selfish pig, Richard Carrington. They agreed to meet in a coffee shop off the Strand half an hour after their date with Finn at the bank.

They entered and saw Carrington at a corner table drinking coffee. In their faces he saw anger, loathing and worse.

'Bad news?' he asked. 'Is he a hermit living in Antarctica?'

Enoch went to order coffee. Sophronia's eyes narrowed giving Carrington the heebie-jeebies. 'No result, no pay, Dickie,' she hissed.

He worried. 'Listen, you know I don't do the actual deed. I pay one of my criminal chums to light the fuse, swing the axe or whatever.'

'You might want to change your routine in this instance.'

'What's happened? What are you talking about?'

Enoch arrived. 'This is your lucky day, Dickie.'

The Earl lost it and spat his demand. 'For God's sake will you tell me what happened?'

Sophronia produced the envelope and placed it on the table in front of Carrington. He pondered it then pondered them. They stared back, their eyes frozen. 'Open it and discover your target,' she said.

He opened the envelope, took out the paper, saw the details and shock lit up his face. He read.

Louisa Faith McClaren, Tudor House, Hampstead London

Chapter 24

The first Down of the day always meant the London papers would be dropped off at Whittleton as well as other stations down the line. Eric brought the bundle to George's office.

'This is interesting, sir,' said the porter.

George looked at the banner headline; *Proposed General Strike.*

'It's not us, it can't be us. The miners are the ones copping it in the neck. They'll strike and it's no certainty it'll do them any good.'

'My brother reckons General means everyone.'

'What? The whole nation will go on strike?'

'Everyone is what he says.'

'Well if the rail workers strike, we aren't any use. The drivers, firemen and signalmen can bring the networks to a dead stop but not us. If the trains are running and we go on strike, people will just walk in and out of here and enjoy a free trip.'

'My brother also reckons there's a depression coming with mass unemployment and businesses going broke.'

'Blimey, your brother sounds like a barrel of laughs. What is he, an undertaker?'

George left Eric in charge for the last three trains of the day as the SM's presence was required elsewhere. Giving away his sister at her wedding now became his number 1 task, and George arrived at the church for the rehearsal entering via a side door.

'At last,' said Emily. We were about to send out a search party.'

'Good evening, Vicar,' said George nodding to the other assembled wedding party members.

'Good evening, Mr Miracle,' replied the vicar. 'It's nice to see you. A station master's job must be so time-consuming.'

George reckoned having a dig at his non-attendance in the local House of God was uncalled for and politely ignored the jibe.

'I'm ready when you are, sir,' he said with his biggest smile. This method of not rising to the bait had served George well when dealing with Gordon the betrayer.

George and his sister headed back down the aisle to the front door with the bridesmaid tagging along. The groom's four-year old niece as flower girl was left free to scamper between the pews and rearrange the hymn books.

Bert and his best man, his brother, took their positions by the altar and the vicar started singing to *la*. It sounded like Mendelssohn's *Wedding March* some of the time.

George glanced at Emily. She whispered, 'The organist is playing bridge tonight. Now come on and don't stand on my dress.'

They set off down the aisle with George wondering how he could stand on Emily's dress which stopped a good six inches from the floor. At the dressmaker's, her wedding dress remained a state secret.

They reached the others and the vicar was forced to stop impersonating the organist in order to give directions.

'Well done, everyone. Now I say, "Dearly beloved and so on and so forth" and when I come to the bit where I ask, "Who gives this woman to this man?" you, Mr Miracle, say, "I do".'

The vicar and then the others stared at George. He twigged.

'I do,' he said.

'And then you step back and sit next to your partner over there. I assume your mother will be your partner.'

'No, Vicar,' said Emily. 'Mr Beckwith will be partnering my mother.'

'Of course,' said the vicar having already been told two of his older parishioners were friends with a hint of emphasis on the word *friends*. There was no discussion on the identity of George's partner.

The vicar carried on and George groaned silently as he sat on the first pew thinking about who would not be by his side.

The rehearsal went ahead with George's mind miles away. The lovely Louisa dominated his thoughts and she only faded when a Down freight running express blasted its whistle approaching the station. George instinctively removed his pocket watch and noted the train was a minute late.

The rehearsal finished after which the vicar spent fifteen minutes picking up hymn books as a result of the flower girl's parlour game.

Getting home, George copped a soaking from heavy rain. He dried himself and waited for Emily. His mother made tea and they discussed the rehearsal with the rain hammering on the station house roof.

Next morning George and Lord Fitzsimons met for further planning of the Open Day at Ripley Hall. George struggled knowing Stephen was keen on Louisa.

Should I tell him we're rivals? If I do, how will it affect our friendship? Will it knock me out of the race to win her hand?

Stephen arrived buzzing with excitement. George died. *He's made contact with Louisa and she's excited to have him take an interest.*

'Good morning, Squire,' said his Lordship. 'I come bearing wonderful news.' George steeled himself. 'We have a travelling zoo for the Open Day.'

George's relief added to his excited response. 'That sounds marvellous but what's a *travelling* zoo?'

'It's a chap who loves animals, pops them in his van and travels around the country setting up at fairs and the like.'

'But Stephen, this is a farming district. Most of the children around here have seen farm animals and even live with them.'

'Ah, but how many alpacas, hedgehogs, tortoises and wallabies do you see in Whittleton?'

George understood and shared his friend's enthusiasm. They went over the details of the event and agreed everything was ready to go.

'Now publicity,' said Stephen. 'Can your London friend write a story we can send to the local papers about the unusual animals?'

'I'm sure Oscar would be more than happy to oblige.'

'He's a damn good friend, George. You seem to attract decent people.'

George smiled inside. *Even a certain female.*

Stephen stood to leave and the men shook hands excited their plans might soon give the village, the manor house and the railway a real boost.

'Oh, by the way,' said Stephen, 'I've invited Lord and Lady Carruthers to come down on the weekend of the Open Day. I told them their friend Louisa is most welcome to come too.' He winked and left. George didn't wink.

Sir Jerome Hamilton-Weir thought he was suffering a heart attack. The pain in his chest became stronger. He sat at his desk and tried to breathe slowly and deeply. His third child, his illegitimate daughter, the woman he'd followed closely from afar for 20 years was inside his home. *How? Why? What does she know about her father?* His mind kept spinning.

For years, Sir Jerome employed a former policeman to report on his third child—her schooling, health, employment and more. He knew she now lived in Hampstead and worked for Lord and Lady Carruthers in Tudor House. The proud father collected photographs of his daughter, taken in secret, and kept in secret far from his family's eyes.

Decades ago, when Louisa's mother revealed her pregnancy, the knight gave her a considerable payment. He explained how for him to acknowledge the child would cause a scandal, and if the mother said nothing about the identity of the father, even and especially to the child, he would pay all expenses for his daughter until she came of age, which he did.

Once Louisa reached 21, Sir Jerome no longer made payments to her mother but instead changed his will making his third child an equal beneficiary with the twins he fathered. Upon his death, his unrecognized daughter would be seriously rich.

His wife knew these details but not the identity of the illegitimate child and agreed to not tell the twins. On her deathbed, she broke her word creating the Enoch and Sophronia conspiracy. Today, Sir Jerome assumed his legitimate children were blissfully ignorant of their half-sibling and her entrée into their father's will.

How wrong he was, and how frightened he became coming face-to-face with his daughter in his own home.

The only consolation he took was when his children discovered the contents of his will, he would not be around to hear their ranting and raving. He stopped those thoughts and pictured the young woman he met outside his study. Her beauty and smile gave him immense pleasure and so much so, his chest pain began to fade.

Richard Carrington needed cash. His father was asset rich but cash poor and such a situation irked him no end. *Damn nuisance* thought the Earl, and damn *unfair as well.*

His fury at being rejected by the divine Louisa changed direction when offered a serious wedge of cash for making her disappear altogether. Asking or tricking Sir Jerome into changing his will was a task way beyond the Earl's imagination or intelligence. This meant murder and body disposal, neither of which he fancied or was good at. Actually he wasn't good at anything, apart from lying and fornicating and even the latter was debatable.

Supping with cutthroats, as he called them, meant employing one such villain to do the deed, but that created a downside. He would have to pay and with such a heinous act, the price would be seriously high. *Damn*, he thought. *I need the cash. I'll do the job myself.*

Carrington used his rat cunning to plot the demise of George Miracle's one true love. The Earl knew planning was essential but nerves played a part. If he failed, he'd earn nowt and possibly suffer horrendous consequences.

He cared not for the potential victim and especially so since the stupid woman rejected him. *The bitch laughed in my face.* Stiffing her would give him intense pleasure.

Emily's wedding loomed large. George worked even more hours to avoid the stress at home. Escaping from the station house helped maintain his sanity. Connie fussed, Emily worried and Spike and Trixie wished the whole thing would be over and done with.

Emily wanted Spike to live in her new married home which was the back room of the Culpepper farmhouse. How lucky was the SM's sister? How many brides get to move in with their in-laws and sleep next door to the hen house?

Connie reckoned it would be cruel for the dog to have to live with so many other animals in and outside the property. This argument between mother and daughter was another reason why George worked late at the station.

The wedding was next Saturday and a week before the Open Day at the manor house. On that weekend, George's godson, Lord and Lady Carruthers and a certain young woman would be in Whittleton. Giving away his sister barely troubled his thinking. Meeting, seeing and speaking to Louisa were thoughts he couldn't escape.

After several days of heavy rain, the weather did the right thing for Emily and Bert and the sun finally put his hat on. This would not be the wedding of the century. It involved a basic service in the village church followed by a reception in the church hall next door. Connie baked for ages to provide the wedding breakfast, and John Beckwith took control of setting up the reception venue.

George went to work in the morning and couldn't escape his mother's words as he reached the cottage door.

'You be back here at 11, George Miracle, and not a minute later.'

'Yes, Ma,' he replied and left for work.

The Crabbie was getting ready for its day's work when George heard a cry of despair. He hurried out of his office and called across the tracks to the crew.

'Good morning, gentlemen. Is everything okay?'

'No,' shouted Madge and swore albeit in a softer voice.

'Pressure problem,' shouted Bobby the fireman.

George headed across the tracks to the island platform. His heart started running. With the Crabbie attracting visitors on weekends, having the locomotive break down would be a nightmare.

He scrambled along the Down and hurried through the pot plants now decorating and dividing the mainline from the branch.

Madge and Bobby were on the job even before George. A steam locomotive needs a decent breakfast and massage way before it starts work. Bobby lit the fire and Madge's oil can began to squirt.

The crew talked to the loco. It was a she and they called her Crabbie. She wasn't crabby, in fact she always went about her business without fuss or bother; that is until today.

Railwaymen tended to be specialists. A chap in a signal box knows everything about block sections, Home Signals, crossover roads and loop lines. A fireman, at least one firing a small loco, would do the fire-lighting well before departure, and ensure the water supply is up to the mark and the tender has the required amount of coal. A driver knows not so much how to drive the locomotive but how to nurse it, coax it, and have it work perfectly in all weathers and on all gradients.

But fixing engine faults needs an expert. If there's a problem with a pipe in the boiler, get a boilermaker or the boys who built it to do the job. Now, at Whittleton, a falling pressure level spells trouble. They needed to know what has happened and more importantly, how it can be fixed; and not tomorrow or next week but now, right now.

George arrived. 'I only want to hear good news. Who's first?'

Driver and fireman stared at the SM and their faces spoke volumes. George's stomach began to churn. Passengers would arrive soon. There would be ramblers, Druid followers, and families on a day out, and those wine lovers who, having been to Ripley Hall, wanted other activities in and around Whittleton. Then there were villagers who liked the idea of their children and grandchildren travelling free on the Crabbie. George would have to tell the paying customers, "I'm so sorry, the train is not running." That's a sentence no railwayman ever wants to utter. This was a potential disaster.

As George was being given an explanation of what the crew reckoned was possibly wrong, a young woman rode up on a horse.

'Mr Miracle,' she called from the field.

George walked to the edge of the platform. 'Hello, how can I help?'

'Part of your railway track is missing this side of the Pickling Halt.'

'Missing?' All three railwaymen stared at her.

'All the rain this past week has caused a flood and the stones under the sleepers have been washed away.'

'Bloody hell,' whispered George. He called. 'Were you able to move in close and to see the damage?'

'My horse shied when we came across the stones on our bridle path. I hopped down for a closer view and there's nothing under several of the sleepers. They're suspended above the ground.'

George struggled with this second bit of terrible news but remembered his manners and called again. 'Thank you so much for riding all this way to tell me. I appreciate your kindness.'

'Good luck,' she called turning her steed and galloping away.

Madge summed up the situation. 'Even if we can get the Crabbie firing, if there's ballast washed away, we're stuck here, boss,' he said, wondering how the young SM would react. All three men wondered what the late Fred Carmody would have done in this situation.

'I'll hop on the blower,' said George, 'and report the matter to head office. You two keep trying to sort the loco.' He set off then stopped. 'Before I report this, please tell me exactly what's wrong with the engine.'

'I can show you,' said Madge. 'Step this way, sir.'

George climbed onto the footplate and Madge pointed to a pressure gauge. 'We need this much pressure but despite the fire been going well over time, see how low the needle is here.'

As the SM moved in close to see, a pipe failed and a burst of steam whacked his face. He yelled in pain, knocked off his cap and Madge thrust out his hands to help the boss.

The driver forgot about the oil can he was holding and in trying to help the groaning SM, managed to depress the button and squirt oil straight onto George's hair.

He invented a new scream, Madge swore and Bobby fought hard not to laugh.

On the day he was to give away his sister at her wedding, George suffered a busted loco, a damaged railway track and now an oil-infested hairstyle.

The crew helped him onto the island platform. Madge handed him a cloth which certainly wasn't suitable for drying anything let alone the SM's greasy follicles. George spluttered. He believed he could handle a cancelled branch line but how could he explain turning up to the church straight from enjoying what looked like a mud bath? His mother and sister would never speak to him again.

'You need Mrs Monty,' said Bobby and Madge agreed. 'If anyone can get anything clean, she's your man.'

'You sure?' asked the bewildered station master.

'Go,' said Monty and gave his boss a shove.

Three minutes later George knocked on the back door of the cottage where signalman Monty and his wife lived. The door was opened by porter Gordon Littleton, resident traitor of the station staff, and lodger of said residence.

Gordon gasped, (a) at seeing his boss call at his abode and (b) at the state of the SM's hair. 'Sir!'

'Is Mrs Monty in?'

She appeared. Her name was Ethel but everyone called her Mrs Monty. Monty called her Mrs Monty, Luv or the Missus.

'What's happened to you, Mr Miracle, Mr Miracle?'

'It's oil, Mrs Monty, and Madge and Bobby said you were an expert at cleaning.'

'Come in, come in,' she said and pointed at Gordon. 'Go out, go out,' she ordered and the porter left for work. 'Sit, sit,' she said and George sat. 'I'm good with clothes, with clothes, Mr Miracle but I ain't never got oil out of hair before, before.'

She fossicked around hunting for bits and bobs, filled a large metal bowl with water and placed items on the table. Soap was not the only part of her armoury. She wrapped an old towel around George's neck who panicked thinking she was about to shave his head.

'I wouldn't normally worry, Missus, but it's my sister's wedding at noon and I dare not arrive at the church like this.'

'The whole village knows it's Miss Miracle's big day, big day. Don't you worry, worry, Mr Miracle. We'll have you right as rain in no time, no time.'

She worked George's hair into a lather. He looked like a snowman with a pointy head. His hair stood stiff. Anyone making a meringue would have been proud of the peaks. His mind came under fire. His panic grew restless. Counselling would help, drugs might be better.

So horrible was his situation, he entertained the thought of no longer being a station master but stopped such thinking when the sound of door knocking interrupted his darkest moments.

'I won't be a jiffy, jiffy, Mr Miracle,' said Mrs Monty who left.

George heard voices and one he recognized. It was his mother. His mind exploded. She'd gone to the SM's office, to the Crabbie and been sent to the signalman's cottage. The incident on the footplate spread like wildfire.

'Ethel, they told me George is here.' His thinking went haywire.

Something is definitely wrong but whatever it is, seeing me looking like a ghostly madman, will ruin her life forever.

Connie appeared and her face copped a whack.

'George!' she exclaimed. 'What's happened to your hair?'

She could talk. The mother of the bride was wearing a dressing gown, and her hair was a mass of white bows all added to create a fashionable hairstyle in preparation for Emily's big day. Mother and son were a sort of matching pair.

George posed his own question. 'Ma, what are *you* doing here?'

'A cow stepped on Bert's foot. He's been taken to the hospital and the wedding's off.'

Chapter 25

The Earl of Fakenham wanted the full fee. He was desperate for filthy lucre and the lure of so much cash, plus the hatred of giving so much of it away to a professional thug, forced his hand. Shooting grouse and hunting foxes were child's play but murdering a human niggled away at what could loosely be described as his conscience, although said niggle fled once he concentrated on making a foolproof plan.

At first he told the twins he needed upfront cash.

'You're getting nothing, Dickie,' said Sophronia, 'until our beloved sibling is unable to receive anything from the old man ever again.'

'But the evil bastard I've hired won't move without a small down payment. You do want this job to work?'

'How small?' she asked.

'Oh give him a pony,' moaned Enoch.

'*You* give it to him,' snapped big sister, older by two hours, and Enoch handed over the £25.

'What's your plan,' asked Enoch.

'Don't tell us,' screamed Sophronia. 'We can't reveal what we don't know. And remember, Dickie, we know nothing of your scheme and even less of the person about to disappear from our dear Papa's will.'

'Understood,' growled Dickie with his nerves starting to jangle.

The Earl knew many people intimately; criminals, scroungers, prostitutes and actresses. The latter were once called prostitutes. A few were cut from the same cloth as Carrington—self-centred hedonists. He called on Lily Bliss, an actress who enjoyed his manliness and title. He gave her a serve of baloney about needing a costume for an important job.

'Do you want to turn heads?' she asked.

Dickie panicked. 'No, no, definitely not; I want an outfit which enables me to move around without being noticed.'

'So you want to be invisible. What are you up to, my Lord?' she asked suspicious of him yet again.

He gave a weak explanation about evaluating a property without being seen, and she let it ride. She liked the thought of him buying property.

His rat cunning and her advice enabled him to disguise himself as a non-descript gent with glasses, a goatee beard, a middle-class person's grey suit, a ubiquitous hat and a plain cane. He developed a slight limp and dusted his hair with powder.

Obviously he knew Louisa's address from his recent visits. He took the train to Hampstead and walked to Tudor House, keeping to the other side of the road. Boredom set in to be replaced by frustration.

More than an hour passed before Mary the housekeeper appeared, the woman who escorted George Miracle through the magnificent house as a wee lad many years ago. Dickie followed Mary at a distance.

She entered a grocery store in the High Street with the disguised Earl following pretending to examine rows of products. He listened. Mary and the woman assistant were old pals, or rather old gossips and Dickie struck gold.

'Her ladyship is expecting again,' said Mary delighting in being the fount of all knowledge. 'And I'll have a bit of time to m'self next week when they trot off to Whittleton to stay with Lord Fitzsimons, the one with all the wine.'

There was more tittle-tattle which Carrington absorbed. He needed to investigate Whittleton, wherever that was, and some Lord called Fitzsimons who apparently was best friends with Bacchus.

George Miracle couldn't think straight. Sitting in the signalman's cottage, he appeared ridiculous, his mother the same. His problems with the branch seemed insurmountable, and his appearance at his sister's wedding looked like a disaster waiting to happen. Now, out of nowhere, the groom has cried off injured and George's oil-stained locks were shunted onto the passing loop.

'That's terrible,' said George. 'How's Em?'

'She's fine. That girl takes adversity in her stride.'

'So what's going to happen?'

'Even if Bert's on crutches, he'll be there same time next week.'

George flinched. 'Next week!'

Connie turned to leave. 'You now have seven days to make yourself beautiful. I'll see myself out, Ethel.'

George's mouth opened. He stared at his hairdresser. 'Next Saturday's the Open Day for the village at the manor house.'

Mrs Monty squeezed the SM's hair. 'We'll have you looking like a movie star, a movie star, by then Mr Miracle.'

Mrs Monty reinforced her reputation as the expert grit and grime remover, and could now add engine oil to her CV, her CV.

'There you go, Mr Miracle, you're as good as new, as new.'

George felt a tremor of happiness on his otherwise dreadful day.

'I can't thank you enough, Mrs Monty. You've saved my life.' He was about to offer her money than remembered how locals in this part of the world considered helping a fellow villager in need to be their duty. To offer money was insulting and embarrassing.

He left continuing to sing her praises. Back at the station his heart sank. There were people on the Down who were not locals. They were here to visit the manor house, possibly the village and even the site once used by the Druids. They would travel on the Crabbie. Damn.

He hurried to the branch line. Bobby shovelled coal. George peered into the cab.

'What's happened?' exclaimed George.

'Pressure's good, boss,' he said. 'We're right to go.'

'But what about the missing ballast? The line's impassable.'

'Not if we stop short, boss. Then we can shunt the Crabbie home.'

'But what about safe working? Aren't you supposed to run around the carriage and travel tender first? What does the company say?'

Bobby had no idea. Madge appeared holding his oil can and George pulled back in fear.

'Sorry, boss,' said the driver. 'Say, your hair looks terrific.' Bobby agreed.

'Never mind about my hair; what are we going to do about all these passengers?' He nodded beyond the pot plants where people moved towards the branch line side of the island platform.

The train crew couldn't help. They suggested taking the Crabbie up the line sans carriage, tackling the line repair then returning for the travelling public. George wasn't sure about LNER regulations concerning damaged track, and having staff performing line repairs definitely sounded wrong and besides, the repairs could take hours. He floundered in his inexperience. Passengers walked closer. George discovered a new form of misery. He turned to face the eager passengers and cleared his throat ready to announce the cancelled service. In all his years on the rail, this was his worst moment.

'Ahoy!' shouted a familiar voice. 'Ahoy there, Mr Stationmaster!'

George stared in the direction of the voice, as did the crew as well as the dozen or so passengers ready to catch the Crabbie.

Sitting on the bench seat of a dray being pulled by two horses was Freda the farmer and now tourist guide. The driver of said vehicle was the irascible farmer, Danny Wight. Between the driver and his female passenger sat a giant wolfhound showing increasing signs of excitement having spotted his favourite railwayman.

The dray came along the road beside the field which backed up against the branch line and its terminus.

George moved to the edge of the platform as the dray pulled to a stop. 'Good morning, Freda, and Mr Wight,' called George wondering what on Earth they were doing. Rufus barked. 'And to you, Rufus.'

Freda called. 'There's a wash-a-way, George, this side of Pickling. The track's done for.'

'Thank you, I've already been told.'

'I see you've got passengers for the Crabbie,' she yelled so loud the folk waiting for the train heard the news. Half the county heard.

Thanks for nothing, Freda, thought George. He felt a real soft spot for the woman and her pooch but wished she didn't announce the bad news to the world. He changed his mind instantly when next she yelled.

'I thought you could run a train replacement service.' George froze. Everyone froze. 'Danny's happy to run a shuttle service between Whitty and his place. The passengers can sit on the bales of hay he's set out here on the dray. Wotcha reckon?'

George couldn't stop a tear. His voice cracked as he shouted his reply. 'What a wonderful offer, Freda. Thank you so much, Mr Wight.'

Danny grunted although you wouldn't know. Freda didn't need to use her blackmail tale from the Christmas 1913 incident, although it was there if needed, but instead told him he would be paid per passenger. Money appealed to Danny. He and the Earl of Fakenham were sort of brothers in that area.

George asked the crew to lead the passengers off the platform, through the gate behind the signal box and along the road to the dray.

'You might need to give people a hand climbing aboard,' said George.

'We're not going too?' asked Madge with a look of horror.

'Take it in turns,' said George. 'Madge you do the first trip and Bobby you do the second.'

Rather than the passengers being disappointed, they looked on it as an adventure, and the children loved the idea of a hay ride in the country. Even the Druid followers saw it as a move back in time to a practice back in time.

George waved from beside the Crabbie as the dray headed off the way it came. Bobby joined the SM.

'I'll fix the fire, boss,' he said and George crossed the tracks to the Up as a London train arrived on the Down. One of the passengers who alighted was a non-descript gent on a surveillance mission.

Eric was on duty. 'Your ticket please, sir.'

The Earl of Disguise handed over the required item. 'Is this Whittleton?' he asked with the station sign shouting at him only a few yards away.

'It is, sir. Where are you heading?'

'To the village and then to the winery.'

Eric gave instructions and the man walked past the station house en route to the village. He was a liar on a spot of reconnaissance.

The week dragged. Emily went to the hospital to visit her true love. He was lucky having suffered bad bruising but no broken bones.

'I'll be fine, Em,' he repeated. 'I might not be much of a partner for the bridal waltz or for carrying you over the threshold but by hook or by crook I'll be there.'

'Stay away from any cows,' she said, kissed him and went home.

In the station house, Emily and her mother couldn't stop talking about the wedding and its changes. There was the cousin who now couldn't come, the florist who may not have Emily's favourite flowers a week later, and the dressmaker who could now add more lace having a few extra days. George wanted out. He spent long hours at the station attending to what seemed like endless paperwork.

Getting Head Office to send a maintenance team to repair the missing ballast was a new experience. He said nothing about the horse and dray service to Pickling and worried he'd be in trouble for running a private railway. He paid Freda out of petty cash so she could pay Danny. Of course it was against company policy but as the train replacement service proved a hit, George felt proud.

Numbers were down that weekend, he hoped because they'd all be coming to the Open Day the coming weekend.

But his mind was dominated by one thing. On the Open Day when everything was due to happen, instead of running the stations on what might be one of the biggest days of the year, he'd be stuck in the village saying, "I do". He suffered heart burn and headaches.

Of course compounding his misery was the fact his best girl would be in town possibly being wooed by his good friend, Lord Fitzsimons. What was there to be happy about?

Chapter 26

The day before the wedding and the Open Day, Stephen arrived at the station sporting a huge grin. 'I'd like an appointment with the station master please.' George tried to hide his sadness.

'Good morning, my Lord,' said the SM with torn emotions. He enjoyed the company of the owner of Ripley Hall and loved working on their joint ventures but felt unease knowing the man had romantic feelings for Louisa. George was sure Stephen didn't know the SM was head over heels in love with the young woman, and that he and His Lordship were now love rivals. George kept putting himself down.

Stand up for yourself, man, he thought. *Faint heart never won fair lady. You're as good as he is.*

'And a very good morning to you, sir,' said Stephen bubbling. 'Everything is set for the Open Day. The animal farm arrives this afternoon. I've arranged for the baker to set up a stall with all sorts of goodies, and the games are being handled by the chaps from the cricket club.'

'Excellent,' said George acting excited.

'And I hear your little loco is now back running on a new track.'

'It is.'

'George,' said the visitor taking the SM to one side of the platform. 'I can't tell you how excited I am about one special visitor.'

Here we go, thought George. *Should I tell him now Louisa is spoken for? Grow a spine, George.*

'Giles Llewellyn is coming tomorrow.' George's face remained blank. 'Of course, you're not a drinker. He's the top wine writer in London and a positive review from Llewellyn could see the cellar at Ripley Hall take off. He could put us on the map.'

'Wonderful,' replied George trying to appear enthusiastic.

'And it will mean more passengers for you, my friend. I'm thinking about turning the lodge in the far field into a sort of weekend getaway venue for people coming to the winery. They can stay overnight and arrive and depart using your wonderful railway; even take a trip on the Crabbie. Life is on the up, George. I'm convinced the Hall and the railway are both about to hit good times.' George forced a smile. 'I'll pop back later today.' He went to leave but stopped. 'Oh, I forgot. Your godson and his family and his mother's divine companion are all arriving by train.'

George copped a metaphorical face slap. 'To Whittleton? When?'

'Tomorrow and I need to ask a favour, my friend. I may be too busy to be here to greet them. With so much happening at the Hall, can I count on you to meet them off the train?'

'Of course,' said George, his pulse pumping.

'Good show,' said His Lordship squeezing his friend's arm. Stephen departed and George called after him.

'What time is their train?'

Stephen called back. 'Lord Carruthers said about noon. Bye.'

Smack! George copped another almighty metaphorical slap in the face. He would not be on hand to welcome Louisa and her entourage. He would be in church responding to the question, "Who giveth this woman to be married to this man?"

George needed help. Forget Louisa, Emily's wedding and the Open Day at the Hall. On an unusually hectic day, there was a station with three platforms to run. If he, the station master, was going to be absent for two hours or more, two porters and a lad porter might not be enough. He dared not ring Head Office and ask for back-up; such action would paint him as incompetent. He searched for a telephone number and made a call.

'Of course I'll come, Mr Miracle. I'd love to be back in harness again. You stay at your wedding as long as you like.'

'Thank you so much, ma'am. I'll meet you off the first Up.'

George felt a huge relief as Audrey, the former station master, mistress, now retired, the SM George's Uncle Fred took over from, happily agreed to lend a hand for the day.

He told Eric who reckoned it was a grand idea.

'Should I tell Head Office?' asked George. 'Is it against company policy for retired employees to come back to work even for only a day, and for me to give her a few bob out of petty cash?'

Eric used his expressionless face. 'Well sir, I won't tell if you don't.'

As the men discussed tomorrow's staffing arrangements, in London, two people were nervous. Louisa McClaren packed her case for a trip to Ripley Hall and a possible meeting with the man she'd fallen madly in love with; a certain humble station master.

Elsewhere in the nation's capital, the Earl of Fakenham packed his case for a trip to Whittleton and his task of murdering Miss McClaren. Were the stars aligning for a poor-man's Shakespearean tragedy? Perhaps not, because as the day of reckoning drew nigh, Dickie's ticker failed. He squibbed it. No, he wouldn't cancel his mission but rather he wouldn't fly solo. He just wasn't up to it.

After his reconnoiter trip to Whittleton, he devised a plan which didn't involve guns or knives and horrible, blood-soaked brutality. He needed a partner in crime and returned to one of his on-again-off-again lovers, the lovely actress, Lily Bliss. He turned on the charm.

'You won't be involved in anything nasty, my girl and of course I'll pay you for your trouble.'

'I've heard it all before, Dickie, but what do you want me to do?'

'A bit of acting; invent a character, dress the part and wander around a manor house. For you, it'll be a walk in the park, literally.'

Being out of work, again, she accepted and the Earl purred. His plan would work and all he needed now was to pay Lily as little as possible. 'So name your fee my darling girl.'

She gave him a stare and he cared not a jot as he would worm his way out of paying yet again. But when she did speak, he worried.

'Nothing,' she said.

Shock whacked the Earl. Dickie gave a weak laugh. 'Come, come, Lily my love, you theatrical ladies are so often out of work. Aren't you currently resting?'

'My fee is a promise of marriage.' The Earl flinched.

'Marriage? Look you know I'm broke but I can pay you for this job from the money I'll be paid.'

Lily went to her dresser and retrieved a piece of note paper. 'I don't want money, I want a title.' She wrote.

The Earl sensed troubled and more so when she handed him the page and said, 'Please sign this, my Lord.' He read.

'I, Richard Meretricious Carrington, Earl of Fakenham, do promise to marry Miss Lily Hortense Bliss on or before Christmas Day this year.' He scoffed. 'Is that it?'

'Now sir, kindly sign and date the document and we can plan your adventure in detail.'

Laughing inside, Dickie signed. Lily secured the document.

George couldn't sleep. His worries were many. Would a big crowd, guaranteed because everyone in the village declared all week they would be going to the Open Day, see something go wrong at his station? Worse, would a disaster occur with him nowhere near his place of duty? Would Lord Carruthers and his clan arrive with the SM nowhere to be seen, and would his absence send a message to Louisa telling her he didn't care? Would Lord Fitzsimons with his vast estate and potentially booming business, not to mention his charm and good looks, sweep the SM's girl off her feet?

What can I offer her; a station house with a backyard privy?

On the big day, he woke before dawn. Little sleep put him on edge. His mother must have been the same as she too was already up. Having to construct her fancy hairdo a second time was a major operation. George entered the kitchen.

'Good morning, Ma,' said George stretching and yawning.

'Good morning, son. I hope you slept better than I did.'

Small talk ensued with George sensing his mother wanted to speak but stopped herself from doing so.

'Are you all right, Ma? You seem on edge.'

'Of course I'm on edge.' She paused. 'There's something you should know, George.' She focused on his eyes and cleared her throat but stopped when the bride-to-be entered, yawning.

'I've just had the most wonderful sleep,' said Emily. 'Is it an omen? Does it mean I'll have a perfect wedding and marriage?'

She sat as her mother fussed.

'Of course,' said Connie.

'It's the beginning of a wonderful, new life, Em,' said George.

'I dreamt Bert's foot miraculously healed itself and we danced all night after the wedding breakfast.' She pointed at her brother. 'And I expect you to dance too, brother dear. None of that old war wound malarkey. Your sister doesn't get married every Saturday.'

Breakfast was of little interest to anyone. Visitors would soon start to arrive at the station house—well-wishers, the dressmaker, the bridesmaid and sundry others—so George made his excuses. His mother repeated her demand from last week.

'You be back here at 11, George Miracle, and not a minute later.'

He entered the Up platform an hour before the first train. His heart copped a thrill. Gordon swept the Down, Eric dusted the station signs and Pip watered the garden.

'Gentlemen,' he called and all three greeted him.

'We know this is an important day, sir,' said Eric so we want you to know we'll do everything for Whittleton village and station.'

A hint of a tear popped into George's eyes. Already under steam, the Crabbie sounded her whistle. The crew waved and George waved back. In his office, he pottered with thoughts jumping in and out of his head.

He checked both the clock and his pocket-watch. The first Up was due in two minutes.

A few locals were heading to London but only one passenger alighted. George waved as Audrey stepped onto the platform. He greeted her with a smile being delighted to see her in full uniform.

'I hope you don't mind, young man, but I wanted to wear my late husband's cap this one last time.'

'Not at all, ma'am, and I'm delighted to see you.'

She met the two new porters, greeted those she once worked with and enjoyed a cup of tea in her former office.

The weather was perfect and gradually people from the village walked towards the station, crossed the tracks and headed to Ripley Hall. Families were everywhere. The first Crabbie carried 22 passengers which was the smallest crowd for the branch all day. Mind you, children travelling for free helped swell numbers. A few parents enjoyed an overnight increase in the size of their family.

Two porters and the visiting SM worked the Down and branch. George worked with Eric on the Up. The minutes ticked by and 11:00 crept ever closer. Whenever a train pulled in from London, George studied the movement on the other platform, hoping to spy the passengers he so wanted to greet. *They might arrive early.*

They didn't and for George, his time was up. He told Audrey his wedding responsibilities were calling, and described the family Carruthers and party.

'We'll be fine,' young man,' said Audrey. 'You run along and enjoy your wedding.'

Emily was breathtakingly beautiful. Her dress, hair, make-up and shoes were simple but elegant. Bert was able to walk with a stick and the church was packed. Those waiting outside for the bride, who walked to the church on her brother's arm, saw her arrive then hurried in for the service. The Open Day activities could wait.

George and his sister made their mother cry. Here were her two little 'uns, all grown up and making their way in the world. Emily's faultless lip reading saw her speak clearly with joy. She was in love.

With the service over, George peeked at his watch. It was 12:44 and another London train arrived at Whittleton. He tried not to imagine Louisa's thinking. Caring for godson George would keep her busy. But she must have been curious, albeit surreptitiously, about the SM. *Where is George?* Thinking about Louisa thinking about him, began to haunt the SM.

The Londoners from Hampstead's Tudor House did arrive and were met by the "new" station mistress.

'Would you be Lord Carruthers, sir?' asked the redhead.

'Indeed,' replied the DSO George.'

'I'm Audrey, your Lordship, helping out for today.'

'And station master Miracle?' enquired George with his wife and her companion all ears.

'Oh he's off at his wedding, sir, in the village.'

There was no outward reaction from the clan Carruthers although inwardly, shock, sadness and even a smidgeon of despair set in as the lady's companion became the one with symptoms worse than her friend's morning sickness.

His wedding!

'I believe Lord Fitzsimons is sending a car for us,' said George glancing at his wife and her companion.

'It's waiting outside the station, m'Lord. If you and your party would follow me, sir,' she said leading the way.

The gardener drove the estate car the short distance to the Hall. Off they went with nary a Miracle in sight. It was no easy job negotiating the manor house driveway with so many locals enjoying the hospitality of the Ripley Hall grounds. There was even an element of danger where the donkey rides crossed the drive soon after the giant rhododendrons.

Lord Carruthers and party were not the only Londoners to alight at Whittleton. The non-descript gent who arrived last week to survey the scene, returned and, from another carriage, stepped a striking woman albeit dressed plainly. She carried a large handbag which, if seen by Lady Bracknell, would have elicited an extraordinary reaction. The couple made their separate ways to Ripley Hall on foot.

Finally the wedding service ended although George knew the reception would follow before he could race back to the station. When the couple sat to sign the nuptial documents, Bert took an age to settle by the table. George bit his tongue to stop calling out, "Come on, come on, you don't want to be late for your wedding night."

From the church, the couple moved outside for confetti and photos. Smiles dominated. Bert's parents were thrilled to see their shy lad marry a lovely lass who they long ago accepted as a daughter.

George groaned inside. He desperately wanted to escape. Then it was time for the happy couple to be photographed with their respective parents. George straightened his tie. Bert's mother and father slipped in beside their son. George went to step forward then froze. His mother popped in alongside his sister but George's spot was taken by Mr Beckwith.

Poleaxed was a good description of George. The villagers weren't shocked in the least. It was well known the older couple were close.

Then the penny dropped.

Ma was super nervous at breakfast because she wanted to tell me there was to be a second wedding in the family. Oh my hat!

George's anxiety became anxious. *Louisa thinks I've dumped her. Lord Fitzsimons is already whispering sweet nothings in her perfect shell-like. I'll soon be living with my stepfather or on my own, and there's still an hour to go with this damn wedding breakfast.*

Finally it was time for the feast. George remembered only a few weeks ago his family teased him about asking Louisa to be his partner at the wedding. Now he was alone.

He made a fine speech well disguising his impatience. Of course he couldn't up and leave. He chatted with his new brother-in-law and his family. He couldn't wait for the dancing to end and for the bridal couple to leave. One dance with his sister was torture.

Outside, he stretched his legs, checked his watch and listened for the trains knowing the Whitty and Crabbie timetables off by heart.

'I enjoyed your speech, George,' said a voice behind him and the SM turned to see John Beckwith smiling.

'Thank you, sir.' George left it there feeling uneasy.

'I'd like to have a chat with you,' said the older man. George's unease moved through the gears. 'I'm in strange territory here and hope you'll understand if I seem a bit … well, strange.'

Still George said nothing. He sensed his job was to listen.

'I have asked your mother to marry me, George, and to my delight she has agreed.'

Beckwith hesitated hoping for a response. George responded. 'Congratulations, sir, and I'm sure you'll both be very happy.'

'Thank you but your mother is most concerned you'll be left alone in the station house.'

'I'll be fine, sir.'

'She mentioned you have become friendly with a young woman from London, and is hoping there might be a future for you and Louise, is it?'

'Louisa,' corrected George now feeling the worst he'd felt all day, although the prospect of having his step-father move into the station house being averted was a massive relief.

A loud whistle sounded as the 14:42 approached the Up platform. George checked his watch. The train was on time and from inside the hall, music and clapping suggested the new Mr and Mrs Culpepper were saying farewell.

George and his future stepfather rejoined the guests. He kissed his sister and shook hands with his brother-in-law. They left to the usual raucous send-off. He went to his mother and told her he needed to return to work.

'Did you have a word with John?'

'We did have a chat, Ma, and congratulations.' She appeared relieved. He kissed her and quietly headed back to the station.

What's happened in my absence, and where is the lovely Louisa?

Chapter 27

George used simple logic. If Louisa arrived on the 12:04, she'd now be settled in the Hall enjoying the Open Day delights and possibly being escorted by the Lord of the manor. George's plan was as follows. Check out the station activities since his absence then find an excuse to slip across to Ripley Hall. If the station had run smoothly in his absence, a second away trip wouldn't make any difference.

The sounds coming from Ripley Hall were startling. Cheers as a game was won, shrieks of delight as people watched an egg and spoon race, and whistles as ... no, that sound was from the returning Crabbie. George watched as the 0-6-0 pulled in tender-end first. Then the relief SM spotted him.

'Here he is,' cried Audrey with her cheeks matching the colour of her red curly hair. 'What a day, young man,' she said. 'It's been the best day of my railway life.'

'Any problems?' asked George waiting for the bad news.

'Yes, too many passengers.'

Eric joined them. 'In my thirty years here, sir, it's never been this busy. Congratulations.'

'Yes, many congratulations,' said Audrey who hugged the young SM and tried to kiss his cheek. Being so short she crash-landed on George's neck.

'And the Crabbie?' he said pointing across the tracks.

'Same,' said Eric. 'You could have used a second carriage.'

George's heart pumped pleasure around his body. But with the station a roaring success, he pondered the excuse he would give his colleagues to check on proceedings at Ripley Hall.

Before he spoke, the latest Down arrived. He popped into his office to be sure everything was ship shape and Bristol fashion when a knock sounded on his door.

'Station master Miracle?' asked a beautifully-dressed older man with impeccably designed and trimmed whiskers.

'Yes sir, how may I help?'

'Sir Laurence Pennington, member of the LNER board,' he said extending his hand.

George's mind exploded. Could his day become any worse? 'How do you do, Sir Laurence and welcome to Whittleton.'

'It appears you have a singular operation here, Mr Miracle. Word has filtered through to board level about wonderful activities happening in this part of the country.'

'May I offer you a cup of tea, sir?'

'Thank you, no, I'd rather see these remarkable changes you've made. May I have a short inspection?'

'But of course, sir. Please follow me.'

As George led the high-ranking LNER official, his employer, his nerves got busy. What surprised him though were his constant thoughts about a young woman currently residing a few hundred yards away. Surely a Head Office heavy would dominate his thinking. And what was even more astonishing, George pondered asking the board member if he, the humble SM, might be excused to go and check on the safety of his girl. Of course he made no such request.

'This garden is wonderful,' said Sir Laurence. 'Is it all your work?'

'Not a single pot or plant, sir,' said George explaining the inspiration of Horace Gardiner from the village and how locals rallied around to create the garden on both platforms.

'And the locals maintain the garden?' queried the visitor.

'They have a roster and are, dare I say, desperate to keep the garden in top condition. If ever the company were to have a best railway station garden competition, you'd find a willing entrant here in Whittleton.'

Sir Laurence nodded as his gaze fixed on the island platform. 'Now I've heard about your wonderful branch line. I must see it for myself.'

George led the way looking enthusiastic while inside his sadness multiplied. First the wedding kept him busy, then the breakfast, and now the visit of a VIP locked him in jail. He despaired of ever catching up with Louisa.

On the island platform, George genuinely panicked. He approached the cab and its two-man crew. 'Gentlemen,' he said with a face begging for good behaviour, 'we are honoured by a London visitor, from the company board, this is Sir Laurence Pennington.'

Madge and Bobby doffed their caps. 'How do, sir,' said Madge. 'I'm driver William Conquer and this 'ere's my fireman, John Smith.' Bobby nodded.

'How do you do, gentlemen and congratulations on the excellent returns from your little branch line.' He peered inside the cab. George died. Madge's shotgun stood silently to attention.

'Well, I've heard so much about the Crabbtree branch, I surely must take a trip.' He smiled at George. 'Have you room for one more, Mr Miracle?'

'Of course, Sir Laurence; after you,' said George indicating the carriage. George looked at the firearm and glared. 'Try and remain on the footplate while the locomotive is moving,' he whispered.

George followed the VIP into the carriage filled with excited passengers. People moved closer to allow the important gents to squeeze in. This trip could take forever and George's love life now headed for a major derailment.

The Crabbie set off with children hanging out the windows and waving to any person or animal in adjacent fields. Most waved back. George decided to raise the important matter himself.

'I must apologize, Sir Laurence, for the shotgun in with the coal. It is definitely not an action I condone and …'

'Well if a rabbit does come along, the crew will never have a stew supper by throwing lumps of coal at it.' He grinned and George felt a massive weight lift from his shoulders.

The man from London wanted to know how George made the branch so successful. George tried to explain the Pickling Halt and dreaded what they would find there.

George Carruthers and his party were welcomed by Stephen Fitzsimons and his mother. Concern was shown for Lady Carruthers being obviously in the family way. Louisa helped Valerie upstairs and settle in her room.

'I'm fine, Lou,' she said. 'You pop along and get yourself sorted.'

Louisa wanted to leave but held back concerned about Valerie. 'I'd rather make sure you are comfortable. What can I get you?'

'Nothing and if you don't go and sort out the nonsense about Mr Miracle and his wedding, you won't be the only one spending a miserable time at Ripley Hall.' The women exchanged glances. Sympathy floated between them.

Louisa forced a grin and went to her room. She changed into more comfortable attire and walked quietly downstairs. She nodded to the butler who seemed to appear out of nowhere.

'Good afternoon, Miss McClaren. His Lordship would like you to join him in the wine tasting cellar when you are free.'

Louisa froze. Stephen Fitzsimons was a kind and attractive man, and the owner of a vast estate but right now she faced a mystery.

The butler explained. 'You walk around to the rear of the house, Miss, and any of the staff will direct you from there.' He opened French doors allowing her to step outside.

'Thank you,' said Louisa and set off around the exterior. Once she rounded a part of the house close to the driveway, she stepped into the garden and headed for the station.

The grounds were filled with happy villagers. She left the manor, walked along the quiet road, turned towards the station, passed the signal box and stepped onto the Down platform. Passengers gathered awaiting the Crabbie.

Pip the lad porter was helping new arrivals from London. When he was free, Louisa approached.

'Excuse me, young man.'

'Yes Miss, how can I help?'

'I was hoping to speak with Mr Miracle.'

'Oh he's especially busy today, Miss. He's been to his wedding and now he's taken the important gentleman from London for a trip on the branch line. Can I give Mr Miracle a message?'

Louisa retreated. 'Thank you, no.' She smiled and walked away, her mind confused and her heart fighting to stay in one piece.

If he's been to his wedding, why is he now back at work?

The Earl of Fakenham and the actress Lily Bliss separately entered the grounds of Ripley Hall. The place was crowded and Dickie asked (read ordered) his accomplice to discreetly explore the grounds and manor house then proceed to the woods to the west of the Hall. Lily left and twenty minutes later headed to the woods.

'Over here,' said Carrington when he saw Lily approach. She moved to him with both now out of sight.

'You have excellent taste, my Lord,' she said. There is the smell of money in Ripley Hall.'

'This is your ten minute call, Miss Bliss,' he replied opening the large bag she carried. He helped her dress then produced a flask and offered it to her. 'Dutch courage,' he said. She swigged. 'Enough,' he said snatching his property. 'Now repeat the script.'

'Please,' said Lily, taunting him. 'A professional knows her lines.'

'Find out everything about Miss Louisa McClaren. I'll mingle with the peasants and we meet back here around 4. Any questions?'

'Yes, when and where are we to marry?'

'Let's do the business first,' he said, picked up his bag and left. She waited as instructed before making her move. Lily transformed herself into a character she'd always wanted to play.

The Crabbie ran well. The crew stopped at the stations and halts with no-one getting on or off. George tried to maintain calm. He worried about finding bedlam at Pickling and far worse, at losing Louisa.

'We're approaching the Pickling Halt, sir,' said the SM. 'I hope you find it interesting.'

The loco stopped and every passenger pushed to leave the carriage. George tried to shield his visitor. They stood on the short, packed earth platform with George playing guard and giving Madge the all clear. The empty Crabbie tootled off to Crabbwell.

Apart from the Halt sign, the old dilapidated carriage doubling as a shelter, and the brick privy with three fire buckets hanging on its outside wall, there were two tables on the platform. Freda stood beside one holding a homemade megaphone and, horror of horrors, Danny Wight, landowner, scruff and misery guts, slouched beside the other.

'This way ladies and gentlemen,' she cried. 'Please follow me.'

She headed to Danny's property and the unusual stones where, according to legend, the Druids once met.

'What have we here?' asked Sir Laurence admiring the tables.

Although quaking in his boots, George tried to sound relaxed. Freda's table contained jars of jam, chutney and pickles with odd lids, odd labels and a homemade sign announcing prices.

'We have members of the farming community doing their bit for the passengers, sir.'

'Fascinating,' said the big wig. 'My wife makes chutney.' George's spirits rose but not for long as Sir Laurence moved to Danny's stall. 'And what have we here, my good man?'

Danny would never make a salesperson. 'These are bits of the tools the Druids used when they come 'ere, years an' years ago.'

He lied without shame. Danny had picked bits of flint from one of the crumbling walls on one of the crumbling buildings on what he called a farm. He pronounced a blessing on building rubble renaming it as precious historical implements. It was tat.

The man from London examined a few samples. 'Local history comes alive,' he said smiling and addressed George. 'This is what the LNER needs; joining with local people with their stories to tell.' His eyes met the farmer's. 'Well done, sir, and long may you continue.'

George glared at Danny warning him not to even think about asking for a sale as he ushered Sir Laurence from the Halt.

'Would you care to see the Druid site, sir?'

'Oh most definitely; please lead on.

They headed into the trees to the now well-known spot where passengers sat on the ground as Freda chatted away explaining solstices and equinoxes and the activities of the Druids. People asked questions with Freda the Oracle sounding forth. She done good.

George walked on egg shells struggling to believe he'd avoided a disaster. The Crabbie returning kick-started his heart as people drifted back to the Halt. As the SM led the London supremo through the trees, a sudden crashing sound exploded. People screamed, George died and turned to be attacked by Rufus the wolfhound.

On his back and being licked to death, George begged for mercy.

Freda came to the SM's rescue and the person laughing the loudest was Sir Laurence. Freda liked him even more when he bought two jars of chutney and said, 'Keep the change, my good woman.'

Lily was wonderful. Her dress and hat screamed aristocracy. Her umbrella when opened became a work of art. She headed towards the front door of Ripley Hall passing villagers heading home who stopped and stared.

'Who's that?' and 'Would you look at her,' they whispered.

She reached the front door, rang the bell and fainted; well, sprawled on the expensive door mat pretending to have fainted.

The butler opened the door, and one wonders if he was trained to react as he did. Without flinching, he gazed at the sprawling Lily and spoke as he always did.

'Does madam require assistance?'

The actress carried on with her thespian routine by lying doggo, forcing the butler to report to a senior member of the household.

'Yes, Fortesque, what is it?' asked Lady Fitzsimons

'There's a woman who has fainted on the front doorstep, m'Lady.'

'She's fainted?'

'Yes, m'Lady.'

'Well don't just stand there man, fetch help.'

With kitchen staff helping, and then George Carruthers who wandered downstairs, Lily was carried inside, given smelling salts, and made comfortable on a chaise longue in the main sitting room.

Watched by several interested bodies, Lord Carruthers took control. 'Please relax, madam. You are safe. How are you feeling?'

Lily performed Act Two. Her pitch perfect Russian accent hooked her audience. 'Oh thank you, so kind you are to me.' She tried to stand and was encouraged to remain seated.

'This is Ripley Hall near the village of Whittleton,' said George trying to help. 'My name is Lord Carruthers.'

'How kind you are. I am the Princess Razumoffski from Saint Petersburg. My dying father told me his cousin, Lord Randolf Fitzsimons would be kind if I was ever to come close to Nearfolk.'

'Norfolk,' politely corrected Carruthers.

'I am sorry,' said Lily. 'My English is very not good.'

George looked up as Louisa, returning from her fruitless trip to the station, heard voices and entered the sitting room. 'Ah Louisa, the ideal person,' said George. He introduced the women and suggested Louisa accompany the visitor upstairs. With a maid assisting, the three women departed.

They settled in Louisa's room and the maid was dismissed. Lily purred inside. She'd not only located the target but was in her room.

My future husband, Dickie the Earl, will be most pleased.

Lily stood. 'I think I am feeling good today now. I must find my driver and turn back to London.'

Louisa encouraged her to stay. 'Please Princess, why not rest a while until you have completely recovered, then you could leave.'

'You are kind to me.' She examined the room. 'What a beautiful house.' She crossed to the window. 'And such a beautiful gardens.'

They admired the grounds in the afternoon sun and where only a few locals remained, helping with the packing. The Open Day was a cracking success. Lily pretended to spy her driver.

'Ah,' she said. 'There I can see my driver. Will you please to tell Lord Randolf Fitzsimons I have called and am so sorry to have missed to see him. I will write from my hotel. Goodbye.'

Louisa didn't feel it was her job to inform the princess her father's cousin was deceased and only recently buried. The actress from South London playing the Russian visitor left and was gone before anyone downstairs saw her depart.

Louisa knocked softly on Valerie's door, entered and explained the recent royal visitor. As interesting as the Russian proved to be, Lady Carruthers only wanted to hear about George Miracle's wedding. Valerie saw Louisa's face and knew the news was bad.

'Not only the woman station master we met when we arrived, but this time a young porter told me about Mr Miracle's wedding.'

The Crabbie arrived at Whittleton with happy passengers including a delighted Sir Laurence. He stood on the platform again praising George to the heavens for the splendid results on the branch.

George obviously took pleasure in receiving such an accolade but his frustration continued at not being able to see Louisa. Now, at last, he could farewell his VIP guest and go true love hunting.

'Mr Miracle, before I take my leave, I was wondering if you could point me in the direction of an address in the village?'

George worried his silent groan wasn't silent. 'Of course, Sir Laurence,' he replied now curious.

'My wife is a keen reader and loves the novels of P. J. Beaufoy.' This time George's soft groan was definitely audible. The visitor opened his satchel and produced a book. 'I'm under strict instructions not to return to London without her copy of this novel being signed by the famous author himself.'

George maintained his faux enthusiasm. 'I can certainly give you the author's address, sir.'

'Excellent, excellent,' bubbled Sir Laurence. George knew the Septimus Oldmeadow address by heart as it was the first home he visited when he arrived in Whittleton nearly six years ago.

The SM nodded at Sir Laurence expecting a farewell handshake. The visitor hesitated and George knew his love life was cooked.

'I don't suppose you know the gentleman?' George's expression said yes. 'I'd count it a great honour, sir, if you would introduce us.'

And so as Lily the pretend Russian princess headed for the woods and a rendezvous with the evil earl, George accompanied the LNER top man to the home of the limerick lover.

No-one called on Septimus and left soon after. Chatting, imbibing and an autograph with a personal message for the devoted reader, kept George away from his job and his girl. When he explained how he needed to become a station master again, he finally won his freedom as late afternoon drifted towards dusk.

He returned to the station where he bade farewell to Sir Laurence, who caught the penultimate Up. George sent Pip, Gordon and Audrey home having thanked them profusely for their sterling service. He and Eric tidied up and tallied up. From a railway point of view, it was a triumph. From a personal and affair-of-the-heart point of view it was a disaster.

He took a minute to duck home. Station House was in darkness. A note on the kitchen table told him his mother was dining with Mr Beckwith and friends. Trixie and Spike were fed and let out. His sister was gone to another life. On his own, George's misery was complete.

The Earl of Fakenham waited till dark. 'So it's the second light from this end on the first floor below that last chimney?'

'It is,' said Lily speaking in her usual Peckham accent. 'What's your plan, Lord Houdini, or shouldn't I ask?'

'I'll climb the ivy to that small balcony and tap on her window.'

'And if you fall, you'll break y'neck.'

Dickie was an adventurer between the sheets, but not at climbing mountains. Lily put him right; after all her title was at stake here.

'I came out through the kitchen. There are back stairs to the roof.' He stared at her, placed a dozen red roses in his shoulder pack and left. He became the murderer on a mission.

Chapter 28

Louisa sat on her bed. She found it incomprehensible that George Miracle, the young man who stole her heart, would up and marry someone, anyone without at least telling his friend Lord Carruthers, let alone her, "his girl".

Why would he speak such loving words to me if he's promised to another? Why at least not leave a message for Lord Carruthers?

She lay on her bed wondering how soon she could leave Ripley Hall. The thought of remaining for days made her misery worse. A light tapping sounded on her door. Louisa sat up not wanting to see anyone or be disturbed. She sensed Lord Fitzsimons wanted to welcome her. She hopped off the bed and stared out the window.

'Come in,' she said and turned to see Milly the maid enter.

'Excuse me, Miss. I'm to turn down your bed. I can come back later if you wish.'

'No, it's fine.'

Louisa stared out across the grounds of the Hall. The celebrations of the Open Day were over and the only lights she could see were from the distant village and closer, the railway station with its platforms bathed in pools of soft light.

Milly potted around feeling embarrassed. 'Excuse me, Miss but Lord Fitzsimons asked me to ask you to pop downstairs for a pre-dinner drink, if you're able.'

'Thank you,' said Louisa.

'His Lordship said if you need to stay with your mistress he would understand.'

'Thank you,' said Louisa again but now determined. She went to her case, put on a coat and a hat and left without saying a word.

Milly shrugged and finished her work. Stephen insisted on there being fresh flowers in all guest bedrooms. In Louisa's case, the petals grew old prematurely and several dropped to the bedside table and even the floor. Milly decided to collect them, remove the flowers and replace them with fresh blooms.

Being a coward, the Earl chose Lily's plan, entered via a back door and crept up the servants' stairs. Dressed in working clothes, if stopped, he would claim he wanted the housekeeper. He saw no-one.

The stairs grew more narrow and continued to the roof, his destination. He reached a small door and pushed hard. It creaked. He was inside the roof. A long, foot-wide board sat atop the joists. In the dim light, he ducked and crept forward.

Where is the bedroom and its small balcony?

He reckoned he was now above the second bedroom from the end so opened a trapdoor beside the chimney. He wanted to think of the money but gazing out on a dark night with the roof sloping in front of him pushed his bravery into retreat.

With the roses in a bag on his chest, lying on his back, he slid slowly towards the edge. The solid guttering offered a smidgeon of security. He reached it and peered down. He was directly above the balcony of the window to Louisa's bedroom. If he fell, he would land on the small balcony only a few yards below. The thought of the payment for his work helped him turn and go feet first over the edge.

His heart rate exploded. His knees hurt as they brushed the edge of the roof. He waggled his feet feeling for the ivy on the wall. Fear made him ultra-careful. He dared to glance down and saw he was on target. Once close to the balcony, he ran out of ivy so dropped the final few feet. The sound seemed massive. He crouched and froze. His right ankle screamed.

Nothing happened inside the room. Pressing hard against the wall, he peered into the bedroom and saw a woman moving about. The red roses in his satchel were removed. They were his bait. He stood ready to tap gently on the glass door.

Get her out here. Get her over the edge. Get away. Get paid.

He tapped. No response. He tapped louder, the woman inside moved, the glass door opened outwards and Dickie's plan ran into an unexpected hurdle.

Louisa in her coat and hat, set off along the drive towards the village. Sitting around in Ripley Hall became frightening. Thinking about the missing station master drove her mad. She knew the station and the station house and whoever was there would know the truth.

As she reached the end of the Ripley Hall drive, she heard what sounded like a man screaming. It came from the manor house but in the dark, she couldn't see a thing. It was not the Russian Princess and besides, Louisa's mission was far too important to turn back.

As the Earl tapped on the glass, Milly the maid decided to empty the fallen petals onto the garden below. She pushed the door, it swung open, hit the off balance Earl whose roses leapt skywards as his arms imitated a windmill on the not-too-distant Norfolk Broads. He fought to maintain his balance. Too late.

Gravity kicked in and Dickie went backwards off the balcony a good 15 yards to the bushy garden below. He missed a solid stone window ledge on the way down but copped a full back attack from a huge rhododendron bush.

The Earl hated failure and being broke but kept quiet so as not to broadcast his disaster. Well he did utter one scream of agony but to be discovered was worse than failure. Lily watched from the woods. She saw him reach the balcony thanks to the lights inside the rooms, and watched him plunge overboard. She ran.

Milly peered over the balcony, her heart racing. 'Are you all right?' she called not being able to see much in the dark. No reply so she raced from the room, hurtled downstairs landing in the kitchen.

The housekeeper, cook and butler prepared the evening meal.

'A man's just fallen off the balcony,' gasped the maid.

This caused the old cat in the corner to stretch and think about pigeons. Panic ensued. A person in authority needed to be informed.

Outside, Lily beat Milly to the victim. 'Dickie, give me your hand.' He groaned. 'We have to leave.' He groaned again. She stepped into the garden, found one of the Earl's arms and pulled. More groans. He fell from the bush and crash-landed on his knees. 'Move,' snapped Lily and the bruised and bloodied aristocrat fell onto the front lawn.

'I'm dying,' he said.

'Shut up and move.' She half dragged and half pushed the limping failure. He would make not a penny from his pathetic sortie, and would even have to repay the upfront pony the twins gave him.

Lily and her noble knight reached the woods and collapsed. 'I take it the woman in question remains in good health?' asked the actress.

It was his turn to snap. 'Shut up, bitch, and you can forget the bloody wedding.'

'We need to return to London, my Lord. Can you make it to the station?' He mumbled. 'Let's go towards the village but stick to the fields.' He wasn't in any mood to argue.

They made slow progress moving through the rural landscape in the dark. Stepping in a fresh cowpat seemed just. They saw lights, crossed a field, climbed a style and Dickie collapsed. He gave a shriek with Lily angry.

'Hello,' called a voice. 'Are you all right?'

They crouched in silence. The speaker opened a gate and crossed the dirt, rarely-used road. 'Can I help?' asked Horace Gardiner, creator of the beautiful gardens at Whittleton station.

Talk about landing on your feet. The elderly gent extended the hospitality of his humble cottage to the wandering, would-be now woeful failed killers.

Of course they were a married couple who became lost on their ramble. They were fed, watered and put up for the night. The words *the Earl of Fakenham* were never mentioned.

Louisa walked along the road beside the field beside the island platform with the 0-6-0 loco sleeping peacefully. Louisa planned to visit the station first and then the SM's cottage.

In his office, George poured over the figures, the ticket sales and counted the cash. He'd never experienced a day like it. 'Eric, this is unbelievable. I need to secure this large amount of money like the Bank of England.'

'And it all happened while the big boss from London was here.'

George checked his watch. The last Down is due in six. Do you mind popping over and seeing it on its way while I finish up here?'

'Of course not,' said the porter now close to retirement.

'And once done, I'm ordering you to go home. I'll stay for the Up freight then lock up. Thanks again, Eric; you and the others have done a brilliant job and with me nowhere to be seen.'

They grinned and Eric set off. 'Good night, sir.'

'Good night, Eric.'

Stephen finally finished tallying and tidying up in the wine-tasting cellar at the rear of the manor house. So many people discovered the wine business at the Hall with people coming from far and wide to taste and buy. Locals told friends who lived far from Whittleton. The Lord of the estate was in good spirits and more so when he pondered the lovely Louisa was a guest in his humble abode.

He entered the kitchen to see people in a flap. The housekeeper explained how a man fell from the first floor balcony of Miss McClaren's room. Stephen exploded. 'What man? What was he doing there? Was anyone hurt? Where is Miss McClaren?'

When told she wasn't hurt but had gone for a walk, Stephen raged. 'Gone for a walk? At this time of the night? Where?'

The staff retreated. Stephen's late father possessed a terrifying temper but his son was a gentleman with a kind and caring nature. To see him flare like this put the fear of God into them.

Without hesitating, Stephen took off.

Louisa approached the station. She decided to go to the closer Down platform. A man in uniform stood there. He would know the whereabouts of the station master, his boss, SM Miracle.

She walked along the platform when Desmond slipped out of his hideaway to close the crossing gates to the road. First one gate then the other clicked into position. Louisa heard the sound of a locomotive approaching from the London end, and all this action persuaded her to pause. She stepped back fading into the shadows.

The locomotive pulled in with all its smoke and steam. Doors were opened and people stepped out. Doors slammed. No-one boarded the train. Eric sent it on its way then collected tickets. George stood in his doorway and waved to his senior porter. Eric waved back and left to go home.

George stared across at the Down as a person stepped out of the shadows and stood under a platform light. He stared. He squinted. It looked like a woman but the hat and coat gave a sort of disguise. Slowly his mind suggested answers. Then his heart clicked into gear. He believed. Could it be Louisa? Was his mind playing tricks? No, it *was* Louisa. He wanted to call out and run across the tracks.

Good job he didn't as the Up freight express pounded its way towards Whittleton and beyond. It rattled through Whitty. With so many wagons, it took an eternity to clear the station.

Louisa saw the SM on the better lit Up platform. She too wanted to cry, call out and wave but rolling stock impeded her view. As the freight finally cleared the station, George hurried to the edge of the platform. The person he saw could only be the woman of his dreams.

On the edge of the platform he called. 'Louisa! Is that you?'

She wanted to reply but choked. The tension and misery which wracked her body since she arrived at noon froze her speech. Her hand went to her mouth which inspired the station master. Desmond opened the gates to the road and didn't see his boss take off.

Ignoring all railway regulations and common sense, George dropped off the platform, hurried across the two sets of tracks and scrambled up onto the Down. Louisa moved towards him. She cried and spoke with tears and spittle.

'They told me you were married.'

He stood staring at her thinking he could never love anyone as much as he loved her.

'Married?'

'Mr Miracle is at his wedding, they said.'

'At his *sister's* wedding,' blurted George. He shouted to the heavens. 'His sister's bloody wedding!' He dropped his voice. 'It's why I wasn't here to greet you off the train. And then a big wig from London arrived unannounced and I've been chauffeuring him around the branch and into the village the rest of the day.' He paused and they stared into one another's eyes. 'I've been so miserable all day.'

'I've been more miserable.'

'Have you, really?' George needed a nudge.

'Surely a clever man like you, Mr Miracle, must know I love you.'

He copped the nudge, threw conversation onto the tracks, took her in his arms and kissed her albeit with a little less passion than Rufus.'

At the climax of their embrace, Lord Fitzsimons reached the signal box and looked along the platform.

'Bugger,' he whispered, turned and walked home.

George walked Louisa back to Ripley Hall. Their misunderstandings about the day turned to subjects of humour. Laughter bounced around the grounds of the manor house. At the steps to the front door, George stopped and held Louisa's hands.

'I won't come in,' he said.

'Oh George, don't tell me you want our love kept secret.'

'Of course not but Lord Fitzsimons has told me of his affection for you, and I would rather be the one to tell him, I'm the lucky suitor.'

'Lucky suitor!' she gasped. 'Am I a trophy, some prize to win?'

'Of course not but I do consider myself lucky to have won the heart of the most beautiful girl in the world.'

She kissed him wanting him to know *he* was the only man in the world for her.

'You do know Miss, a station master will never be wealthy, works all the hours God sends, and often lives in a small railway cottage.'

'Sounds wonderful,' she whispered pushing her nose against his.

'There are other men with wealth, property and prestige who would love to marry you.' He paused. 'You do have a choice, Miss.'

'Are you trying to back out, George Miracle?'

He slowly shook his head. 'Never in a million years.'

He kissed her tending more towards the Freda and Rufus routine, squeezed her hands and set off home. After about a hundred yards, he turned back and she was still in the same spot. He could see her far better than she him. He waved and she waved back. The station master reckoned today was the best day of his life.

George wanted to knock off but there was still much to be done. He entered his office and made doubly sure the safe and all cupboards were securely locked. His office door contained two locks.

When he opened the cottage front door, his mother's voice floated up the hallway. 'Is that you, son?'

George entered the kitchen. 'Well who were you expecting, Ma, or shouldn't I ask?'

Connie poured her son a cup of tea. He sensed she wanted to talk. He sensed the topic was marriage but reckoned her news was not as striking as his.

'It was a wonderful day, George. Thank you for all you did.'

'It was nothing, Ma.'

'How was the Open Day?'

'It was a spectacular success and you'll never guess who turned up from London.'

Clearly Maggie wasn't listening. 'George, I need to discuss your domestic situation, your meals and washing.' The SM froze. 'John has asked me to marry him.'

George moved and kissed her. 'You're getting absent-minded, Ma. I've already congratulated you and Mr Beckwith.'

She remembered and realized the big day had overwhelmed her.

'Of course but we're both concerned about you.'

'Me, Ma? Whatever for?'

'Stop being clever, George. You can't possibly survive on your own. Emily and I have cooked your meals and done your washing, even darned your socks ever since you left school.'

'Excuse me, Ma. When I lived in a trench with German bombs and bullets for company, who do you think did my washing and cooking then? Well? Oh of course, silly me, it was my batman.'

She ignored his sarcasm. 'And since then you've been waited on hand and foot. With me and Em married, you can't run a railway station and feed yourself.'

George paused. 'I think you're right, Ma.'

She exhaled with relief. 'At last, thank you for seeing sense.'

'So when are you and Mr Beckwith thinking of getting married?'

'As soon as you can find a housekeeper.'

He built the tension. 'Does it have to be a housekeeper?'

Connie hesitated. It sounded like a reasonable question. 'What do you mean?'

'It's simple, Ma. Instead of finding a housekeeper, would you be happy if I found a wife?'

Connie copped a whack. 'A wife? What do mean a wife?'

'You know, one of those feminine creatures who falls in love with a humble and impoverished station master.'

Connie wanted to threaten her son but sensed he was about to tell her something secret and important. When he succinctly explained the last hour of his life, she cried with relief and happiness. Their embrace was warm and long but interrupted with many questions.

If Emily had been there, her list of questions would have kept them up all night.

Chapter 29

The next day, Sunday, George did more than his fair share of station work. He saw the first Up depart and turned to see Stephen Fitzsimons standing beside his office door.

'A station master works seven days a week,' said the landowner.

George's stomach started churning. When Stephen told George of his feelings for a certain lady, George said nowt. He was wrong. It worried him. Stephen was a friend. George should have spoken about *his* feelings for Louisa and now, it was too late. All night he thought about when and how he'd explain his relationship with Louisa to the Lord of the Manor. Now there was no choice.

'Good morning, my Lord. I trust your Open Day was a big success.'

'Thanks to you, George, it was a minor triumph. But I'm here for a special reason.' The sinking feeling in George's stomach dropped even further. 'I wish to apologize for possibly putting pressure on a particular lady I have recently discovered is attached to a certain station master of this parish.'

George cringed. Not only because he'd failed to inform Stephen of his love for Louisa, but also because she'd gone against his wish not to tell anyone of their love until George broke the news.

'I apologize, Stephen.'

'Stuff and nonsense, man; you have nothing to apologize for.'

'I asked Louisa to give me time to speak to you first.'

'Louisa told me nothing. *You* told me everything.' George struggled to understand. 'There was an odd incident at the Hall last night and Louisa went for a walk after dark. I went to find her and arrived in time to see you and your girl under a platform light, how shall I put it, greeting one another.'

George smiled with relief. Stephen stepped forward extending a hand. The men shook hands both applying powerful pressure.

'Well played, sir, and the very best to you both. And by the by, I happen to know a chap who can supply top quality wine for a wedding breakfast at a highly competitive price.'

They laughed and George's heart pumped with pleasure.

'I've arranged a small dinner party tonight at the Hall. It's to toast two people I'm proud to call my friends. Find cover for your railway, George, and we *won't* be dressing for dinner.' They laughed and Stephen departed, calling, '7.30 for 8.'

George entered his office but returned immediately when certain sounds grabbed his attention. A man with homemade bandages on his head and hands and sitting in a wheelchair, was pushed onto the Up platform by a young woman. He groaned and she groaned at his groans.

'Good morning,' said the SM. 'Are you travelling to London?'

'Yes,' said the woman, 'only we can't find our tickets.'

'I've been in an accident,' moaned the man, 'a terrible accident.'

'I'm sorry to hear of your misfortune,' said George studying the wheelchair. 'Your wheelchair is much like the one the station gardener uses.'

The woman jumped in. 'Yes, Mr Gardiner said we could borrow it and that Mr Miracle would look after it for him. Do you know Mr Miracle?'

'I do indeed,' said George, 'and I'll pass on your message.'

The young SM remembered advice his late uncle gave when facing passengers with excuses about not paying to travel. Looking at the gent, his life seemed a sad and sorry one. George wrote on a card and handed it to the woman.

'This will take you both to London.'

The woman, a human, was sincerely grateful. The man, a coward and failed criminal, said nothing. If George knew the Earl of Fakenham had travelled to Whittleton expressly to murder his beloved, the SM might well have pushed the wheelchair and its occupant off the platform as an express came thundering through.

The next Up arrived and the Londoners departed. The platforms were empty; a typical quiet early Sunday morning in Whittleton. George parked the wheelchair in his office and greeted Eric.

'I gave you the morning off, Eric.'

'I know, sir, but I thought you'd have a mountain of work to do after yesterday.'

'I do indeed and …' George didn't finish his reply.

In an instant his and Eric's world changed. Two masked men brandishing Webley Mk IV revolvers, standard issue for British officers in the Great War, burst onto the platform and pushed Eric into the office.

'Get over there,' spat the smaller man pointing his gun at the senior porter.

'You,' screamed the other man pointing his gun at George. 'Give us the money now or we'll kill you both.' George hesitated more from shock and fear than bravery. 'Now!' screamed the second gunman.

George moved to the safe. 'All right, all right, don't shoot.'

The tension exploded. The criminals were desperate. Each hand holding a gun shook. Two trigger fingers sweated.

The second gunman, guarding George, pulled a canvas bag from his jacket and threw it at the SM. 'In there, all of it, and *hurry!*'

George tried to glance at Eric and realized a second horrific pain.

If the loyal porter had stayed home as I ordered he'd be safe.

The large sum of money was placed in the bag. George counted it twice last night and knew exactly how much was there. He held out the bag to the crim who snatched it.

The raid was over in a few seconds.

Connie awoke buzzing. Her daughter looked a picture on her wedding day and was now on her honeymoon. The mother of the bride too was soon to wed and best of all, her boy, the youngest station master in England, seems to have found a girl. No, *has* found himself a girl.

Connie was sure George skipped a proper breakfast. She boiled two eggs, buttered two pieces of toast, topped them with sliced fresh tomatoes and pepper, made a pot of tea, placed the lot on a tray and set off on the short walk to the SM's office. She was at the top of the slight ramp when she heard the gunshot.

Eric, brave and loyal fool that he was, grabbed at the first man as he ran after his partner fleeing with the cash. Off balance, the criminal instinctively fired at the porter. Eric clutched his shoulder dropping to his knees. George leapt to his side but froze when he heard a scream.

Connie arrived with her tray of goodies. The gunman with the cash crashed into the SM's mother sending her son's breakfast flying. George looked up to see his mother being manhandled by a gunman.

'No!' screamed George. 'Let her go!' he raced to confront the men. The one who shot Eric pointed the gun at George.

'You want the same as your mate?' he yelled pointing his weapon only a few inches from George's temple.

The man with the cash and the hostage shouted. 'You call the cops and she gets it.'

The robbers and the terrified mother of the bride disappeared. George dropped to his knees beside Eric. 'You go,' said the porter trying to stop the flow of his blood. 'George, go!'

It was the first time Eric ever called the SM by his first name.

George raced onto the platform and headed towards the gates. He reckoned the gang would never escape through the village but into the surrounding countryside with any number of lanes and roads.

He screamed at the signal box. 'Monty!' He may not have even been there. Of course he was there and already on the phone.

George jumped off the end of the Up platform and banged on the gatekeeper's hideaway. 'Desmond!' He came out wondering why people were hunting this close to the village.

George went to the gate closer to the criminals to close it for a train. Desmond followed his boss. George shouted. 'We've been robbed and be careful, they're armed. Eric's been shot.'

The gate closer to the village swung across the tracks blocking motor vehicles. The getaway car roared around the corner screeching to a stop. The massive crossing gate blocked their way. The crim in the front passenger seat pointed his gun and fired.

George and Desmond ducked for cover. But shooting railwaymen wouldn't help the thieves. The boss in the back holding the money and controlling Connie shouted orders. The front seat passenger hopped out and struggled to move the gate.

While he struggled, Desmond crept forward and attacked the gate on the Down line. It swung into position. Fury erupted in the car. Desmond fled. The car was free to start crossing the tracks but then stopped thanks to the second gate now locked ready for a train. The car lurched forward stopping a foot or so from their latest barrier.

'Go back!' screamed the criminal acting as gatekeeper. He couldn't move the gate because the car was too close. Swearing filled the Sabbath sky. The car reversed. The gate swung back giving the crooks a clear passage. Leaping aboard the car, the gatekeeper with a gun started firing at anything so as to keep the railwaymen at bay.

The vehicle's engine revved and the car lurched forward when a terrifying explosion was heard by everyone from the village to Ripley Hall. Madge came late to the battle but when he did, he and his shotgun made a terrible mess of the radiator of the gunmen's stolen Aeroford four-seater. A second cartridge exploded and the front passenger side tyre collapsed.

Reloading both smoking barrels, the Crabbie driver walked to the end of the Down and aimed his weapon at the windscreen of the car. He didn't speak. He didn't need to. The driver and front seat passenger dived out, sans weapons with their hands reaching for the sky.

They whimpered. George came alive. His mother was in the back of that car. Was she hurt? He didn't hesitate and rushed the German trench. With his imaginary bayonet at the ready, he charged into battle.

A single revolver shot rang out from inside the car and George's heart copped a terrible pain. He reached the car, grabbed the nearest handle, and flung open the door.

To be continued

The Stationmaster Miracle Series Book 3 ~ *The Miracle Royal*

The Detective Joanna Best Mysteries

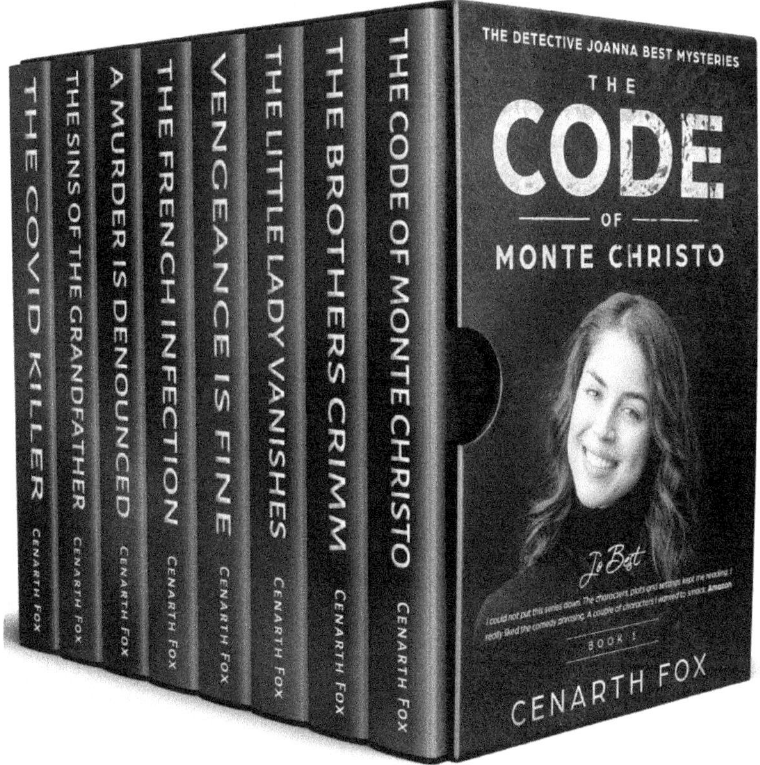

www.cenfoxbooks.com

Joanna Best is the youngest homicide detective in town. Smart, feisty and gorgeous, she's brilliant at cracking cases and rubbing people up the wrong way. Some jealous colleagues are desperate to undermine her. Certain criminals want her dead. Juggling a career with Victoria Police, having three men madly in love with her, and a strange family, Jo Best's adventures will drag you in. Her second banana is an Australian born Chinese IT guru who makes computers sing. Her best pal is a female 60ish police surgeon, a forensic genius and chocoholic.

I could not put this series down. The characters, plots, settings, kept me reading. I really liked the word comedy phrasing. A couple of characters I wanted to smack. **Amazon**

Sherlock Holmes

The great man is soon to retire. On his last night at Baker Street, the loyal landlady drops a bombshell. Holmes is staggered. Mrs Hudson has done what!? Sherlock Holmes never panics—until now. Dr Watson arrives and is stunned. It's their greatest challenge. Sir Arthur Conan Doyle is furious. A famous author turned WW1 counter—intelligence spy is on the case. *The Strand Magazine* smells a scoop. Inspector Lestrade from Scotland Yard plans revenge, and at stake is the brilliant reputation of the world's most famous consulting detective. His only hope is to 'play the game'.

www.cenfoxbooks.com

A delightfully imaginative pastiche. Recommended. **Peter Blau BSI**
An extraordinary book, one of the most enjoyable pieces of Holmesian fiction I've read in a long time ... a complex, ingenious and deliciously funny story of intersecting realities, and the conclusion is entirely satisfactory. I love it! **Roger Johnson**
Commissioning Editor: *The Sherlock Holmes Journal*

A Sweeping Saga

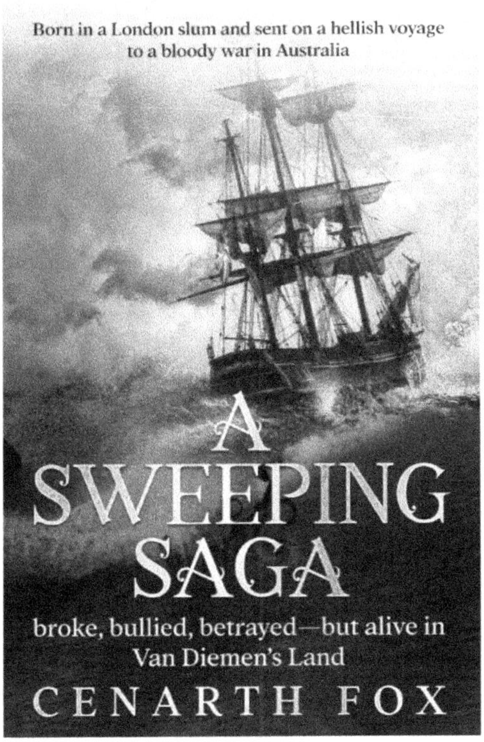

Jonathon Sweeping became Oliver Twist before Dickens was born. In a London slum, his young parents battled poverty, disease and heartache. Forget schooling. Shove the child up a chimney. Make young Sweeping a sweep. Threaten him, injure him but under no circumstances pay him. No wonder death and stealing dominated society when even children fronted the Old Bailey. What hope for the boy? Jonathon moved from prison hulk to convict ship to the other side of the world where Van Diemen's Land with its stunning natural beauty became a war zone. It was kill or be killed as genocide exploded. The boy became a man fighting injustice, cruelty and bushfires. He started a family and together they lived, loved and built a new nation in what became Tasmania. This is Jonathon Sweeping's sweeping saga.

A combination of fine scholarship and effective prose make A Sweeping Saga a great pleasure to read.
Emeritus Professor Michael Roe University of Tasmania

The Queen of Crime

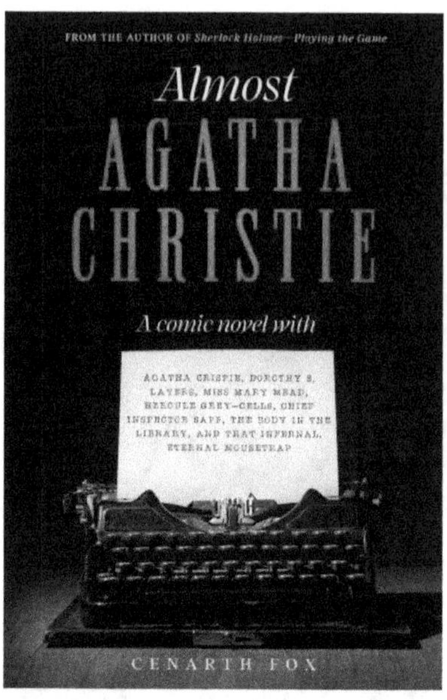

In the south of England after WW1, Agatha Crispie writes her mysteries – *Murder on the Oriental Express, Witness for the Defence* and *The Rat Trap*. Her second husband and his family despise her work. A writer, Dorothy S. Layers, pays a visit and Archibald is bowled over. The lights go out and Archie finds a body with a peg on its nose in the library. The old spinster, Miss Mary Mead, has a reputation for solving crimes. Then Agatha disappears. Has she been murdered! The new Belgian butler arrives. Hercules Grey-Cells is more like a detective. Enter Chief Inspector Sap from Scotland Yard. And when Miss Mary Mead returns, the family are in a spin. A comedy made hilarious if you know anything of the great Dame Agatha and her tales.

I enjoyed this book a lot. It is extremely funny I would recommend it to anyone who is a fan of Agatha Christie. **Amazon 5 stars**
An hilarious spoof on the writings of Agatha Christie. All the characters are extremely stupid and the plot is as improbable as those of the original Agatha, but it is cleverly constructed and will have you laughing out loud at those ridiculous references to Christie's book titles. **Yass Repertory Theatre**

Three World War Two Thrillers

In 1939 Germany is smashing through the Low Countries and the British, Belgian and French forces are trapped at Dunkirk. Louise Wellesley is a gorgeous and aristocratic young Englishwoman desperate to become an actress. But her upbringing demands she go to finishing school, the Buckingham Palace debutante ball and remain at home until the right chap comes along. Such young ladies most definitely do not cavort semi-naked upon the wicked stage. But war brings change. People tell lies. Rules are broken. So when you're in a foreign country and living by your wits while facing arrest, torture and death from the French police, Resistance, Gestapo and a double—agent, you bloody well better remember your lines, act out of your skin and never ever bump into the furniture. Oh and it helps if your new best friend is Edith Piaf.

A Plum Jewel is the third in the series about a beautiful young actress turned spy. In the opinion of this reader it may be the best. Cenarth Fox has loaded this tale with so many twists and obstacles the reader may feel the need to take notes. Mr. Fox's knowledge of the working of wartime Britain and France is remarkable. The reader is right in the middle of the action. I can't recommend this book strongly enough.
Scott Skipper

The Plum Trilogy – www.cenfoxbooks.com

www.ingramcontent.com/pod-product-compliance
Lightning Source LLC
Chambersburg PA
CBHW070607120726
47909CB00007B/2470